In the Shadow of the Conquistador
a novel

Shane Joseph

Library and Archives Canada Cataloguing in Publication

Joseph, Shane, 1955-, author
      In the Shadow of the Conquistador / Shane Joseph.

Issued in print and electronic formats.
ISBN 978-1-927882-10-8 (paperback).--ISBN 978-1-927882-14-6 (Kindle).--
ISBN 978-1-927882-15-3 (epub)

      I. Title.

PS8619.O846I52 2015   C813'.6
C2015-905591-1   C2015-905592-X

Dedication

To those who seek their fortune in lands far away. May you be armed with courage, fueled with hope, and may your endeavours leave this world a better place.

Other Works by Shane Joseph

<u>Novels</u>

Redemption in Paradise

After the Flood

The Ulysses Man

<u>Short Story Collections</u>

Fringe Dwellers

Paradise Revisited

Table of Contents

One—In the Land of Gold

Jimmy

We were meeting after twenty years. George Walton strode through the lobby of the Imperial Hotel in Lima, hand outstretched.

"Jeremy!" He pumped my hand. I wondered why he was using my formal name; what happened to Jimmy? "Glad you made it!" he said.

His hair was still thick and wavy though streaked with grey, making him look dramatic when he shucked it sideways. His wild eyes and weak chin continued to give him an air of fragility, while his posture retained confidence; how much he was hiding, one could never tell.

"Thanks for inviting me." Peru in the rainy season may not be every tourist's idea of fun, and I realised that my ebullience was artificial. My palm was clammy in his dry grip.

He held me at arm's length. "Still bone thin, eh?"

"I hit the gym regularly in preparation for this trip."

He waved his hand in the air. "Yeah—that stuff they tell you about altitude sickness—it's all crap."

I countered in a reflex that George had always brought out in me. "People have died on Dead Woman's Pass. That's what the travel books say—the honest ones."

"You plan meticulously, Jimmy. Gotta leave room for the unexpected."

I was glad to hear him call me by my familiar name again. He had developed a paunch since our last meeting. Middle age was sobering.

"Had anything to eat?" he asked.

"Aircraft food."

"Let's go out. We have lots to catch up."

He was already leading me firmly by the arm towards the revolving exit doors. I nixed suggesting that we eat in the hotel after a tiring fourteen hour journey via Miami.

A green waist-coated money changer, patrolling the street, readily took our dollars for sol—a capitalist convenience we did not have back in Canada. It had rained earlier in the day, but rainwater had quickly evaporated, retaining humidity mixed with pollution from the exhaust fumes of honking motor traffic.

Prostitutes hovered outside the hotel. A police car was parked in the vicinity, protecting the girls, it seemed. No one was being arrested. There were plenty of offers, overt and covert, as we headed toward the brightly lit Jose Pardo Boulevard, the safe tourist drag. The women looked like they had finished the cooking, fed the children and left them in the care of husbands before going out for their night's work: respectable, some even be-spectacled and wearing conservative clothes—very middle class.

"Fancy a piece of Latin American spice afterwards?" George said, looking askance at me.

"You know I don't go in for that kind of stuff."

"You go in for stuff that's more risqué, Jimmy." His voice had turned hard, and I was surprised that after all these years the bitterness still came through.

I stopped walking. I had promised myself before setting out on this trip not to fall into his emotional traps again. "I didn't come all this way to have an argument."

He smiled. "Sorry. My enthusiasm still gets the better of me at times."

We crossed over to the pedestrian boulevard in the centre and continued walking along Jose Pardo in silence, as traffic roared on both sides of this tree-lined oasis of respite. Young couples sat on benches on the central walkway, sharing secrets on a moonless night.

Fragments of how we met up again swept past me. There was the e-mail received out of the blue:

Jeremy—how are you? Decided to dust up your old business card, and tracked you down via the College's bulletin board. Professor emeritus, eh? Seems like you took the early package. I'm done with academia. Had it with unruly youth who were not listening. And panting virgins wanting to get laid by their professor. And schools being run as businesses—all that shit. I'm into Colonial History in a big way now—answers a lot of life's questions for me. Remember Peru? I'm writing a book set there, one I've stopped and started over the years, and I'm going to Machu Picchu in two months to immerse myself in the setting. Thought you might like to come along. To catch up. Let me know if that works for you—George

A string of e-mails followed, threads of the past stitched together, culminating in this decision to join my life-long friend. For my part, it was the guilt of not staying in touch that made me reveal more information than required.

We pulled into a smoke-filled bar off Jose Pardo, appropriately called Puma. After a couple of bottles of Quesqina beer, George opened up, his hair falling over his forehead more than a few times. He desperately wanted to talk, I gathered. As for me, being on Diamox for altitude sickness, I wasn't drinking alcohol.

He talked about old times: growing up in Scarborough, our mutual bond of being born before our parents were married, our fathers' deaths so close upon each other that had marked us indelibly, university days, mutual college professorships, the abortive political campaign—events that had drawn us together. We stayed away from the one subject that had split us apart.

"You must be on a good pension now, eh?" Bitterness had crept into his voice.

"So would you, I imagine?"

"Yeah." He ordered another beer and went to the washroom for the third time.

I ordered Ceviche, hoping the rawness of the fish would be countered by the lime and raw onions. The servers were courteous and attentive; Latin smiles, infectious and disarming.

"I got no bloody pension!" George said, downing his third beer. He was staring down at the table, face covered by that unruly mane of hair.

"Don't you see? The bastards were out to get us, Jimmy. They want the poor immigrants—pay 'em less, work 'em hard—no one complains."

"You did the same, remember?"

"I paid a fair wage. What I got rid of in my contract staff was the feeling of entitlement. The new owners pay what the 'market can bear'—markets in the bloody Third World. How does one protect the education business from globalization when courses could be done online now?"

"But I thought you owned the business?"

"I brought in angel investors as the school started to grow. Soon they were running the place. And like the old Spanish emperors, asking for more than their fifth share. My standards were not good enough for the growth they expected. Angels, my ass!"

"We were the spoilt generation, George. The unions softened us. It was a luxury life in an un-globalized world." I didn't want to ask him why he had been fired.

"You're right on that. Globalization fucked us. Empires with walls were far better."

He had several more beers after that, interspersed with as many trips to the washroom. And I thought *I* had the frequent urination problem, because of the Diamox. He insisted that I listen to all his antics in Vancouver: the boathouse he now lived on, the mountain chalet in Kananaskis, the parties, the women—always lots of women.

"It's been a great life, Jimmy. A damned lonely one. You know—when the party is over, you are left cleaning up ashtrays, empty bottles and plugged condoms."

I knew about the lonely part, not the rest.

He was staggering when we left the bar and stepped back into the noise of traffic and leaded gasoline fumes. When we paused at a cross-light, a bus with passengers clinging to its doorway swung by and nearly swiped George, who had one foot on the road and the other on the sidewalk. I pulled him back instinctively. It struck me that he might be a liability on the trek.

"I'll be okay on the trail, Jimmy," he said, as if reading my thoughts, staring after the errant bus and resuming his lurch back to the hotel.

"You always were," I reminded him, "the life of the party."

He grinned. His eyes tried to focus on me. "You remember those times, eh Jimmy. Remember Mrs. Brown?" He was like a boy again. His zest for life and his energy had been boundless. The boy who beat me in every sport. Even on the academic side, George was the thoroughbred, while I was the plodder. I would pour through my copious lecture notes, spend hours in the library on research, while he would be goofing off somewhere, drinking with the boys; then he'd show up for the exam and ace it. Sometimes I felt I clung onto him just to taste what success would be like.

And in the romance department...well...

That night, after a shower that still left me smelling of various street fumes, I lay on my four poster bed. Amidst muffled sounds of traffic trying to creep in through the shuttered Spanish windows protruding into the street, I wondered if George would finally forgive my transgression, and whether his invitation to accompany him to Machu Picchu was with reconciliation in mind.

For my part, had I come because, after all these years, I wanted to put my shame and deceit behind me?

The following day we toured Lima together. George was smartly dressed: polo shirt, khaki pants, walking shoes, and shades that hid the previous night's drinking. He was exuberant again and ready to absorb the day's sights.

There was no rain today but the skies were overcast in Lima—they were overcast for ten months of the year the guide said—El Nino apparently.

"Pollution, more likely," George said.

I asked him about the book he was writing.

"I am sticking to the historical record while trying to put a human face on Pizarro," he said. "History has treated him badly. But I understand him. So much of my life resonates with his." He didn't elaborate further.

Shanty towns surrounding the hills over the city threatened encroachment. We drove by one on our way out of the city. Electrical wires, expropriated from the main road, ran haphazardly across some huts. Water from a broken sewer leaked onto the main road, more a cart path, dividing the makeshift lean-to buildings; dogs, chickens and a donkey weaved in and out of half-naked children playing merrily in the mud. A '60's model Mercedes Benz sat in front of one house, still in immaculate condition, and I wondered how the heck it not only got there but stayed without being plucked clean. Perhaps the local mafia chief of the shanty town owned it.

Yet the suburbs of Baranca and Miraflores, just ten minutes away, were enclaves of order and calm, despite gated haciendas with armed guards patrolling outside high gates. The rich lived well, as in all developing nations. The architecture in these suburbs was varied: common elements were outward jutting ornate wooden windows, marble or ceramic covered front gardens and wrought iron balconies. There were originals too—like an aircraft fuselage connecting two wings of a house. I wondered who had owned the plane originally and how it had ended up supporting the house. The Peruvians had taken Spanish architecture beyond its limits.

"The Spaniards gave them architecture," George exclaimed, when we passed through the affluent suburb of San Isidoro. Elegantly dressed men and women overflowed the doors of a packed church, reminding me that it was Sunday. "I'm tired of the locals complaining of the bastardization of their culture. Heck they wear European clothes now and speak Spanish!"

The guide took deliberate aim at George's comments on our return later when he pointed out various bombed-out buildings in the city: testament to the Shining Path rebellion of the recent past, spawned by the marginalization of rural folk. These events were unimaginable at the time of the Inca, he explained, who had built their society on the ethos of community service.

In the ancient ruins of Pachcamac, just outside the city and within yards of another encroaching shanty town, George got animated again as we walked among rows of altars once dedicated to human sacrifice.

"Young virgins—think of the power in the hands of the man who took their lives." He swooped down an imaginary knife, pupils dilated, face in a contortion of pain and pleasure.

"You are making a spectacle of yourself," I said.

"I am on holiday. I can do what I damn well please," he replied, skipping over the steps of the ruins that led down to the ocean, hands outstretched to the heavens. I wondered if he had lived a past life here—he seemed so much at home. Was he faking it, as usual; or did young blood still excite him like it had done so many times before in the past?

We asked to be dropped off at the Plaza de Armas in the city centre, a busy square connected on all sides to narrow traffic-choked streets. We sat at an outdoor café and ordered café con leche.

Within minutes of our arrival, mounted riot police and armed guards began filtering in from one of the side streets and taking position in front of the Congress building, pushing pedestrians and onlookers away. An air of expectation descended on the square, and George's fluent Spanish picked up the reason from hurried comments in the background uttered by other patrons.

"Labour demonstration. Teachers. Not paid enough."

"We didn't have that problem," I said.

"Oh yeah?"

"You could afford a boat and a chalet—what are you complaining about?"

He ignored my comment and stood up suddenly, grabbing his camera. A parade of demonstrators, waving placards, was filing into the square.

George grabbed my hand. "Come on—I need to get a shot of this and send it back to those bastards at the college."

"Don't—you'll get into trouble with the cops."

"Oh, fuck the cops—they won't harm a pair of gringos." He was already stumbling into the now-deserted square, running into its centre, camera at the ready.

A mounted policeman broke ranks and galloped over to intercept George, swooping low, baton waving. I heard him yell, "No photographie!"

"Fuck you!" George retorted. The baton made contact with his camera, sending it spinning along the cobblestones. The horse reared on its hind legs as the rider wrestled it down, slamming the animal into George in the process. I was on my feet and running to George's assistance. During the blur of getting to him, with loudspeakers opening up all around us, I recalled a similar incident, years ago, of picking up George outside a pub on College Street in Toronto on St. Patrick's Day during our university days; he had taken on a pack of boisterous and drunk Irish immigrant kids, calling them potato peelers and leeches of Great Britain and the Dominion of Canada. A bottle was broken on his head and I picked him off the sidewalk, bleeding, with George still determined to go inside again and "finish the job."

This time, I managed to wrestle a heavier George off the square and into the safe confines of the café. Helpful

Peruvians picked up his camera, which was never to shoot another photograph again.

"Save the memory card," was all he could think of as he fell exhausted into his chair and closed his eyes, panting. "I'm gonna send it to those bastards at the board—show them what will happen with their belt tightening."

"You should have stayed in politics," I said, partly to vent my frustration, partly to calm my nerves. "That act of yours would've made a better picture for your last campaign compared to the ones that did."

Despite his pain, he managed a smile. "No. We were the idealists Jimmy. We wanted to change the world. Politicians are crooked. We've had this argument many times before."

I remembered them well: the long evenings of intellectual discourse, the chink of beer bottles and the haze of cigarette smoke that accompanied those discussions, oh so many years ago. I also remembered the sexual detours he had taken when his ideals were inevitably thwarted.

I ordered him a beer, and he appeared to relax after draining half the bottle. Fortunately there were no cuts, just an ugly bruise on his shoulder where the horse had bumped him. The loudspeakers drowned out further conversation, and we sat, lost in our thoughts.

George was late for dinner that evening, and I lingered over a large Inca Cola, yellow and smelling of bubble gum. After a few sips I laid the drink aside. I longed for a beer. This being November and the low season in Peru, tourists were few; two women at a table in the centre were the only other diners in the Imperial's cavernous dining room. I focused on them for lack of anything else interesting.

After a while, the animated gestures of the blond woman, recounting something to her more subdued brunette companion, drew my attention. The blond was of curvaceous build and wore a red bandana over her hair; sharp nose and blue eyes; a healthy tan covered her bare arms. The rest of her clothes were comfortable designer hiking gear: khaki pants, sleeveless white vest that squeezed and accentuated her body. The companion had her back to me and was slimmer, more conservatively dressed, with short dark hair gathered in an elastic band at the back; she nodded several times and seemed to acquiesce with everything her more animated companion was saying. I wondered why I was staring at them so much. The blond woman had triggered off a memory somewhere. Then it dawned on me: apart from the tan and the trail gear, the blond reminded me of Denise.

My reverie was broken by George, who came stumbling in. The women stopped talking and looked at his rakish figure that had brought a shift in energy into the room.

"Sorry, had to buy some last minute supplies." He threw himself down on the chair and looked about him for the waiter, licking his dry lips. He caught the eye of the blond woman, started, then held her gaze. He breathed unevenly. The waiter came over. The spell was broken, and the woman turned back to her companion.

"Cervesa, por favour! Cervesa grande!"

After the waiter departed, George motioned. "Who's that woman?"

"Don't know. Tourists, I suppose. Like us."

"I thought I had seen a ghost," he said.

"So did I."

He pulled his eyes away and fished out a plastic packet from his hiking waistcoat. "*My* remedy for altitude sickness. After all, the Coca tea of the Inca has a cocaine base too."

I sucked in my breath when I saw what he had in the cup of his hand. "You are still at it?"

"Never really gave it up. There are lot of places off Jose Pardo that sell it. I did *my* research."

We had smoked-up in the seventies, not just tobacco. I quit when smoking went out of fashion and one had to huddle outdoors in cold weather for a nicotine fix. I hadn't seen George smoke on this trip so far and had assumed he had given it up as well. Not his weed, apparently.

We ordered beef steaks, Peruvian style, with potatoes and beans. George glanced occasionally at the two women. So did I. There was an unspoken barrier preventing us from voicing the memory that the blond woman was invoking. Between beers, he fiddled with the new digital camera he had bought. Not bad for a guy without a pension, I figured, but kept my thoughts to myself.

The women rose to leave, and George smiled and called out. "Let me guess—you folks are going to...Machu Picchu?"

The blond woman smiled, open, provocative. "Good guess. How did you know?"

"There isn't much else for tourists in Peru. Cheers!" George raised his fourth bottle of beer to them.

"Oh no? What about Lake Titikaka or the Amazon jungle?" She was flirting, and I shuddered, knowing from experience where this would lead.

"All passé compared to old Machu," George said.

"I hope so. We've been to the other places on our trip so far. Left Machu Picchu for the grand finale. Eight a.m. flight to Cusco tomorrow."

"Maybe we could change ours and join you. Jimmy, could we do that?

"We have the 10.30. The tickets are non-changeable and non-refundable, remember?"

Her companion had risen and was collecting their things. She wore glasses and was shorter, diminished against her more outgoing friend. Facing her, I caught a glimpse of a scar running down her cheek from ear to jaw, giving her features an edge. "Come along Ali, we have an early start tomorrow." She looked annoyed at our imposition, as if she had to protect Ali from men like us on their travels. I guess I was a kindred spirit with her when it came to protecting George.

"See you on the trail," George said.

"Perhaps," said Ali, winking at George. "Good luck!" She passed us, leaving a trace of perfume in the air. Even the scent matched and took me back to the past.

As the women left, George turned to me, a crooked smile on his face. "Ghosts apart, they haven't had sex in a long while. You can see it on Ali's face. I bet I could be in her bed tonight if not for her friend."

I couldn't resist. "Don't be so damned sure. Maybe they are getting it on together. Not every woman needs you, George."

"Fuck you!" His snap was sharp and sudden. "Just because you fucked my wife—that does not give you a lock on women. And that's no ghost. You got it? She's no ghost!" His fists clenched the table tightly and a nerve bulged in his neck.

Here it comes! I steeled myself from blurting out the retort that would have ended our trip then and there. Instead, I remained silent, submitting to the hammer of retribution. I think he could see the pain in my face, for as quickly as he had erupted, he deflated and his inimitable smile resurfaced.

"Why am I raking up old shit? Forgive me, old buddy. We should get a good night's sleep."

With great difficulty I rose from my chair. "I'll see you in the morning. In the lobby at eight?"

"Roger that."

I left him ordering another beer and went up to my room.

***

George

He sat nursing his beer long after Jimmy left the restaurant. He knew he shouldn't be drinking so much; it didn't go with the physical exertion still to come. But the desire to live on the edge was strong, stronger than it had ever been in recent years. He felt his life was heading towards its climax and it would happen here in Peru, amidst the ghosts and skeletons of the conquistadors who had blatantly raped and pillaged to achieve their selfish ends, but who had built their empires and left their stamp on the world. It was exhilarating too, this feeling of connectedness with history, to realize that he was not alone, despite the delinquent life he had led. *Mankind is a derelict ship, on a one-way trip to extinction, despite the best endeavours of the occasional transformational leader who springs up to steer it.* History had offered up these leaders from time to time: Moses, Jesus, Gandhi, Martin Luther—yeah, but they were all mere contradictory blips against a tide that was genetically bred—survival of the fittest, dog-eat-dog—ending always in death. The anti-leaders were more inspiring, like Pizarro, for the Spaniard had been after gold, and fuck everybody else! Pizarro had been clear in his intentions, instead of cloaking it in impossibly noble gestures about saving the world. Men like Pizarro made history instead.

"Cerveza, senor?" The waiter was looking at his watch as it was past closing time.

"Non gracias," he answered, struggling to rise, the wash of alcohol consumed this evening weighing him down. *Head for the door. You have to conserve your strength till the end of this trip, George.* He signed his name and room number on the bill and staggered for the door, banging into furniture in his way. *Derelict ship, I am one!*

***

Francisco Pizarro

An extract from *Conquistador*—a novel by George Walton

As his raft neared the shore of Tumbez, Francisco Pizarro stood on the bow and imagined the land that had slipped away from him on two previously aborted expeditions: a tropical land of aqueducts, roads and bridges, and ably governed natives; a land of untold wealth yet to be acquired. Peru—a narrow strip of land locked between the ocean and the cordilleras.

A sense of triumph swept him as he recalled the many obstacles that had hitherto thwarted him and which he had now overcome: storms at sea, jealous governors, the lack of money, soldiers and sailors who had fallen prey to the easy life in the tropical islands en-route and had not wished to venture further south, suspicious natives who had never seen a horse or a gun. And yet, with the help of his dear comrades-in-arms Almagro and Padre Luce, they had scrambled together this third and final voyage, and his raft was now a mere swimming distance from the Land of Gold.

He did not wait for the boat to strike ground, but jumped overboard and waded onto the beach. The water was warm. His advance party of rafts that had carried baggage and military stores were already drawn further up the beach, and the men were unloading cargo. He walked swiftly towards the town, hand on his sword, boots crunching on the stones. His band of men had quickly assembled and followed him, armour clanking, voices loosening from the long sea voyage. He recalled similar walks through villages in Spain, but back then in his impoverished youth, his companions had been hogs, and his sandals had been worn down to their heels. Tonight he would eat guinea pig and potatoes served by delectable local women, when but a few years ago stale bread and onions from the kitchen of a generous innkeeper would have been a feast.

Something was wrong.

The streets were deserted and some of the buildings looked sacked.

"Draw arms," he commanded. Steel scraped scabbards and muskets were cocked.

He drew his sword and slowed his walk to a cautious step.

A scurrying sound increased in a side street, and suddenly three of his men from the advance troop came rushing towards his party. They were panting heavily.

"Captain," the lead soldier pulled up, sweat pouring from under his helmet. "The natives have fled. They have killed our men inland."

"Fled?" asked Francisco.

"Yes, Captain. And they have taken all that is valuable with them. We came across our three advance guardsmen strung up beside the road with their throats slit."

A vice gripped Francisco's heart. "I thought they would show us hospitality. And yet they choose violence. Bring up more troops from the ship. We will find those savages, and their gold, and they will pay in blood."

The die was cast. This was not going to be any easier than the first two expeditions. But who had imagined that conquest would be easy?

Suddenly those mountains ahead looked menacing.

Two—The Making of a Conquistador

Jimmy

Memories of the past return in flashes, mostly the ones we want to remember; others remain suppressed, until someone drags them out of you. Meeting George in Lima had opened long-sealed floodgates.

My parents were teachers who led a very ordered life: school, homework, household chores, mass on Sunday, a trip to Algonquin Park or cottage country in the summer, community theatre regularly and—perhaps once a year—a splurge at a choral concert in downtown Toronto. Mom and Dad communicated through ritual tasks; when she placed his dinner down silently, he only had to move his newspaper slightly to acknowledge it, and if she didn't do it right, it was greatly disconcerting to him. Likewise, if he did not arrive with the groceries at exactly 6:30 p.m. on a Wednesday evening, she would be frantic.

I was adopted by my parents, I discovered later. I was the child from a surreptitious teen pregnancy and would never discover my real parents' identity—the church from whence I was "sourced" saw to that. My adoptive parents however left a stronger mark on me than any genetics would. I was conditioned from as early as I could remember to be neat and tidy; my room had to be cleaned before I left for school; homework was from 4.30 p.m.—6 p.m., TV was limited to thirty minutes, visiting the library was left for Saturday mornings where I was allowed to take out only the number of books that I would actually read, just as I could not put more food on my plate than I would eat. These habits dog me even today and have been my cocoon in times of stress.

My father was a creature of habit, but I sensed that underneath his air of middle-class respectability there was a bubbling anger, instilled in him by the rigid discipline of the boarding school he had grown up in, and the fact that he had lost his parents early in life. I saw his anger expressed in the way he chewed on his cigarette after a hard day at school and when he fumed while marking school papers. Expressions like, "Bloody idiots, can't spell!" leaked from him frequently.

My father was my judge and jailor when examinations drew near. He shut me up in my room to study and checked on me every hour to see if I had completed the assignments he had set for me, assignments, he claimed, that would guarantee me an excellent showing at the exam. I developed headaches during that time and hated those periods of solitary confinement.

My mother, on the other hand, retreated to church for her sanity. It was home, school or church for her. She was a frail, kind woman who believed that a woman's job was to support her husband and her family. One evening, I found her stuffing a pile of chits into her handbag, a look of glee on her face. This intrigued me and I was determined to find out what else made my mother happy. A few days later, when she was in the kitchen getting dinner ready, I stole over to her handbag which was lying on her private desk in the study she shared with my father—his desk was on one side and hers on the other—and took a peek inside. The chits were unrecognizable at first, smeared and crushed with faint print. I got a shock when I realized what they were. And I thought she had been spending her leisure hours in church!

Apart from this indiscretion, which I decided to keep a secret, I watched the two of them go about their lives mechanically and wondered what spark of romance had brought them together in the beginning. Had I been adopted out of a duty to the community, or to prevent their sterile relationship from coming unglued?

George's home, by contrast, was organized bedlam. His father was its supreme commander. He ran a construction business when not working as a member of the provincial parliament (he had two stints as an MPP with a period in between when he was out of office but had been more active than ever during that hiatus planning his comeback). Their house on a normal day was a parade of builders, constituents, realtors, engineers, business people and other unidentifiable citizens, coming and going at all hours. George's overworked mother rushed to and fro replenishing tea, cookies and other refreshments for all comers. As a teenager growing up in Scarborough, I was drawn to his home, if only to escape the sterility of mine. George was full of grandiose plans even then, despite his ambivalent relationship with his father. George hated his father shouting at his mother, yet admired the elder Walton's business and political savvy. George's ambition back then was to be better than his father—he was going to be prime minister of Canada when he grew up, he vowed—a powerful magnate to someone like me who was looking for a role model.

George's mother, unlike mine, was not very educated and was a stay-at-home housewife, kind hearted, always having milk and cookies out for me when I visited. Mrs. Walton liked to gossip and smoke, especially at the ladies bingo club, and my mother stayed away from her to guard her own privacy. There were many times when I would be at George's and hear his parents quarrelling: his father yelling at his mother for yapping to the women in the neighbourhood and revealing his political plans that she'd overhear from the many visitors he received, and she yelling back at him that it was bloody difficult to buy groceries for a household when one did not know how many visitors were going to "drop in" the next day. George would be embarrassed at his parents' outbursts and curse under his breath, "Don't mind them—the shouts are normal. When they start throwing things at each other, that's when it gets weird."

"They are better than mine," I replied. "The silence at my home is louder than your parents' shouting."

"Dad resents Mom because he was forced to marry her to save face. He knocked her up when she was working in his office as a receptionist."

"I guess that makes two of us, born at the wrong time."

I think it was our "unwanted" status that drew George and me into each other's orbit and kept us bonded like brothers in those early days of growing up in Scarborough.

George's house was a monstrosity in our neighbourhood. The houses were mainly post war, single story bungalows, all pretty much looking the same. But Mr. Walton, being a builder, was constantly making enhancements to his house. First came the second floor—the house was like a bomb shelter one summer while that floor went up. George was rewarded with an upstairs room, while his old bedroom was converted into a library. Then came the pool; when Mrs. Walton complained about the maintenance, it was filled in the next year and replaced with a tennis court, which was ripped out the following year in favour of a manicured lawn and a fountain, which seemed to settle Mrs. Walton, who could now entertain her friends from the ladies club, outdoors.

The interior of the house was regal—a curved staircase, oak panelled walls in the study and the library, a finished basement containing many rooms where we played hide-and-seek, a wine cellar, a sun room on the main floor that had windows on all sides, piped-in music in some rooms and a large deck spilling out into the garden—annual projects that Mr. Walton had his construction crew work on every summer.

George had a large collection of toy guns, and when we were in our single digit years, playing conquistadors and Indians was a regular activity. His interest in Spanish colonial exploits had been sparked by a book his father had given him for his eighth birthday. George was always the conquistador, which left me with little else but to play Indian. But I was an Indian who wanted to live at the end of our game, and I would 'rise from the dead' and shoot back, after George had cornered me and mouth-shot me over a thousand times with his imaginary bullets.

"You're supposed to be dead," he'd scream at me.

"No I'm not!"

It was still better to be shot at by George, than going back to my silent house.

Our games got more serious as we grew older...

One summer day, during the school break, I went to George's as we had arranged to go to the park to fly our kites. Mr. Walton answered my knock on the front door. He was busy talking to one of his many visitors, a man in a business suit. Mr. Walton scarcely paid me any notice other than to hold the door open and say, "George is doing his homework at the moment." I ducked under his arm and headed for George's bedroom as he turned to talk to his guest. George was at his desk, papers spread out about him.

"You've changed your mind?" I asked.

"I can't. Dad won't let me go until I finish my homework."

"During the holidays?"

"Dad says, I've got to brush up on trigonometry, because it's part of next year's program. 'Got to keep the mind active, my boy!' "

"But it must be hard; we've not even read up on it yet."

"It's easy. Just a bunch of silly calculations. And it's done. I've figured it out."

"You are a genius! So if you are done, what is the problem?"

"Dad wanted me to spend two hours on this assignment—that's how long he thinks it will take to 'do it justice' as he says."

"He doesn't know you're smarter than that?"

"He doesn't know much. But I've got a plan. When that man called over, I slipped into Dad's study and moved the clock forward by half an hour. He's going back into his study when he sees the man off. Go around the back and wait for me. I'll hand in my assignment, and then we have to skedaddle."

I took the kites and went around the back of the house. I paused by the open study window and peeked in. Mr. Walton had sent his guest away and was smoking at his desk, deeply wrapped up in what looked like building diagrams. George entered.

"Here, you are. It's done," he said in a flat voice.

"Humph." His father did not even look up.

"It's done, Dad."

Mr. Walton looked up, not at his son but at the clock. "Humph. Five o'clock. About time too. Leave it there. I'll review it when I am done." George turned and left the room rapidly. Within seconds he was grabbing my hand in the garden and pulling me away. "Run!" Only when we were a few yards down the driveway did the neighbourhood church ring its bell announcing to all and sundry—the half hour. I'm glad they outlawed church bells soon after that.

I remember the time we went hunting racoons. George's house overlooked a ravine, and in the summer, racoons crept over the fence and attacked the garbage. His mother was forever swearing at the trails of foul smelling chicken bones strewn around that she had to clean up before George's father's many constituents called over. Sometimes she didn't make it in time, and George Sr. would be incensed and yell at her.

When I went over to his place that day, he was in the backyard carving a V-shaped stick from a pile of freshly broken branches off the giant sugar maple.

"Slingshot," he explained.

I sat on the stoop and watched. He methodically slit an old inner tube of a bicycle tire to produce two, quarter inch-wide rubber strips, each about a foot in length; he tied an end of each strip to each upper end of the V branch using smaller strips cut off the tube. The tongue of an old shoe provided the sling, to which the other ends of the rubber strips were attached, one on either side. He checked the aim by putting a pebble into the sling, closing and gripping it fast in his hand, then pulling back and releasing the stone through the V at a tin can twenty five feet away. He hit the can on the third try.

"It's pulling left. Here, you can have this one." He tossed the slingshot at me and picked up another V branch to carve. "The next will be perfect."

Two hours later we were armed with a slingshot each.

"Come on let's go hunt those bastards."

But racoons are never around when you want them. We scoured the ravine in the midday heat along the banks of the creek that was stagnant in patches. George practised by taking trial shots at dogs out for exercise, while their owners talked to each other and momentarily took their eyes off their pets. When the animals yelped and ran like the world was ending, the owners were jerked out of their chatting to embrace the consequences of their negligence, and two eleven-year old boys were stumbling through the bushes, falling into mud on the soft banks of the creek, running as fast as the dogs, in the opposite direction.

"Maybe we'll find them in the early morning, or in the evening. They must be asleep now," I said. I was panting from our last getaway and rapidly tiring of the hunt for racoons, and of the chases by pet owners.

But George did not listen to me, and we continued to spend the next two hours looking for our prey. At one point, he made us hide behind some branches in the smelliest part of the creek where a big blob of rapidly decomposing fruit was lodged against an overhanging branch. The smell was beginning to make me sick to my stomach.

George had remained highly agitated throughout the hunt and there was a fire in his eyes. "That smell—it's the same as a garbage can. They'll come soon."

And then we heard the shaking of branches and saw the clumsy stumble of the scavenger: a full-size racoon, as big as a dog, making its way down the bank on the other side, stopping occasionally to ferret out invisible scraps in empty food wrappers and used Styrofoam cups littering the area.

I wished that son-of-a-bitch racoon had come five minutes earlier. The sickly sweet smell of the degenerating fruit and the sight of that warbling grey fur-ball adding its own stench to the scene took me over the edge. I retched loudly.

The animal pricked up its ears and started backing up the hill. George broke cover, pulled his sling back and let fly, but the animal was moving, and I lost sight of what happened next as I was throwing up into the bushes.

"Sorry," I said and retched again. But George was gone in a crash of branches and a splash of water, as he ran across the shallow creek, yelling, "Come back, you bastard. Come back and die!"

When I had emptied my stomach sufficiently and crawled back up the bank to the other side, out of smell-shot of the rotting fruit, I heard him returning, swearing under his breath, "Son-of-a-bitch! Why the fuck did you have to do that, moron?"

"I told you, I was getting sick from the minute we got there. Did you get him?" I thought he was going to shoot me next, he looked so mad.

"No. But I'll get him tomorrow."

***

George

The next morning he went out alone. Jimmy merely got in the way. He was waiting behind the shed at 5 o'clock. The birds had started a few minutes ago and awoken him. His parents were still asleep; laboured snores followed him as he tiptoed out the back door.

He breathed in the cool air; dew covered the leaves in the trees that fell down the hill into the ravine; the shed was just at the drop-off point—easy prey for scavengers coming off the creek below. This was his home; no one—animal or human—was going to take it away from him by upsetting the delicate balance of his parents' relationship, even more strained as it had been these last few years since his father had entered politics.

His mother's tired looks at the end of a day of frenzied activity around the house, his father drinking his daily scotch, elevated to a double now. Things had definitely changed at home, for the worse. Sometimes he wondered if his father cared for his mother anymore, or was she just a servant now?

His frustration fell away as he narrowed his sights on the animal scurrying up the hill in the dark, moving towards the shed.

The stones weighed heavily in his pocket; they had been carefully selected for weight and balance after he had returned from his fruitless quest the day before. He aimed at the middle of the ambling shadow.

The first stone stunned the creature; it froze then deflated. The second stone must have hurt for it elicited a faint bleat-like sound. He left the shelter of the tree and advanced on his quarry, third stone drawn. A second four-legged shadow was hurrying up the hill—enemy reinforcements. He stuck to the fallen one—hit them where they are weakest, do not fight on many fronts—lessons from the books he had read on the military strategy of colonial conquests. The third stone hit the wounded animal with a flat *thunk*, and the second shadow squealed and went scurrying down the hill, and branches on the creek bank flittered in a diminishing wave.

He paused and waited for the injured racoon to move. It started limping slowly. He followed it. It paused by the shed. A plank had been placed leaning against the roof at a forty-five degree angle; the animal started to advance along it. *Good. Just where I want you.*

He waited until the racoon was almost at the roof level and shot the fourth stone. With a cry, almost human, the creature rolled off the plank and onto the roof—marooned now, unable to descend until his attacker left.

Daylight was advancing rapidly. He climbed the tall maple tree next to the shed, the bag of stones banging against his thigh. He was eye-level with the forager, four feet away. Foxy face, fear written everywhere, even in the foul smell emanating from it.

"Don't fuck with my property, you bastard," he said and shot the fifth stone—he saw the blood spurt this time, from the mouth, splattering the roof.

He heard footsteps below.

Jimmy!

"What the heck are you doing here so early?" he yelled at his scared-looking friend.

Jimmy was in his pyjamas; he looked like he had left his house in a hurry. "I had a dream that you were hunting racoons again."

"I thought you'd had enough yesterday."

"Yes, but something bad was happening in this dream. I came to warn you."

That was when the racoon made a desperate attempt to escape and leapt off the roof, hit the plank, couldn't hold on and fell with a thud onto the upward looking Jimmy.

Both animal and boy went down in a heap. There was human and animal squealing, and he couldn't make out one from the other. In the bid to free themselves they seemed to be locked tighter to each other. He let go the sixth stone at the soft brown furry side of the boy-animal. He missed, and Jimmy screamed in agony. The shot helped dislodge the animal however, and it limped across the yard and went rolling down the hill, crashing into the underbrush below.

He jumped down from the maple and went to his friend's assistance. Jimmy had scratch marks on his face, his clothes were torn and a welt was forming on his forehead.

"You shouldn't have come," he said to the dazed Jimmy, who had lapsed into a bout of shivering. "I had the whole thing under control."

"George! What the hell is going on?" His father was on the back deck and advancing, a dressing gown hastily thrown over his pyjamas. Mom was peeking from behind, a look of shock on her face. She was already on her first cigarette for the day. She looked so fragile, and that scared him.

"It was the racoon," he said. But that did not prevent the slap that his father gave him.

"We weren't fighting, Mr. Walton." Jimmy rallied weakly.

"It was the racoon," he insisted to his father. "We shot the racoon!"

His father had him by the ear and was hauling him indoors, while his mother bent over Jimmy.

"Get inside you idiot. What would the neighbours think of us?" his father said.

He kept insisting. He had been the victor. His father was the idiot for not understanding. "We shot the racoon. So you would not shout at Mom anymore."

***

Jimmy

When we were in high school, we met Mrs. Brown. She was our library assistant for one summer—divorced, in her mid forties, busty and full hipped—she exuded a sexuality that got a resounding response from the library patrons, male and female alike. There were several rumours: that she was getting laid by married men, that she was a Wiccan, that she preferred younger men, particularly students. Her eyes melted whenever she met George who always touched hands with her while exchanging books. Me, she treated with a quizzical look—perhaps I was not as easy to classify as my hornier friend.

When the subject of Mrs. Brown came up one day, I boldly speculated, "I wonder whether her breasts are real or fake."

"They are real," George replied.

"How do you know?"

"I've felt them and sucked them."

"Oh, come on ... " I paused. Maybe ... maybe George had been stealing one on us—*doing*, while the rest of us talked and wanked. Perhaps, that's why he had skipped debate practice after school on the last few occasions ...

I took a deep breath and said, "So now you are going to tell me that you are one of her lovers."

George had an amused look on his face. "Yes, I am. And it's my secret. You are the only one to know."

I felt offended. "And I have to carry this heavy secret with me now? And it could all be make-believe, just to make me feel bad."

"It's not made up. Do you want to see for yourself?"

"How will I do that?"

"Come with me. Mrs. Brown and I have a date every Thursday evening."

"And does she have someone else for every other day of the week?"

"Who cares? She's hot on Thursdays."

That Thursday we drove down a street overlooking the Rouge Valley. George explained to me on the drive that Mrs. Brown needed seclusion and privacy because her coven practiced in her basement on the weekends and she did not want nosy neighbours complaining.

"She does not want anyone seeing who's screwing her, that's why," I said viciously. Ever since George had revealed his secret to me, I had been viewing Mrs. Brown with an extra heavy dose of lust when visiting the library. In fact, I had started borrowing more books than I could possibly read, breaking a lifelong habit.

We parked George's beat-up Honda two streets away and walked down a dead end road to Mrs. Brown's house—a two storey, turn of the last century, red brick farm house with a steep sloping roof and dormer windows on all sides. It looked run-down and due for demolishing to make way for the mass produced subdivisions taking over Scarborough. She must have rented it for a steal.

Just as we rounded the long driveway, George asked me to step behind a giant oak tree and wait until he was indoors.

"Now remember—I'll make sure the front door is unlocked. The stairs creak, so stay on the right edge by the banister. The master bedroom is the far right room—it's got a broomstick door knocker. Got all that?"

I nodded, peering at the house. My palms were clammy and my underarms were drenched.

"Give us about fifteen minutes before you come in. She likes to get worked up before she lets me into it. She plays with me a lot."

"How come you don't jerk off when she does that?"

"Control, brother. Control ... " And then he was off, jauntily swaggering down the path towards the stone steps leading up to those flesh coloured doors that were pulsating at me, drawing me like a red hot vulva.

I paced back and forth looking at my watch, willing the minutes to go by. Finally, at the fourteenth minute, assuming one minute to get inside, I couldn't wait any longer. I crouched and ran down the driveway and leaped up the steps, my heart about to burst with excitement and fear. I paused to catch my breath in front of the large birch double doors—if I walked in now I was sure they'd hear my pounding heart. After I had calmed down a bit, I pushed the door open gently. It swung silently as if oiled just for my entry. I stepped in and smelled incense—pungent clouds of it all over the house. I stifled a sneeze that threatened to explode the house. I found the stairway and walked on its right side, ascending the clouds of incense as if I was rising up to heaven. The stairwell was decorated with pictures: Mrs. Brown with various men at different stages of her life, Mrs. Brown in a witch's costume replete with hat and broom, a close-up of Mrs. Brown staring into the camera, her eyes bloodshot with lips barred. No family pictures of parents, children or siblings—weird!

I heard sounds in one of the upstairs rooms—Mrs. Brown must be warming up. And then on the landing in front of me, its whiskers bared like its mistress in the picture, stood a Siamese cat, a slow, menacing purr emanating from its mouth, its body crouched as if about to spring at me.

I froze. *Of course you idiot—a witch has to have a cat! But why didn't George warn me?*

I extended a trembling hand to pet it, while in the background I heard a peal of pleasure emanate from Mrs. Brown, a foreign sound compared to those with which I had associated her in the library, but more in context with how I had imagined her in my wet dreams. My shaking hands stroked the soft fur of the cat, and it purred—we were both melting in relief that the other was not on the attack.

The door with the broomstick knocker was ajar and a lot of panting and grunting was going on inside. Unbridled energy gushed out of the room, enveloping me and the cat. The cat suddenly froze, baring its mouth, tail riding high; then it snapped viciously and took off in the opposite direction, down the stairs, disappearing into the incense haze below.

I peered through the crack in the bedroom door. What I saw: Mrs. Brown dressed in a black bra with her huge breasts hanging out of them; her only other accoutrements were black fishnet stockings and stiletto heels. She was kneeling in front of George's crotch, and by the long strokes she was making he seemed to have a giant erection, although in the locker room I had thought him quite average.

"Sugar me now, honey," she said coming off him, rolling over on the carpet and opening her legs, revealing a dense bush of red hair. For a moment I imagined George entering her and bursting into flames. In fact, for all his bravado, he sank amateurishly into her, and she helped him by putting her strong hands on his buttocks and swinging him in and out vigorously. He seemed to gather confidence the more she squealed with delight at his performance.

"Now, from behind," she commanded, pushing him out; she rolled on her knees and crouched facing the door. George struggled from behind to get back into position. Finally he did, and she bucked backward into him like an athlete on the blocks waiting to take off at the sound of the starter's pistol, only she did it repeatedly, and no gun went off. Her eyes were glazed and bloodshot like in the picture on the wall, a trail of saliva drooled down her mouth, and her breasts dangled and banged into each other with every thrust. *Those can't be fake; they must be real.* George, was riding harder now, his face contorted as if he was about to lose control. He tried to focus elsewhere and for a moment he turned toward the open door.

"Stay a bit longer, honey," Mrs. Brown cooed and slowed her stroke, as if sensing her lover's impending climax. But George yelled, "I can't fucking hold it anymore."

"Stay!"

"I'm coming!"

And I felt the stickiness in *my* pants. I'd had the starter's gun in my hand during this whole scenario, without even realizing it. And dammit! I had shot *before* George! He'd beaten me by a hair's breath—again! I held my wet pants and slunk downstairs to echoes from Mrs. Brown saying, "Oh, you are a such good little lover boy, Georgie."

George had it all arranged, he told me the next week. He knew how keen I was to lay Mrs. Brown. He'd spoken to her about me.

"She remembers you," he said chuckling. "'The tall skinny one' she calls you."

I blushed. "She's playing with fire."

"She's doing me a favour. I told her you are my best friend. And, she likes us. Don't worry, it will be very private."

"I'll handle it. Just get me in there." Now that the die had been cast, I was determined to be better than him.

The following Thursday we took the same route in his car. We stopped at our favourite hamburger shop for sustenance. I ordered a triple burger, hoping that meat correlated with lust.

When we arrived, I asked, "Are you staying in the car?" I wanted his protection and yet wanted to be alone with Mrs. Brown. I guess, I didn't know what I wanted right then.

George yawned as he pulled on the handbrake. "I'll introduce you and hang around downstairs in the lobby. She might want me for Round Two."

"I'll make sure she doesn't need that. But thanks for coming along."

"You nervous?" He tilted his head at me, the toothpick from the hastily eaten sandwich sticking between his teeth.

"No." I exhaled, and he laughed.

"Remember to work her up. She is like putty after that."

The walk from the car, up the driveway to the front door, was the longest one I had ever taken; my feet dragged like leaden weights.

Mrs. Brown met us at the front door, a glass of red wine in her hand. She was dressed in a black ankle-length dress; from her various bodily protrusions, I gathered that she was wearing nothing underneath.

"Hello, boys—what took you?" She was flirty, yet businesslike, as if we had just missed the 6 p.m. fuck.

"Traffic," I said.

"We stopped to eat," George said.

"Whatever," Mrs. Brown said disinterestedly. "Are you boys old enough for a drink?" We were not.

"Never mind." She seemed to read our minds.

She sat on the couch, legs splayed, surveying us. She was a cat surveying two very juicy mice. Her eyes turned to me. "So you want me to help you become a man, eh?"

I tried to hold onto my escaping blush, unsuccessfully. George came to my rescue. "He's done it before," he lied on my behalf, and I blushed again.

Mrs. Brown downed her glass, went over to a sideboard, picked up a half empty bottle of wine and headed upstairs. "Georgie, you can light the incense. We need some good energy for what we are about to perform." Then she glanced over at me, her lips curling, eyes narrowing. She hooked a finger. "Come along, honey. Let's see to your education."

I followed her up the stairs, mesmerised, her luscious ass in my face, warbling hypnotically, summoning me into its nether regions.

As we entered the room with the broomstick on its door, the cat darted out, and I jumped involuntarily. She laughed. "Relax, honey. You will never do anything unless you relax."

"You okay, Jimmy?" George's voice came from downstairs. For the first time he sounded concerned; perhaps he was regretting putting me into a situation that was increasingly obvious as being out of my league. I was determined to show him that I was definitely *in* the league.

Mrs. Brown lit a row of candles that ran around the room. Then she lazily unzipped her dress and shook it off her and turned to survey the impact she had on me. Satisfied, she lay on the bed, her high heeled shoes dangling off it. "Come here, Jimmy," she purred softly as candle smoke filled the room and she began to blur in front of me.

To go into the rest of what happened is humiliating and I will be brief. She commanded (yes, that was the word) me to touch, stroke and pinch certain areas of her anatomy. I liked her breasts the best; her bush was a soggy mess in seconds as she cooed and moaned and started to writhe on the bed. Then she suddenly turned on me and started ripping off my clothes. My belt got stuck, and when she pulled it off frenziedly, it slapped against my crotch, sending me into a crouch of pain.

"Do it, now!" Her voice roared in my ears. When I looked down, my cock had disappeared—only a rosebud of a protuberance stuck out between my legs.

I heard her calling, "Georgie—you'll have to take over. Your friend can't do it." My humiliation was total.

I jumped on top of her and pressed my body to hers, willing my member to rise and do its duty. But that was never going to happen—at least not today, not under these circumstances. We rolled in an embrace. She began ripping my back with her finger nails. The anger in her face was mushrooming by the second. Then with a vicious shove, she sent me reeling off the bed and strode to the door, yelling, "Georgie!"

"Georgie" had arrived in the room and was taking in the situation.

"George," I panted, covering my lost manhood. "It's not what you think."

Then George did something I never expected of him. He shoved a clinging Mrs. Brown aside and came over to me.

"Aren't you going to look after me, Georgie?" I heard her pained voice.

"Fuck yourself!" was George's angry answer.

Mrs. Brown recoiled and hissed at him, "Young bastards! You're all the same!"

George helped me rise, ignoring her.

"Get out of my house, both of you!" Mrs. Brown was slipping on her black dress, her face twisted in frustrated wrath. I picked up my mangled clothes.

"We are leaving," George said. He ripped the broomstick from the door and tossed it to her as we exited. "Use this."

She flung it back at us, and we ran down the stairs—the cat appeared from somewhere and followed us, as if trying to escape along with us—through the door and out into the yard. Mrs. Brown's screams followed us to the car. The cat stopped short of the car and snarled at us, then turned on its heel and scampered back to the house. As we pulled away, I realized I was still naked.

"Just get your pants on—you can do the rest up later," George ordered as he swung the car with a screech onto the main road.

"It's not as you think," I kept saying to him.

"It's okay, Jimmy. This was a bad deal. I should not have got you into this."

His concern made me feel all the more miserable. George had well and truly beaten me in the game of love, lust, or whatever you call what had happened back at Mrs. Brown's house.

At the end of the summer, Mrs. Brown left the library despite a sudden spike in enrollments. Various reasons were rumoured, among them "being a bad role model in the community."

The next summer George's father died—suddenly. He was campaigning for his re-election and was returning from a party meeting in Waterloo late at night. His car skidded off the ramp and plunged into a ditch. George Walton Sr. died instantly of massive head injuries, so went the news story that morning.

I ran over to George's house the moment I saw the news on TV. His mother was sitting, nursing a cup of tea, an ashtray already full of cigarette butts, looking numb. Her first words when I got there was to embrace me and moan, "Oh Jimmy, how will we manage?"

"Where's George?" I asked, pulling myself away from her. Her eyes were dry. She looked more confused than in grief.

"Oh, he's somewhere in the house," she said drifting back to her tea and cigarette.

I eventually found him in his father's study. He was sitting in his father's dressing gown, a glass of scotch on the desk.

"George!"

He was drunk already. "Sit down Jimmy, my old friend. You are now looking at the head of this household."

"But George—your dad just died!"

"I know. He was a tight-assed idiot who wouldn't cry. He wouldn't want us to cry. So I am taking over now." But he was brandishing the glass half-heartedly, sloshing the contents on the desk, over papers.

"Look at this shit—more bills than assets. My old man sold us up the creek," he yelled. "My mother is going to have to declare bankruptcy."

"Hey—not so fast! Your dad had political connections—they'll help."

"We'll see."

"You'd better get dressed and sober up. The house will be full of people coming to pay their respects soon. Your mother needs you. And you are hiding up here ... getting drunk?"

He rose shakily. "We have to go down to the coroner's office first." He came towards me, and his body was shaking. The glass fell from his hands and crashed to the floor. I held his shaking body.

"This is new to me, Jimmy," he cried, deep sobs welling from him. "I'm fucking scared."

The funeral was a grand affair—all the political stripes were present. George Sr. must have planned for a glorious exit, for a premium funeral policy covered the expenses. George fumed and cursed while I stood beside him. He scowled at the party faithful, and I shuddered at his outright scorn. I later found out why: his mother's request for financial assistance had been turned down by the big-wigs who had been in and out of the Walton home in the past.

Things went downhill for the surviving Waltons after that. The four-wheel drive vehicle was repossessed. Mrs. Walton, who had never worked since George was born, was seen on the bus every morning, heading into the city. She had got a job as a filing clerk in Etobicoke. The building company was the next to go—over-leveraged by debt and sold for a pittance to a rival builder.

George continued to rail in school, which is where I saw him most days, not wanting to visit the old house which was looking more unkempt and unloved by the day. Kids stayed away from George during those days because he walked around with a permanent sneer on his face. Finding the time to meet him also became difficult for George had got a job in the local grocery store, unpacking produce in the back room. I'd catch occasional glimpses of him whenever I shopped at the store: wearing a red apron, shucking back his hair as he piled cases on top of each other, wheeling them out on a dolly, stacking empty shelves and making a quick exit to the back room. I pretended not to notice him for I knew how embarrassed he was by the job he was doing.

"I'll teach those bastards," he said one rare day when we were chilling in the schoolyard. "They do not know what the word 'loyalty' means."

The following week, he announced that his mother was selling the house, it was too much to maintain, despite their dual incomes.

"That's the only source of my university tuition now."

"Where will you stay?"

"Mom's looking for an apartment on the west end, close to her work."

"We'll never see each other again."

"I'll be back." But he kept his face downcast when he said that.

That's when I decided to broach the subject with my parents about renting our basement to the Waltons.

It was after dinner one evening. Dad was at his customary seat in the living room, smoking and reading the newspaper. Mom was preparing for her class the next day.

"Why don't you rent Mrs. Walton the basement?" I said, surprised at my boldness.

Dad flicked his cigarette and said nothing.

Mom looked up from her work. "I don't like that woman. She smokes too much."

"She's lost her husband, Mom."

Mom put on her prim look, her eyes going aslant and her lips pursing. "Still, that is not an excuse. She's also a nosy parker."

Dad still hadn't said a word.

"What do you say, Dad?" I felt I was running out of options fast.

Without looking up, Dad turned a page in his newspaper and said, "Your mother is right. They are too much bother."

I was fed up with their intransigence. "What are you worried about, Dad? Your peace and quiet? And you, Mom—won't you get more money from the rent to pay for your gambling?"

Dad looked up sharply. "Gambling?"

Mom had her eyes averted. "Jeremy—how dare you. I will not have any more of this conversation."

But I had reached my limit at that point. "Go on, Mom—tell him—tell him about the chits and your 'church' visits. Where the priests are bookies and the audience is a bunch of bettors screaming at a pack of four-legged creatures running their asses off. Go on, tell him!"

"Rita," Dad was standing at his full, portly height now. "What the devil is going on here?"

I stormed out of the room, allowing them to sort it out. I stood just outside the door, listening to them tear into each other. They surprised me—the pent up reserve they had built around themselves had exploded—they were louder than the Waltons. I heard snippets like:

"You cashed the Canada Savings Bonds?"

"I can earn much higher returns than that—bloody swindling government."

"How dare you do that without telling me, Rita?"

"Why do I have to tell you everything—I earn a living too. And since when did you ever want to talk to me?"

"That goes for you too!"

Things got rowdier when I heard objects flying around the room and the crashing of furniture. I remembered George's words, " ... when they start throwing things at each other, that's when it gets weird."

Despite my apprehension, I wrung my hands together in glee, "At last—there's some life in this place. It will be good for their relationship ... " I was heading out the door, still disappointed in my inability to help George and his mother, when I heard my mother scream, "Jimmy—help! Your father ... !"

I rushed back into the living room, which was a mess of overturned furniture. My mother's lecture notes were littered all over, and the porcelain side lamp had fallen off its perch and shattered. My father lay on the floor, clutching his heart, and Mom was pulling her hair out, screaming, "Get an ambulance. Help!"

I visited my father in hospital once; he was unable to pull through the several heart attacks that came at him as he lay wired up in bed with all sorts of tubes sticking out of him. Mom had been unable to visit; she spent the days crying uncontrollably, something new in my experience, so I stayed away from her.

On that hospital visit, two days after his first heart attack, I sat opposite Dad in the visitor's chair, and we remained for a long time in the comfortable silence that had been symbolic of our relationship. I did not know what to say to him at a moment like this. I remember the clock ticking, the background sounds of nurses and orderlies walking the corridors, talking routinely about patient conditions; the occasional "code red" and "code blue" announcements over the PA system when everyone quickened their pace outside and voices dropped a notch.

I looked at Dad's gnarled hand; one day I guess I would end up like him. Despite my efforts to be different, and despite different genes flowing in my body, I was probably going to die like this. His fingers started to twitch, and I rose from my chair and inched closer to the bed. He raised his hand to the oxygen mask and made to pull it off. I panicked. Should I call the nurse? Then his other hand gripped me and pulled me closer. He had managed to get the mask partially off his face. "Jimmy ... .Jimmy ... " his voice rasped.

I leaned over him. His dry breath, with a trace of stale nicotine in it, was weak but pleasant. "Jimmy ... "

"Yes, Dad?"

"Let it out, Jimmy."

"Let what out?"

"Don't ... don't keep it inside ... "

"Mom's crying at home. Is that good?"

"She crying? That's good. She never cried ... "

"You never cried either, Dad."

"Yes. A shame. Couldn't, you see. Wouldn't let us, in my time ... "

"Should I cry too?"

But he began running out of breath, and the mask slipped back into place. He sucked deeply on it. I never had the chance to speak to him again.

George was waiting for me outside the hospital, sitting on a bench in the driveway, throwing pebbles at an empty pop can. I was surprised to see him show up. I hadn't seen him since he told me he was moving out of Scarborough.

"How's he doing?" he asked.

"Not very well." I took a seat on the bench next to him.

"I came as soon as I heard," he said.

"Thanks."

"I heard they had a row."

"Word gets around fast."

"I dropped by your place. Your mom told me. She also told me she was sorry. I didn't know what she was talking about."

"Mom's growing up," I said.

"You'd better go to her. She was breaking down all the time."

"That's good for her. My dad told me not to keep it in. That's only real lesson I learned from him."

"It takes a while to miss a dad. I'm still not over mine. I felt he robbed us." He connected with the pop bottle this time and sent it spinning across the pavement.

"I asked them if you and your mom could rent our basement."

"You did?"

"Yeah."

"It didn't work out, I guess."

"No." I didn't want to tell him that my father lay in a comatose condition partly because of George and his mom. Why complicate things at this stage?

George put his arm around my shoulder. "It's okay. My mom's found a place. We are moving at the end of the month. Thanks for trying."

"Everyone I know and care about is leaving."

"Your dad's not gone yet. Mine is. I'll be in touch."

"No you won't. People get busy."

"You've still got your mom, Jimmy. Like I've got mine."

I rose. This conversation was getting morbid. "I guess I'd better go and console her then, eh?"

"They get hysterical and incoherent. Stay the course, it gets better. And try to let it out. I did it by getting angry. I'm still angry."

We headed towards his old car. "I'll give you a ride home."

We drove home at a reckless speed, with George yelling out the window at motorists who were "driving like silly bastards." At one point, he tailgated a nervous motor cyclist for fifteen minutes, until the poor fellow ducked into a side street. He honked his horn liberally while I looked around nervously for cops.

"This is how I get rid of my anger," he chuckled as we drove past his house with its "For Sale" sign on the lawn and pulled into mine.

"Remember," he said, "You've got your mom. And you've always got me."

Three—Early Battles

Jimmy

It was a time of political turmoil when I entered university in Toronto in late 1968. It was a time of being infatuated with a swinger Prime Minister who stood for the noble freedoms that were yet to exact an economic toll on our country—a fertile period in the universities and in the minds of my generation.

The ferment continued through the following two years as I pursued my first degree, a BA. I had involuntarily fallen into the trap of following my father. I felt I would make a good English professor; my father's proclivity to read incessantly, write elegantly and hide behind the artificial world of academia seemed to fit me well. I couldn't bear to be in the midst of conflict like the dashing Mr. Trudeau.

Then the unthinkable happened: separatists kidnapped a foreign diplomat, and a minister was found dead in a car trunk. The air was filled with uncertainty. People talked in huddles all over the city. *This is not our Canada, this cannot be happening to us!*

I remember that day well. For it was on that very day, during the heart of the October Crisis, as I walked between lectures on the campus grounds, that a voice hailed me, "Jeremy! Jimmy Spence!"

I swung around to see a long haired hippy walking towards me, a wide smile creasing his face.

"George Walton!" I exclaimed, the last couple of years falling off me.

"Sorry, I never kept in touch," he said, shaking my hand.

I grinned, relieved for some familiarity in the midst of a world turning unfamiliar. "Neither did I. People get busy."

He had filled out and his long hair was supplemented with thick sideburns. He was also wearing thin rimmed circular glasses, but they seemed more for effect than for sight: he took them off and tucked them away in his pocket.

He punched me playfully. "Look at you! God, it's good to see you."

"Likewise," I said, and meant it too.

"I transferred from York. The women are better here," he said chuckling, looking at two female students who were hurrying past, noses in the air, reacting to his hungry look. "What are you taking?"

"English. You? Sexology?"

"Politics."

"I should have guessed."

"It's a great time to be in politics."

"You end up in the back of a car trunk."

"Ha, ha!"

I was happy to see him. We agreed to meet in the student pub that evening to catch up.

Over several beers that evening, amidst jostling students staring at the news from Montreal, we caught up on scraps of our lives.

"I've joined the provincial socialists—youth wing," he said, as we watched grainy footage of troops patrolling Vieux-Montreal.

"I thought you were a capitalist?"

"My father was. See where that got him? They dropped him like stock in a bankrupt company."

"You'll be up against stiff competition. The conservatives have a lock in Ontario."

"We'll see. I'm not a total leftie like some of the guys in our youth wing. You might say I'm an enlightened capitalist." He gestured at the TV. "Everyone is over-reacting, even Trudeau. I like his lifestyle, not his politics."

We watched the news blare away. Everyone had a viewpoint about words like "bleeding hearts" that the PM had just uttered that morning.

George shook his head. "People are such wimps. How's your mother?"

I felt comfortable unburdening. Perhaps it was the beer, but I wouldn't have done this with anyone else. "She took early retirement this year. Dad left some money, in my name, which paid for my tuition. He must have distrusted her all along—about the gambling and all. I still live at home with her—it saves on rent. We see each other around meal times, and then too, we don't talk much. It seems that I have substituted for my father. How is *your* mother?"

"Passed away—last year."

"Shit, I didn't know ... "

"We didn't keep in touch, remember?"

"But you could have called me."

"Could have, should have, what does it matter now? She took our drop in status hard. They get weird in widowhood—mothers. No more enigma, or challenge, just a tired old woman. She died of a broken heart. She had a good life insurance policy, though."

George and I had engaged in a couple of phone calls after he and his mother moved out of our neighbourhood two years ago, a couple of weeks after my father passed away. But one of us was always busy, and getting together had been difficult. After a while, it was easier to pretend that we would call each other one day, and not do it. And the longer it took, the guiltier I felt, and the easier it was not to call.

"Those who fall off the treadmill need help. Like our mothers." George said, his face tightening in suppressed emotion. "I support Plewes's call for rent control. That's another reason I joined his party."

"You are sure it's not for revenge?"

"That too. Those conservatives have been in power for too long."

"You are too young to be an MPP. Isn't there a pecking order?"

"There is. And I am considered a 'high potential.'"

"What does that mean?"

"Progressive positions up the party ladder over time. I am on the organizing committee for the elections next year. I've got my sights to run in 1975. Heck, Plewes first got elected at twenty. And he didn't quite make it through university either."

George's eyes were aglow with a fierce light as he recounted his plans. He had it all mapped out, finish university next year and get a teaching appointment. That would give him the latitude for his political activity, and the credentials.

"You should come out to a party meeting one of these days. Plewes is a charismatic candidate for leader."

"You are pretty serious about politics, then?"

"Remember my desire to become the Prime Minister of Canada?"

"Yeah," I smiled at the memory.

"Bet you, I'll do a better job than him," he motioned to the screen where Trudeau was making his "Just watch me!" statement in the umpteenth replay.

It was more than a year later when I attended one of George's meetings—during the party's provincial leadership campaign. In the party echelons, Plewes was opposing Saxon, the ultra-leftist leader of the Muffin splinter group within the socialists. Many students were interested in Muffin, as in anything counter-culture, and it was a debate on how "left" should one go. George seemed the lone opponent of the pro-leftist student group at the university and had warned me that the session was going to be a fierce one.

I sat in a corner toward the back of the packed auditorium comprised of students of all parties who had come out mostly for an afternoon's entertainment. Two podia faced each other on the stage. George was in one, his hair slicked back and tied in a ponytail, moustache and sideburns neatly trimmed for the occasion, he was wearing a blue blazer and party tie. Mike Thomas, a hairy two hundred fifty pound, deep voiced, fourth year student and Muffin supporter, was at the other podium. As proceedings heated up, I doubted the views expressed ever reflected the conduct or beliefs of Plewes and Saxon, but it was entertaining.

The two debaters sparred with each other for the first thirty minutes, rhyming off facts to support their arguments: George was advocating a free economy with controls only for the disadvantaged like widows, orphans, the sick and disenfranchised, while Mike went full bore for nationalization of corporations, retaining a hundred percent control in Canadian hands and driving out foreigners, particularly the Americans. All this was pretty ho-hum stuff and there was much chair scraping as people constantly headed for the vending machines, or to the washrooms, or for smokes, some even headed home.

Suddenly Mike lashed out, "Foreigners control this country like it is another colony. Nothing has changed since the days of imperialism."

George shot back. "And what is wrong with imperialism? Would you have the Canada of today if it had been peopled by a bunch of foraging nomads?"

"Sir, you are being racist."

"Bullshit. Answer my question, Thomas."

"I am talking about modern multi-national corporations, not imperialist states."

"They are just another form of the other, I'll grant you. Our largest automakers have economies larger than the old imperialist states. And their 'empires' stretch over more of the earth than the old one that Queen Victoria reigned over."

"They also suck our capital away. We haven't had a balance of payment surplus since God knows when."

"But would you trade that for jobs and a lifestyle that you aspire to, Thomas? Does a balance of payments bother you? Does it bother Joe Blow on the street?"

I noticed that the format of letting each speaker make his point for a period of time before the other countered had been dropped by the moderator, perhaps deliberately so, because the chair scraping had stopped, and audience members were craning their necks from side to side as each verbal broadside was launched by the debaters.

Mike Thomas looked down at his papers for a moment, regrouped and came in from another angle: "Capitalism unleashes the worst excesses on the subjugated masses. Look at the Korean 'pleasure women' in Japan, and the same thing happening now in Thailand and Vietnam with the Americans—"

"Oh sure," George shot back. "And have they been keeping their cocks at bay in Russia?" A guffaw rippled over the audience as people exhaled the tension and began to enjoy this repartee. This was more like what they had come out for. Even a couple of wolf-whistles broke out on the side.

"Or in China?" George was going in for the kill. "Or the orphans in Romania—whose bloody children are those? People are going to have sex no matter what regime they live under. We happen to put our sexual exploits in the media— the ultras keep theirs in their bedrooms."

"We are not talking specifically about sex ... " Mike Thomas tried to reign in the discussion; but there was no stopping George who had now left the podium, microphone in hand, pacing in front of his opponent.

"Why not sex, Thomas? You brought up the topic. Why? Aren't *you* getting enough?"

The auditorium burst out into laughter.

"I beg your pardon?" Thomas went red in the face and looked pleadingly towards the moderator who finally decided to step in.

"Mr. Walton, please state your point without insulting Mr. Thomas. And do you mind addressing the audience from your podium, please?"

George held his ground and addressed the audience "Mr. Moderator, my esteemed colleague here has relegated capitalism to unbridled and corruptible sex—"

"I never said anything of the sort!" Thomas yelled back.

"Then what's your point?" George held his hands open to the audience with a question on his face.

"Never mind," Thomas said in disgust and looked down at his papers for more ammunition. "This is a futile argument that you spin off into absurdities."

"Let me give you issues that the present government dismisses as absurdities, Mr. Thomas, and those are what I propose we press for in this election, and not trade in absurdist allegations of free enterprise fuelling sex. Rent control, that's what I am preaching for here, so that poor widows and single mothers have roofs over their heads. Landlords make money hand over fist, there is absolutely no reason that rents go up arbitrarily in this city every year. And here's another for you, Mr. Thomas, my father was a builder, and every time he climbed that scaffolding he took his life in his hands. If he fell, he could not get help from anyone—no one gave a rat's ass. Workplace safety is pathetic in this province—that is something I would fight for and not worry about unbridled sex. In fact, America is peaceful these days because they are 'making love, not war' at Woodstock and other love-ins. We need more love, Mr. Thomas. More sex, Mr. Thomas, not less of it!"

The room broke into cheers as George walked back to his podium, resumed his seat and glared pugnaciously at Mike Thomas.

The moderator mercifully called for a break at that point, and I left the hall knowing that a victor, albeit a popular one, had already been declared.

I could also see why George was considered a 'high potential'. He was parroting the same platform issues of the moderates under Plewes.

A month later, Plewes won the party leadership, and George was 'in'.

***

Atahualpa

An extract from *Conquistador*—a novel by George Walton

Francisco Pizarro was tired from days of marching over the cordillera before arriving in this lush valley. Like in Tumbez, the natives had obligingly vanished from their city, Caxamalca, giving his paltry band of a hundred seventy-seven men the run of the place. He stood in the Plaza de Armas beside his lieutenant, De Soto, and brother Hernando, squinting against the occasional glint from the chainmail of his men who were hiding strategically around the plaza and waiting for him to drop his handkerchief. Pathetically outnumbered, surprise was their only advantage, and guns. They had attended mass that morning, and the men had been given an extra large breakfast; now they longed to kill.

And now, Atahualpa, King of the Inca, and his entourage were outside the gates of Caxamalca, invited to dinner by the Spaniards.

The Inca were colourful in tunics of white and red; the vanguard swept the path in front of their ruler and his party with large tree branches. Three battalions followed, from among the tens of thousands of troops encamped outside the city, littering the plain. They stood tall, signifying noble birth, and their breastplates and helmets glinted, casting Franscisco's troops' tell-tale signs into shadow. There were five, perhaps six thousand Inca in the square as the sun began to go over the city's ramparts.

The press of humanity parted and Atahualpa appeared on a throne borne upon a litter with the magnificent plumes of his diadem fanning the air around him. His haughty manner demanded privilege and obeisance as his birthright. His men bowed their heads in his presence, and he squinted quizzically at these white men who merely stared him down.

Friar Vicente, who had conducted mass that morning, stepped between the Inca and the Spaniards, and with raised cross in one hand and a Bible in the other, said, "It is God's will that you be the friend of our commander."

Atahualpa shot back through his interpreter, "Your men have mistreated us. You have stolen from our storehouses."

Vicente protested at this affront, stamping his foot in the dusty square, going so far as to say, "You will submit to the authority of the King of Spain, become a Christian and abandon your idolatry of the sun that sinks each day, unlike our God in Heaven."

"I will never be a Christian," was the translated reply. "Your master may be my friend, and we accept his offer of hospitality, but I will never give up my god." Atahualpa inclined his head towards the setting sun.

Francisco seized his opportunity while the priest and king were locked in ideological debate. Pulling his tunic around him and drawing his sword, he darted across the square, waving his handkerchief.

Arriving at the Inca's litter, he pulled the startled king off his perch and yelled "Santiago," the code for "shoot at will."

The plaza exploded in gunfire, coming from all directions, picking off the Inca like dazed ducks. Pausing to reload was the only determinant of how many died how fast. All the while, Francisco held on to his prize hostage, who was not as strong as his royal bluster had projected.

The Spanish cavalry emerged in the wake of their guns, slashing left and right, yelling, spilling blood that flew across the square as heads parted bodies and rolled in the dust. The trapped Inca tried to retreat to the gate which had closed behind them. The surprise was total.

The nobles in Atahualpa's entourage made one brave attempt to surround their leader and fend off the Spaniards but they too were mowed down relentlessly by the pressing cavalry.

The square fell quiet as the life of the Inca was taken out of it. The groans of the dying were relentlessly extinguished by a slashing sabre or a fired gun, or a horse hoof grinding down on bone.

Atahualpa was led away into captivity, in shock, his feathers drooping and trailing behind him like broken wings. His troops outside the walls began retreating in disarray.

"Remember," a triumphant Francisco called after him. "Supper is at eight. I keep my appointments."

***

Jimmy

I met Denise at the student exhibition put on by the university arts guild in '72. Various Nuevo-modern techniques were on display: print media mixed with painting mixed with photography. The students were experimenting with many forms and had ended up confusing everyone. Visitors surrounded exhibitors in small clusters around the cavernous double gymnasium turned exhibition hall to try and understand these hideous creations that were supposed to be appreciated as art. And of course, no one wanted to be making premature judgements, in case the next Picasso was to be found among these amateurs.

I had come on George's invitation; he was one of the organizers that year. I hadn't seen him since we had parted for the summer holidays, and I had been busy since the new semester began a month ago. I thought this would be a great way to catch up.

I found him holding forth to an awed group of visitors on the importance of stretching conventional boundaries of what we had hitherto considered the confines of modern art. I don't know when or where he had developed this new-found interest. Despite his many other talents, George hadn't held a paintbrush in his life.

It looked like it would be awhile before I could capture George for myself, so I strolled about the exhibits. The Quebec crisis was old hat by now, Vietnam was news. Yes, hideous they were: images of half-naked bodies, dismembered body parts juxtaposed with pictures of the Indo-China war, and rock musicians with shaggy hair; we were in the throes of Flower Power and bell bottoms. The colours were dark blues, maroons, reds and black.

Then a section to the side caught my attention. A string of conventional paintings of working class people in various day-to-day settings: a man on the subway, a woman breastfeeding her daughter in the park while a dog pees on a flagpole nearby, children trailing backpacks in the dust and walking down country roads after school, the apprehension of a middle-aged man sitting in a doctor's waiting room. The figures were well-proportioned, the colours warm and optimistic despite the situations being depicted—this was a relief from the doomsday scenarios adorning the rest of the room. I was drawn to these paintings because there was no one milling around them and because they got me away from their melodramatic cousins.

"Ah, I see you have hit upon the secret payload," George had pulled himself away and was heading over to me. "Aren't they beautiful?"

"They are a breather from the blood and guts. Who's bold enough to exhibit this stuff alongside the gore?"

"Ah, that was my decision. I wanted to give Denise a backdrop to shine against."

"Denise?"

"I'll introduce you. Come along." He dragged me over to the other end of the room where an artist was sketching one of the visitors. As we strolled over, the study was just rising; he inspected the sketch as the artist put away her pencils, then fished in his wallet for change, paid her and departed, looking satisfied at his likeness on paper.

"Denise, I'd like you to meet my old friend Jeremy."

I looked into her blue eyes as she stood up to shake hands with me; liquid, probing, and the warm smile that parted her wide cheeks. Her hand was cool and gentle, melting in mine. She was dressed in a loose white tent shirt open at the neck that revealed a soft cleavage of milky white flesh, down which plunged a giant string of black beads. She shook back thick, waist long strands of blond hair. "Hello ... Jeremy."

I fell in love on sight.

I struggled for words. "Hi!" I managed.

"Shall I sketch you?" she asked.

"Why ... yes!" I thought that was a brilliant idea. Now I would get to admire this vision without being accused of staring.

George intervened. "Jeremy was marvelling at your paintings, honey. I told you it was a brilliant idea to be in this show."

She smiled and her mouth revealed pearly teeth, evenly placed. "I'm a traditionalist. Thank you, Jeremy. I am glad that someone appreciates conservatism in this changing world."

"It's Jimmy." I had regained my composure. "And yes, I would like my picture sketched."

"Sit here on this stool, then. George, why don't you run along and try and sell some of my paintings." She took me by the hand, sat me down on the stool, and returned to her pencils. George stood hesitantly, as if unwilling to leave me with her. She shooed him away, smiling. "I don't get many customers, George."

"I'll catch up with you later, Jimmy," George turned around slowly to return to the crush of visitors. I think he looked back a couple of times but I had already dismissed him from my mind; my eyes were riveted on Denise, on her graceful hands as they picked up a pencil, the way she composed herself, staring at me, absorbing me as she prepared to render my essence on paper.

We talked as she sketched. She was a fine arts student in her final year; raised by a single mother living in Montreal, she was heavily leveraged on grants and student loans. It was easy talking to her. I found myself telling her all about me. I had never done this before with other women, it had always been some safe, academic subject in which we found mutual interest to focus our conversation. But with Denise it was different; I couldn't put my finger on it, but with her I felt safe.

The best part of that sitting was when she would look up from her work, stare straight at me, study my contours and suck me into some space in her mind where she could remold me and bring out my finer features for the world to see. In this exercise she was placing me on the pedestal that no one had ever placed me before.

"I'm also an only child," I offered.

"So's George," she said. "Are we spoilt children?"

I laughed. I felt light. I wanted to stay there, long after the exhibition closed for the day and the lights went out. I imagined her and me alone in this cavernous place, shrinking it to just the space between us, she sketching, me admiring her.

"There, almost done," she said, giving her head a shake and looking satisfied. "You are a good study. Very patient."

You are mesmerizing. You immobilize me. "Why aren't you with your paintings?" I asked.

"I'm a horrible salesperson. Besides George thought it would be best if the artist was unseen. Prompt curiosity, if any, you know."

"Yours are the best paintings in the room. You should know that."

She blushed. "Thank you. Not many say that, other than George. Here—come look at your picture." She extended the sketch to me and stood back as I surveyed it.

I caught my breath. Staring back at me was a handsome man with long shoulder length hair, curling along the collar. The thick moustache (shaved now) curved over the lips making me look very masculine, although I had always battled the stoop I began to develop while young and which now permanently distinguished me. My eyes exuded confidence and the smile on my face was alien to me.

"The smile ... do I look like that?"

She laughed. "It's in your face. Just under the surface. You keep it concealed, I can tell. I took creative liberty there. Not something I do usually."

I must have thrown off all caution at that point. "Can I see you after the exhibition? Go for a drink? Talk about art?"

"Oh, slow down!" she said. "I've just met you."

"It's like I've known you all my life. You've been hiding from me, like my smile."

Her face grew serious. "George and I are dating. I'm sure he would not approve."

I looked down at my picture and it helped keep my eyes averted from her. Inside, I was frothing. *George, George— why do you always beat me to the finish line?*

***

An extract from the novel *Conquistador*—by George Walton

"If you set me free, I will give you a room filled with gold," the promise of the captive Inca king rang through his slumber and Francisco woke with a start. What was he doing sleeping at such a momentous time? Then he remembered the Inca woman, Atahualpa's sister, who had been in his cot earlier in the afternoon; he had poured wine over her burnished body and lapped every drop, ingesting her heavy musk. He had meant to woo and rouse her that way, but she had remained detached, an ice princess. He would continue his campaign on her, later. The conquest of the Inca had to be complete.

The wine and the forced lovemaking had put him to sleep. She must have slipped out of the chamber afterwards and was probably licking her hurt with the other Inca women. As he buttoned his tunic and slipped into his black cloak, he regretted what he had to do next.

"They are amassing an army and will set upon you. Thirty thousand Caribs within their ranks will eat you alive. You have to cut off the head. Kill Atahualpa!" Voices of his lieutenants including the trusted Almagro, or just the voices in his head?

But all was well, Hernando was returning from Cusco, the Inca capital, with gold enough to fill several rooms. The elusive gold had finally been discovered, and Atahualpa had paid his dues, despite the rumours about his duplicity. Almagro, Francisco's trusted commander had arrived from Panama with two hundred reinforcements. All was well, indeed. Atahualpa was now dispensable. The trial on charges of treason and fratricide went swiftly, for there was no one to speak in the Inca's defense.

Torch light flickered in the square as Francisco stepped out. A tall stake stood in the centre. Atahualpa was tied to it, naked, except for a loin cloth, with faggots piled up around him. Soldiers guarded the perimeter, and a silence had descended that made the sweat break out under Francisco's tunic. Tears glinted in the condemned king's eyes and they seemed to plead, "Why are you doing this to me when I gave you everything you asked for?"

Francisco averted his gaze from those tearful eyes, grateful for the gloom and the erratic firelight. The Inca's intelligence had surprised him during these months of captivity. Atahualpa had learned chess and cards, and his ability to read and write Spanish had quickly surpassed Francisco's.

Friar Vicente stepped forward again, more confident than he had been during a similar meeting months ago in this very place. "Do you renounce idolatry and embrace Christ?"

The Inca hung his head.

"If you do so, you will be spared burning and die like a Christian."

The beaten Inca sighed and nodded imperceptibly.

The monk poured water on the prisoner and performed the rite of baptism. "May God have mercy upon your soul, my son."

Francisco caught a flicker of gold amidst the crowd. The Princess in her royal costume and gold regalia, flanked by her personal servants, was in attendance, determined not to hide from the fate of her people. A wave of pride overtook his gloom; he had conquered the Land of Gold, all the proof was before him.

He stepped forward and signalled towards the executioner. "Now, you may use the garrotte."

***

George

He sprawled on the grass and looked at her. She was special, not like the other women he had bedded. In fact he had not bedded Denise yet. It was like he was saving her for a special occasion. Even Jimmy had a crush on her, which made her all the more desirable.

It was a warm day for early fall. Leaves littered the hill they were lying on at Edwards Gardens, overlooking the old water wheel spinning in the fast moving creek. The park was almost empty as schools were still in session; only a small seniors group hovered by the limestone statue of the lady with an urn on her shoulder and her other hand eternally pouring from a pitcher into a petal shaped basin at her feet.

He had managed to spirit Denise away between classes at the university to grab the moment. She wanted to paint his picture against this backdrop of wildflowers and rhododendrons in the valley.

Her paints were strewn about the ground, and her face was a study in concentration as she dabbed colour onto the easel between glances his way.

He lay back and daydreamed.

"Stay still," she said. "You are the most difficult study."

"Sorry," he said and shifted weight.

She would be perfect as a politician's wife—beautiful, demure, caring, artistic, and compassionate. She accentuates my unique position among the dull and stodgy party faithful.

"It's a perfect day," he murmured, teasing. He wanted to test her limits. "A day for passion."

She arched an eyebrow. "Oh no, Mr. Walton—I know what you are thinking. You are not getting into my panties."

He could almost feel her biting off the last word from that sentence " *... yet.*"

"*When* do I get into your panties, dear lady?"

She didn't answer but made a half-hearted effort at concentrating on the painting.

She wants me, but does not want to initiate the move. This is delightful!

"What's the thing you want most in life now, Denise?"

"Doing what I am doing right now."

"Being with me?"

"Painting." She looked up immediately, unsure if she had hurt his feelings, and then quickly added. "You are very pleasant company too."

"Thank you." He was enjoying this dalliance: a long drawn out act of foreplay, if you could call it that. It was so delicious that he did not want to eat, instead just look at the treats. She was a box of chocolates that would begin to lose its excitement the moment the first bite was taken and the mystery transferred from the visual to the sensual.

"Will you support me in the next election?"

"I didn't know you were running. Isn't it a bit early for you? Politicians are usually middle aged farts. At least, the ones I have met."

"I have to run. I'm the only one they salvaged from the youth wing. Plewes is going to show those blasted Tories a thing or two in the next election."

"Winning is important to you then?"

"There is no other option. I don't participate just to say I showed up. Winning is everything."

She looked up and stared closely at him. "I wonder how I can capture that in you, George."

"Capture what?"

"Capture the killer instinct that lurks behind the façade of a suave lady's man. And the fear that drives that instinct. It's important that it comes out in this portrait, otherwise I would not have done justice to you."

"Well, you are the artist. Show me."

"You frighten me, George Walton. Sometimes I think I walk a tightrope with you."

"Well, we haven't been out much. If you'll let me take you out more, perhaps you could judge that better for yourself."

"That's what I am worried about. The more I find out about you, the more it frightens me."

She began putting away her paints. "I think I have done enough painting for today. Take me for a walk around the gardens. I want to see the all-season tree."

"You didn't answer my question."

"I am not sure I have the strength to support you emotionally, George. You are a like a volcano—those who are close to you get burned in the lava."

"Well I am flattered. Talk to my friend ... our friend ... Jeremy. He's been around for a long time with me. He hasn't been burned."

He rose and came towards her. He took her around the waist and pulled her towards him. She resisted strongly and pulled away. "Don't. We shouldn't have had that conversation. I can't go from cold to hot just like that."

He pulled her again, and this time she lost her balance and fell into his arms. He crushed his mouth on hers, probing with his tongue pulling hers out, entangling his in hers. His passion was unquenchable and radiant. She melted under his assault, and they kissed with abandon. When he let her go suddenly, he saw her lips reaching thirstily for his, desire unleashed. The seniors had stopped watching the limestone lady and were watching them instead.

Denise wiped her lips and shuddered, turning away. "I told you, George Walton, you frighten me!"

"See, you can go between extremes," he said, the rakish smile on his face turning to a resonating laugh that echoed across the grounds, as he cradled her waist and walked towards the gnarled all-season tree at the top of the hill.

***

Nov 15th 1972

Darling Mother,

I trust the new apartment is working out for you. I miss you and am looking forward to spending Christmas with you, even though I may have to put up with Stella and her family.

I can't wait until I finish university and start making some real money, so I could repay you for all you've done for me. I'm getting you a separate phone—that's what I am going to do first. Raising me was no mean feat, especially when the teachers said you had a 'gifted' child on your hand—one that had to be trained in the fine art of painting, with the best teachers that your money could barely buy. Yet, you persevered.

I am really excited, because my art professor introduced me to a guy who runs a gallery in Yorkville. This gallery owner, Fred, likes my pastoral scenes and has offered to display "Dragging Books on Country Roads" and "Breastfeeding while the Idle Dog Pees," given their off-kilter themes rendered in conventional style. He says the waiting rooms of specialist doctors' offices have demand for these paintings, as they alleviate stress for patients. Very soon, I'll be making my own money. Beats waiting tables.

Another source of my excitement these days (and also my consternation) is the two men who have entered my life, almost simultaneously. Yes, yes, remind me—I took an oath to focus on my studies after my long relationship with Henri ended. Henri was a bad experience—going nowhere, no ambition except for his rock band that could only manage gigs in nightclubs in Montreal. Even then, I knew he would end up with an alcohol problem. Leaving you and Montreal to come here to university was palatable, because I was also leaving him. Chalk it down to the experience of a lonely and naïve high-school girl, who was then, as now, your beloved daughter.

But to the new men: now make sure you read this whole letter before you pass judgement. The first one's name is George Walton. Oh, he fancies himself—loves colonial history. He is overconfident, and the girls here love him, which makes me jealous—so I must have feelings for him, as much as I pretend not to. He is six feet tall, athletically built, long wavy hair that blows beautifully in the wind, usually sports a five-day scruff of beard when he's not out campaigning. Oh yes—the campaigning—he wants to be the next prime minister. Serious! And he has such fire and passion when he engages in debates, that I think he *will* one day. Mother, George is passion personified. I am scared to get too involved with him, not knowing what cliff I will fall over. And yet, there is a vulnerable side to him—just like you told me my father had, before he ran away with your best friend. Deep inside, George seems to be alone and wants to be surrounded with activity and people. I suspect he also fears women despite his bravado. I suspect he fears me as I do him. I wrestle with trying to paint his picture and feel that I cannot yet do justice to it. Tell me I am making a fool of myself over George, Mummy ...

The other guy is George's best friend, Jimmy Spence. Now, if ever there was a detached, loyal one—it's Jimmy. He's a lanky guy, even taller than George. A very organized person, his digs are spotless, while George's are a mess. Don't worry, I haven't been sleeping with either of them—just visiting, as one is supposed to do with one's batch buddies. Jimmy is studying to be an English professor. Every time he sees me he invites me out, but I keep putting him off, because I feel we might spend the whole evening looking at the sunset and not saying a word. He is comfortable in his silence, but his eyes are sad, and I feel there is a whole world of emotion bubbling to get to the surface. He's the kind of guy you could call on a whim and ask to help carry your bags home from the grocery store. He will also thank you for giving him the opportunity to bear your burden. Another very difficult subject to paint, although he is very pleased with the sketches I have done of him. He thinks I make him out to be better than he is. He would make a good husband I think, to some dull woman.

So there you are, Mother Dearest, the men in my life!

Please send me your thoughts, for you know how much I value them, even though I may not take your advice. How can I? I am your daughter, remember—I am supposed to rebel.

Lots of love and hugs!
Denise

***

Diego de Almagro

An extract from *Conquistador*—a novel by George Walton

Hernando looked haggard as he went down on one knee in front of his brother Francisco.

"The journey from Castile was long, this time?" asked Francisco, looking down at his kneeling brother from his elevated chair in the governing chamber.

"Yes. Many died."

"I heard the emperor knighted you." Francisco did not wish to dwell on the casualties. Conquest involved loss, and the weak perished.

Hernando bowed in acknowledgement.

"Was the emperor happy with his fifth share?"

Hernando straightened up. The elder of the two brothers, and born of the official family lineage, Hernando still showed deference towards his younger half-brother on political matters, respecting Francisco as the true discoverer of Peru. "His Excellency was very happy. And lavish with his gifts."

Hernando fished out a parchment from his coat and extended it towards his brother, then withdrew it, realizing that his brother was still semi-illiterate. He had been away from Peru for too long, or the return journey from Spain had taken its toll on his memory. "Emperor Charles has appointed you Governor of Peru."

A look of triumph crossed Francisco's face. "About time."

"And he has recognized the efforts of Diego de Almagro as well, conferring the honour of 'Don' upon him and giving him the lands to the south."

Francisco's face darkened. "What!"

"Yes, my brother. Up to six hundred miles to the south of your lands."

"But that is impossible. Almagro will claim Cusco as well."

"Is he there now?"

"Yes, I sent him to deal with the Inca while I built here in Ciudad de Los Reyes."

"He will know about this grant already as I had some of his men among my troops, and they made haste for Cusco as soon as our ship arrived in port."

"I must send a message to Juan and Gonzalo to withstand him if he gets too ambitious."

"In fairness, Francisco, our brothers are no match for Don Diego."

Francisco rose from his chairs and paced the room. Hernando was right. Don Diego needed to be lured with a prize far greater than what the emperor had granted. The lands of Chile, further south from Peru, that's where he would send Almagro; dangle the golden carrot in front of his old ally's fading eyes...

***

George

It was graduation night, class of '73, five years of university and two degrees behind him, he was glad to be moving from the benches to the lectern in the classroom; he had secured a teaching position in a college nearby, all in keeping with his plan.

One piece of unfinished work remained: what to do about Denise? They had dallied with each other over this last school year, igniting passions but never consummating, fanning them like smouldering fires that had now, for him, turned into an active volcano.

He had also seen her go out occasionally with Jimmy; perhaps she was trying to make him jealous. But he never felt threatened by Jimmy. In fact, Jimmy took the pressure off so he could indulge in his baser dalliances. He had not wanted to bed Denise like he had done so many others here on campus, but now the other women were becoming less appealing.

Just last week, when he had visited the new ethics professor in her apartment across the city, he had imagined making love to Denise instead. The professor had very strong "ethics" when it came to sex: woman on top. This did not sit well with him, as Denise would never be this aggressive, so he reversed position and conjured up Denise's face beneath him. The professor sensed this betrayal, got mad and called him "an immature prick." Angered, he slapped the professor, spun her around and entered her from behind holding her forcibly down, riding her doggie style. She went ballistic when he broke away, and began throwing things at him. He calmly finished his drink, picked up his clothes and went out into the hallway, shutting the door in her face. Absent-mindedly he began dressing, only to be disturbed by a neighbour who stepped out of the elevator at that point, shrieked and dropped her grocery bag, then hugged the wall and scurried into her apartment, a look of horror on her face.

Yes, he was getting bored with the other women.

He entered the hotel and headed towards the ballroom following the signs leading to the graduation party. There was a charity casino theme this year, and he had rented a tuxedo with a black bowtie and cummerbund to match. Denise had said she was arriving alone and would meet him there. Instead he met Jimmy at the door, looking spiffy in a similar tuxedo but white in colour, his beard trimmed for the occasion.

"Meeting someone?" he asked.

"Yes," Jimmy replied, looking nervously about him towards the doorways through which chattering graduates were entering the ballroom, ushering in streams of perfumes and scents of various kinds, raising the decibel level by the second.

"What have you done with the hairstyle?"

"Getting ready for the real world," Jimmy shouted back, still looking about him.

"Buy you a drink, Jimmy?" Blackjack and poker tables lined the left side of the room with very few takers this early in the evening; the roulette wheel and baccarat table on the opposite end, however, were starting to attract guests. The bar and the finger food table in the centre were being liberally patronized.

"She's late," Jimmy said looking at his watch.

"Didn't know you had a date?"

"Denise agreed to meet me."

"She said the same to me."

They looked at each other. Jimmy swore in exasperation. "This has been going on far too long, George. Why don't you lay off her? You've got so many other flings in your bag."

"She's the best, Jimmy—you know it."

"What will it take to get you to leave now?" Jimmy rarely lost his calm, but his breathing was laboured and there was pain etched all over his face.

"How about a game of poker? Winner take all?"

"Damn you! I'll have that drink first."

***

Jimmy

I don't know why I agreed to the poker game with George. Maybe I felt the stakes were so high, I had to beat him, for once, especially today. We took our drinks and headed towards a table where the dealer was playing by himself.

"Business slow?" George chimed.

"Seems like it." The dealer studied us. "You boys wanna play?"

"Yeah. But we would like a twist on the rules. We are going for one game between him and me—winner take all. You keep dealing each time we discard, until one of us calls."

The dealer shook his head and sighed. "You guys betting on a girl?"

"How do you know?" I asked.

"See it all the time. Kinda sad when women become chips."

"Deal," George said, slipping him a ten-dollar bill. "We don't have much time."

"Call a wild card," said the dealer.

"Twos," George said. "You okay with that, Jimmy?"

I nodded.

The first five cards I got were king of diamonds, king of hearts, two of clubs, three and four of spades. I was looking good—sitting on three of a kind with the wild card to help.

I looked at George; he had a scowl on his face. I was tempted to call, but George was a wily card player. I knew he was bluffing. I threw my three and four of spades. George discarded one card only. *Shit.*

My replacement cards were two sevens. I was now on a full house. Better do it now than later, I thought, and was about to tap when I saw George grinning.

"What was that line by Kipling, Jimmy, 'If you can risk all your life's possessions on one game of pitch and toss?' I buy that line, you know."

"I prefer 'a fool and his money are soon parted'— Bridges, circa sixteenth century."

"What about Pizarro and Almagro duking it out over Cusco? Read that part of Inca history, Jimmy?"

"You boys finished with the literature bit and ready to call?" asked the dealer who was now looking anxiously at a fresh bunch of guests who had crowded around.

"I'll call," George said, and I felt a clutch at my heart. How could he do better than a full house in just two serves?

"Lay your cards down," the dealer ordered George.

He put them down, one at a time: ace of hearts, ace of clubs, two of spades, two of hearts, and his replacement card which was still lying where the dealer had placed it face down, the six of hearts. He had trumped me with four of a kind.

"Twos are great wild cards, eh Jimmy?" George grinned at me across the table as I chucked my hand face down on the table and stalked out of the room.

I heard him calling after me, but it was not the voice of the George who cared, he was just going through the motions then. *Sonofabitch!*

***

George

After Jimmy left, he checked his watch—*Good, she should be showing up any time now.* He slipped the dealer another twenty dollars for his work in arranging the distribution of wild cards and went outside the ballroom and waited in front of the main entrance doors. He had asked her for an extra hour to help them decide who should be her companion tonight. Well, he hadn't exactly gone into the details of how that would be accomplished; he had simply told her that he and Jimmy would have a gentlemanly chat about it and the best option, from her vantage point, would be decided. After all, Jimmy had been his oldest friend and they had made many life altering decisions in the past in a civilized manner. She had been grateful for being relieved of having to make the decision herself.

Then he saw her coming towards him, dressed in a burgundy evening dress, hair pulled back arranged in coiffure that trailed two long curls down the sides of her face. A pendant on a simple chain adorned her neck and nestled on the swell of her bosom, amply displayed over the low-cut dress.

She saw him, and her face lit up; the air of anxiety surrounding her immediately lifted for her gait quickened as she hurried towards him.

"Oh, George," was all she could manage as she looked into his eyes.

"It's all right. We decided. He left."

"I'm glad it wasn't you that left," she whispered, as if praying to herself.

As he took her arm firmly and led her inside. He knew he would have her tonight. He had earned the privilege.

***

May 1st 1973
Dearest Mother,
Oh, such wonderful news to share—all good, all good!

First off—school is over. I graduated! Your only child finally did you proud! Pity you couldn't come to the graduation due to your attack of the flu. Hope you are feeling better now.

Second—Fred sold my paintings at the exhibition he organized last month. He wants more work now and is also talking about getting me a commission from a medical consortium down in the US who wants some specific scenes captured. The director was down for Fred's exhibition and said that he was drawn by the way in which I rendered these ordinary scenes with extraordinary character. Isn't that great, Mum? Remember your comments to me as a child that ran along the same lines? I am so glad you saw that in me and helped bring it out so others could appreciate my gift.

Now for the grandest news—George and I are engaged. Yes, that sounds like a very grown-up, old fashioned thing to say, but I made sure it happened after I graduated.

He was waiting for me at the graduation party. Thanks for the money for the burgundy dress—it was perfect. And your pendant was just the icing on the cake—George couldn't take his eyes off it—or was it my breasts he was ogling? Who knows? But my accessories were just perfect.

The food at the party was quickly gobbled up by our starving student population; these parties are so stingily organized. And here we were in all our finery. So we left early and headed to a French restaurant on King St. George must be bankrupt now or he must have won some money at the casino before I arrived. He was flushed with cash and ordered champagne along with our four-course meal.

I was tipsy but not drunk. He took us for a drive along the QEW, made the limo driver stop by the lake somewhere, and kissed me under a crescent moon out on the water. Then the driver took us to George's apartment, which must have been professionally cleaned for the occasion because I have not seen it in such a spanking state.

George put on the most romantic Humperdink and Bacharach music, and we waltzed in-between the packed furniture, falling down numerous times onto the ottoman, the loveseat, even brushing against the bookcase and toppling over his tomes on political history. He opened another bottle of wine, red this time, and by now I wanted him more than ever.

Am I embarrassing you mother? But this is your daughter's coming of age date. My three years with Henri means nothing to me now after that first night with George. George is so passionate, and you know what? Experienced! He leaves you wanting more. Ah well—I'm sure you know all these things, Mother Dearest—I need not give you the gory details.

I said that I have 'all good' news to share. But there is one not-so-good item, and that is, Jimmy. I haven't seen him since the graduation party—did not see him at the party either. You see, apparently Jimmy and George came to an agreement as to who would escort me to the graduation party, and Jimmy, for all the noble reasons, backed down—a very gentlemanly gesture. Yet, he hasn't returned any of my subsequent phone calls. I went to see him yesterday, and the landlady told me that he had left with no forwarding address. We will all be leaving one of these days, now that the glorious days of university are done. George must know Jimmy's whereabouts. When the dust has settled on their "duel," I will ask George. Jimmy is, and always will be, a dear, dear friend. I feel like a piece of land these two men fought over—a colonial goldmine. It's a pity there has to be a victor and a vanquished.

I'm looking forward to seeing you and spending a well earned vacation in Montreal. But dear Mother, here is the decision I have reached: I am moving back to Toronto this summer. I need to be near George. He is special to me, and I don't want to lose him.

I'll let you digest on all this, and will see you shortly.

Love!

Dee

***

Jimmy

Something happens when one crosses the threshold from student to teacher. I started to become more forgiving, less black-and-white about things. I had students from all walks of life in my new college English program that fall, many from impoverished or broken homes, getting by on student loans. The more I empathized with them, the more I was able to let go of my bitterness towards George.

And there was no avoiding him. He had joined the college too, in the same liberal arts faculty, teaching political science, history, economics and ethics.

During the next two years, I watched his political star rise; he was quoted in the national newspapers as someone to watch. He wrote regular columns in those same newspapers, expanding on his theory of "enlightened capitalism" and was the party watchdog on rent control issues.

He invited me over to his new apartment in the Annex for weekend soirees but I rarely attended. I knew that Denise would be there, and as much as I yearned for her, it broke my heart to see them together.

Still, I got to do small things for Denise, which I attended to with delight. For instance, when she finally called from Montreal after getting my number from George, I was elated. She apologized profusely for neglecting to stay in touch and warmed my heart with her words. I was ecstatic when she told me she was returning to Toronto, albeit to be with George (she was going to be near me too!). We ended that call with me offering to help her settle in.

I helped unload her truck and decorate her new apartment. I took time off to paint the place in the pastel shades she liked. She then added to it by painting wall murals of her own creation over my plain backdrops. When she had to go down to Buffalo to meet with the medical consortium that had commissioned her to do a series of paintings, I drove her down because George was tied up in meetings with the trade unions. I treated her to dinner on our way back to Toronto, to celebrate her winning a lucrative and challenging commission to paint a dozen portraits over the next twelve months. I was content with the scraps, lap dog that I was.

My mother and I parted ways when she decided to move to Victoria to live with her sister. It was a relief for both of us to add distance to the silence between us. She wrote me formal letters regularly, and I did the same. Our correspondence was very much the same as what we had talked about when we lived together: the price of goods, the annual women's bazaar, health, finances, books we were reading—safe subjects from a safe distance.

My aloofness from George during that period must have hurt him for he did not have me as his sounding board any more. He needed an audience, and I had been his best one, until he met Denise. For the next few months, I forced George and Denise from my consciousness and concentrated on my career, and even tried to date various women unsuccessfully, and most importantly, I buried the hollowness in my heart over the loss of the two people who were closest to me while they continued to strengthen their relationship with each other. I would get the occasional letter from Denise, with an accompanying photograph of the couple: in the Rockies on holiday, in Mexico on the beach, and even at the party convention wearing promotional tee shirts and waving posters.

It was two years later, when George called me one afternoon, just before the 1975 provincial election campaign got underway.

"Jimmy, I got the nod—I'm running."

"Congratulations!" I said half-heartedly.

"Can I count on you as one of my campaign organizers?"

"Why me? You've got so many others in your party apparatus."

"Because I can trust you, Jimmy. You and Denise are the only people I trust."

But you'll cut my throat at the drop of a hat, or the draw of a card.

I agreed to help him. I had come to the realization by then that George was thicker than family. In fact, he was my only family, despite his innate ability to hurt me.

***

George

The campaign was nearing the end, and he was exhausted. Today had been gruelling: visiting a seniors' home, a school badly in need of repair, an overcrowded hospital that was transferring every fourth emergency patient to other hospitals, and finally, a meeting with city council—all in one day. He was wiped.

Switching from the right wingers to the left wingers made no iota of difference; it was clear to him by now that money—and how much of it you could wield—was what did the trick in the end. The right wingers *had* the money while the left *desired* it, only to do the same things their opponents did when they got their hands on it.

And to cap it all off, that son-of-a-bitch Greg Lawson, his father's old right-wing party buddy, was on his tail, heavily funded with corporate money, with a bus bearing Lawson's campaign slogan, and a swanky image of Greg dominating its gleaming exterior. Lawson had been to the same venues and promised the seniors protection of their pensions from stagflation, promised an overhaul of the school replete with a new gym. Lord knows what Lawson had promised the hospital—more patients? Lawson was full of promises he couldn't keep. It's a pity voters found out only *after* an election. Yet Greg Lawson had been an enduring fixture on the political circuit for over twenty years—there must be some magic in how the man survived.

He had decided to stay at the hotel on the airport strip, given his early start the following day on the west side of Toronto. Tomorrow's programme included a daycare centre (make sure to carry as many babies and smile, while they dribble all over your suit and poop on your arm), a new immigrant and small business owner who couldn't speak much English (gesticulate like crazy—and smile!), and a student conference at the university in the afternoon (get ready to talk about abortion, gay rights and the erosion of the planet). After that, he would be heading home for a well earned rest, before the home stretch of campaigning. The election was in a week and yet it seemed so far away.

His handlers and hangers-on had been good and had served him well. After all, he was the promising new blood, and the party elders had laid out their best protection as a gesture of their investment in him. But the handlers were tired too, and he had sent everyone home for the day. He was weary of people in general and wanted to be alone to recharge. He wished Denise was with him, but she was busy in another part of the city, getting ready for the election and the post-election festivities. He didn't underestimate the amount of organizing required for that event—win or lose. He was grateful that Jimmy had offered to help her. His tiredness and frustration with the futility of politics also made him horny; Denise would have been a safe outlet tonight.

He fished under the torn lining of his overnight bag and pulled out a pouch. He had been guarding this one. Now, with no one around, he could finally indulge. He pulled out blank cigarette papers, spread the marijuana and rolled a few joints. Then he sat back and enjoyed the first one. As exhalation trickled through his nostrils, he felt the constraints fall away. He was tired of playing Mr. Goody Two Shoes politician—he wasn't so in real life, and this whole campaign had been one of putting on the act. Yet he needed the feeling of power, the need to win, the adulation of the masses, and being in politics kept him on the treadmill. He resented the fact that he couldn't be free with women anymore, and that it wasn't only Denise he had to worry about, but the whole campaign. After the second joint, he felt really relaxed. He walked down to the bar.

It was ten o'clock, and the place was humming. A three-piece band played in a corner, but no one was dancing. This was a business hotel, and the guests were strangers to each other—more men in suits than women. From the accents and voices, they were mainly foreigners passing through; southern drawls added to the diversity and the anonymity.

He had shed his signature blue suit and dressed in an open necked casual red shirt. He had switched his contacts for the horned rimmed glasses he never wore to public events. For additional camouflage, he'd shaved off his moustache—he had to have a post-election image, and damn if he was going to be stereotyped! He hoped no one would recognize him in this transient pit-stop, despite the TV appearances, campaign posters and public meetings over the last four weeks.

He ordered a drink, sat on a bar stool and ogled the woman serving behind the bar—fortyish, trace of shadow in her armpits as she reached up for glasses, breasts jostling for freedom from the tight tank top, short blue-red hair and a nose ring. Her hips wobbled as she moved behind the counter, serving drinks with a lazy nonchalance, chewing gum.

"Whiskey sour," he ordered, slipping the glasses onto the bridge of his nose and looking deep into her eyes, smiling slowly. She showed interest, even faint recognition, and then a mask of professional courtesy took over.

"Which city are you from, honey?"

"Calgary," he lied. "Oil business."

She looked into his eyes, searching somewhere in memory, as she slid the drink over to him. Then she moved down the bar and chatted with a male colleague serving at the other end. Her voice carried, and he overheard how she had to look for another job soon because home expenses were getting out of control. Marty, her teenage son, was on drugs again and needed counselling, and Jolene, the daughter, had to have another abortion. As he learned her life story, his lust for her mounted.

A commotion rose in the back, and he turned around to see a boisterous group of suited men walk in, surrounding a man in the centre: Greg Lawson. *The son-of-a bitch even follows me to my place of rest.* He kept his head averted and swivelled back on his stool—he was severely outgunned and did not want a face-off tonight.

Lawson signalled to the woman behind the bar, and she waved back to him, a wide smile on her face. She picked up a tray and ushered Lawson's party into a glass-doored room at the back, switching the "reserved" sign outside the door to one reading "private." Lawson gave her a big hug, then a politician's caring look, and introduced her casually to his colleagues while she took orders, smiling at everyone.

When the drinks were dispensed, she took them over, and Lawson tucked a note into her jeans belt, while his other hand gently circled her bottom.

At the bar, he ordered another drink when the woman returned from serving Lawson's party. When she placed it front of him, she paused, seeing the fifty dollar bill on the counter.

"You tip big, mister. Thanks!"

"There's more if you do what I tell you."

She squinted, the bill halfway into her pocket. An angry streak crossed her brow. "What's on your mind, mister?"

"Who's Lawson to you?" he pressed on, ignoring her reaction.

"He helped my mother get an apartment when I was a teenager. Single mothers don't get things easily."

"I bet you, she paid him in kind for that. Or you did."

Now she looked really angry. "How dare you!" she hissed. The band was drowning out most of the sound so he felt safe talking.

He reached out and grabbed her hand, pulling her over, smiling as he did. Her protest was a pretense of false modesty—he knew her type. Suddenly, he wanted this woman—wanted what Greg Lawson had had. It was good that she did not recognize him.

"Listen—there's a lot of money to be earned tonight. At least ten more of those bills for starters." He didn't know how he was going to justify his expense account, but right now he didn't really care. He'd figure something out later.

Her face was up against his. He could smell the nicotine in her breath, partially drowned with mint from the gum, but still strong. She was listening. He read fear in her eyes. *The docility and servility of the masses in the presence of dominant personalities has occurred throughout the ages.* There was also greed in her eyes. *Money talks, especially to the impoverished.*

When he finished whispering his demands and let go her hand, she grinned wickedly and straightened her hair, thrusting her breasts at him. "I'll think about it," she said.

He watched her ferry drinks to Lawson's party for the next hour, while he nursed a couple more scotches. The alcohol helped deaden the pain. The pain of disillusionment upon realizing that other than for the power it gave him, politics held no appeal to him anymore. He had been naïve enough to think he could change the world. The hidden conquistador in him had hit another dead end. He was secretly hoping he wouldn't win, although losing would hurt him too. He did not like to lose.

She was ending her shift. She came up to him with his tab.

"Shall I sign this to your room? What's your room number?"

"I'll pay cash."

"What's your room number?"

He put down another fifty dollar bill, scribbled his room number on a napkin and got off his stool. "Don't keep me waiting."

When he inched out of the side entrance, something told him that Lawson was watching him, but he couldn't turn back to verify. His tired body was coming alive again—the game was underway. At least, this was a way of giving Lawson an indirect kick in the balls, and having fun while doing it.

She did not keep him waiting. He had scarcely got back to his room and brushed his teeth, when his door swung open. She slipped in, a plastic key card in hand.

"I expected you to knock," he said.

"I work in this hotel. I don't hang around hallways."

"Make yourself comfortable. Drink?"

"Why not? I've had a long day helping guys drink yourselves into lust." She made for the mini-bar, grabbed two miniatures, broke their seals and drank them neat off the bottles. She wrinkled her cheeks and advanced towards him. "Now, where's the money?"

"Advanced payment, huh?" He smiled. He knew her type. "There's half on the bed. The rest—after your performance."

He pulled up a chair and threw his feet up on the desk. "Show me what Lawson got you to do."

"It wasn't much. He was very careful. He had me dance with my clothes off."

"Go on, show me."

"Got anything stronger to get me in the mood?"

He tossed the remaining joints at her. She lit one, took two long puffs and left the smoking cigarette smouldering in the ashtray. "That's more like it."

She tucked the money into her bag, which she then tossed on the floor. She began wriggling her hips slowly, eyes closed, hands rising in the air and twirling in waves. His excitement mounted.

When she was down to her underwear, she stopped. "I need another drink." He watched her lean over the mini-bar, full hips, G-string panties. She must do this a lot on the side, he figured—helping Marty and Jolene with their expenses.

When she had half swigged the third miniature, she turned around. "You know, you remind me of someone I met when I was in the entertainment business. The time I met Greg."

"Can't be. Different time, different town."

She resumed her dance. He was getting bored with this foreplay. "What else did Lawson do?"

"He just watched."

"What do you charge for extras?"

She paused. "That wasn't part of the agreement."

"I don't think Lawson went only for eye candy."

"Why don't you call him and find out?" She picked up the joint and took another couple of puffs.

She started removing her bra releasing her breasts, firm with only a slight sag. She brought them up to his face. "They are real, honey." She retreated teasingly just as he reached to touch her.

"Take it all off!"

"Hey, slow down," she cooed as she continued to run her hands over her beasts and pout her lips at him.

He rose and advanced on her, and a look of fear crossed her face.

Then the door crashed open and flashlights started going on off, blinding him. He heard a voice commanding, "Focus on the woman. Now, get them both."

There were three men in the room: two clicking cameras and one suited guy shouting orders, all whom he recognized as being in Lawson's party downstairs.

"What the hell are you doing here?" he managed to say.

Then realization dawned. He swung around on the woman who was already gathering her clothes and purse and making for the door, head shielded against the flashing cameras. "How many *more* keys did you make?" he yelled after her.

"Smells like a hashish den in here," the suited one said, waving his hands in front of his nose.

He took a swing at the man, but the flash blinded him again, and the men, their mission accomplished, were running out of the room. The door slammed in his face, and they were gone. He held back the urge to give chase. What use would that do—create more photo opportunities?

He swivelled and punched his fist into the wall. The pain running up his arm helped ease the frustration. He felt like his head would burst. He hit the wall again and cried out in pain. He staggered over to the mini-bar and helped himself to the last remaining miniature. He scooped ice from the tray, threw the cubes into a hotel laundry-bag and held it over his swelling fist.

He sat on the bed for a long time, many possibilities running through his head. They all led to the conclusion that he was finished. Perhaps the "out" he had been wishing for had just been granted to him.

There was a tap on the door. He swore—was he not going to have any more privacy tonight? But when he had *chosen* to enter the public arena, his life had lost its privacy. This was a hand of poker where the bets had worked against him.

He walked up to the door and looked through the peephole. Greg Lawson stood outside, alone, hands in his pockets, looking sad.

He opened the door. "What do you want, Lawson? Come to gloat over my bones?"

"Can I come in?" the old man said. "These hallways are loud."

He held the door open. Lawson, a squat man, stepped inside, hands still in his pockets as if he was afraid to touch anything.

Lawson stopped in the centre of the room and turned around. "You know, you are just like your father. Liked to live on the edge, he did."

"I'm not interested in the morality lecture."

"Obviously not. I came to tell you that there will be no newspaper article tomorrow. You are going to lose this election anyway. But out of respect for your father, those pictures are going only to your party bosses. I'll let them deal with you."

He laughed hollowly. "What's this—honesty among thieves?"

The old man sighed. He looked tired. Perhaps the campaigning had gotten to him too. "Listen George—your father bedded that woman, when she was a minor, while we were on the election trail. He was a master at covering his tracks. But he got it in the end, right? Do you know that he was drunk when his car went off the road? We hushed it up. I do not want to see history repeating itself."

He was stunned by this news about his father. But it all added up. It explained why the party had cut the surviving Waltons loose after George Sr.'s death.

Lawson continued while walking out of the room. "I will not be running again after this new term. We need young people like you at the helm, whichever side of the political spectrum you sit on. Don't fuck it up the next time."

"I'm fucked up anyway."

"Part of a good politician's make up is the 'comeback,' the reinvention. Focus on that four years from now." Lawson paused on the threshold. "Goodnight, George. Have a good night's rest."

***

An extract from *Conquistador*—a novel by GeorgeWalton

The soldier's chest was a mass of wounds, some gangrenous. He wouldn't last more than a few days. Francisco held the torch above the injured man in the cot. Surrounding him stood a friar, an overworked physician, and guards from the Rimac garrison.

"What happened this time?" Francisco barked, unable to keep the frustration out of his voice.

"Thousands, Your Excellency." The man's voice was inaudible, hoarse, parched. The doctor held a jug to the dry lips.

"How far did you get?"

"We saw Cusco in the distance. But the plain surrounding was full of Manco's men. Thousands."

"And ours?"

"We saw none. But the Spanish flag was still flying over the ramparts."

Juan is dead and Hernando is trapped inside. How many more days can they hold out until the food runs out completely?

He did not want to ask the dying soldier what had happened. Let the man save his breath for his greater battle with looming death. He knew the answer: Cusco had fallen and the remnant Spaniards were besieged inside, and this time Manco would not fall for the same trap that his father Atahualpa had succumbed to.

"Give him more water," Francisco ordered. Then turning to the priest, he yelled, "And pray for his soul, and for my brothers. And may that Inca bastard, whom I tried to civilize, rot in hell!"

He strode across the barracks towards his quarters. Peru was under siege, not merely Cusco. Just days ago he had repulsed an attack here in Los Reyes. The Inca were smarter and wilier this time, and would give no quarter. If only they had not let Manco escape with his tall story of another gold mine that only he could lead them to. Was this the end of his Peruvian Dream?

He missed Alamagro. Almagro, who was blissfully unaware of all that was happening in Peru and was on his way to Chile, on an expedition that he, Francisco, had engineered to get rid of his best friend.

***

Jimmy

Five days before the election, we were summoned. I received a phone call from Denise saying that something was up, and that we should be down at party HQ in Toronto for an important announcement. She said that George was already down there, so I picked her up from her apartment. Despite their holidays in exotic destinations together, Denise was still hanging on to her independence and had not moved in with George. Somehow, that gave me some hope that she was still attainable.

It was 8.30 a.m. on a crisp September morning heralding the fall when we walked into the party office downtown. The reception area was crammed with journalists and photographers, and the staff guarded the doors to the leader's offices. We had to mingle with the press. They recognized us as the supporting cast and pried us for information while we waited. I decided to escape and get coffee downstairs, while Denise kept repeating that she knew as much as they did at the moment. When I returned, the party secretary had just entered the reception and was being attacked by microphones from all sides—a spotlight was trained on him. Despite the early hour, he was impeccably dressed right up to the silk handkerchief in his lapel. In his calm, methodical and gentle way, he explained that the candidate for Scarborough North, Mr. George Walton, would not be running due to personal reasons, and that retired MPP Harry Palin would be replacing Mr. Walton.

It was a short announcement, no further explanations were given. As the secretary stepped away, George emerged from the inner office, pale and subdued. He put on a grin for the cameras, thanked everyone for helping him in his campaign and said that after giving the matter deep consideration he felt he could not deliver on the expectations of the party and would step down in favour of the more experienced Mr. Palin. Then he shook the secretary's hand and they retreated into the inner sanctum again.

We stood in shocked silence as the mumbling press departed slowly, cheated of the salacious details of their scoop.

"But all the preparations ... " Denise bit her lip, the coffee going cold in her hand. "Jimmy, there's more to this."

"Let's wait for George. He can't hide in there all day."

He came out an hour later. I was late for classes, but phoned-in from a call box to say I was being delayed. He looked forlorn as he crossed the street where we were waiting for him in my car.

Denise got out of the passenger seat and ran to him, and they embraced in the middle of the street amidst tooting traffic. I tooted too, wanting them to break that silly embrace that was making me embarrassed and get the hell out of the downtown traffic that could run them down at any moment. Finally, they broke away and walked towards me, amidst yelling drivers and curious pedestrians.

I pulled the car away, trying to put some distance from that embarrassing scene, while they remained locked in an embrace in the back seat, saying nothing.

"Can we talk later today?" I said into the rear view mirror. "I'm late for classes. This warrants talking about, right?"

George looked at me. He had aged ten years since I last saw him two days ago at the charity bazaar put on by the party's fundraising committee.

"There is no need for any more talking, Jimmy. I'm finished."

"Are you going to tell us about what happened, at least?"

"I don't want to talk about it. Let's say that I was set up by Lawson."

"And that's all you're going to say to the people who have invested their time and sweat in you?"

"I'm sorry—okay?" His voice rose notches as he spoke. "What do you guys want from me? Blood?"

Denise butted in, her hands tightly clutched in his. "Jimmy, now is not the time. There will be plenty of time to talk about this later."

I drove in silence towards his apartment, where I was going to drop them both off. When I turned off the highway and looked in the rear view mirror again, they were locked in embrace, kissing passionately. When I broke the second red light along his street, I realized that I'd had my leg pressed down on the accelerator.

***

George

He knew he was washed up when he began losing control of his students back at the college. A mercy call came from the party faithful, or perhaps from the trade union boss, and he had managed to hang onto his teaching job.

He had returned with new insights on politics that he was determined to impart to his students. Perhaps, he would write a book on his experiences. "Backroom dealings" was a good element to inject into his lectures, and the students would lap it up, he thought—anything for intrigue and double dealing. But the topic didn't fly, because the tips were coming from *him*, George Walton, failed political novice. "Sour grapes," he heard a student sniggering during one of his sessions.

When the social democrats became the official opposition following the election, students hinted that the seat lost by he-whose-name-could-not-be-mentioned had cost that party from overthrowing the conservatives and ruling Ontario for the first time, even though the margin of seats won by the ruling party over the opposing parties far exceeded one. When Harry Palin lost his seat in Scarborough North, the college's heartland, they blamed it on George Walton.

He was a pariah, trying to claw back some dignity. His past indiscretions with faculty started to surface now that he was in the shit house. There were rumours circulating, making their way directly back to him through the viciously efficient college grapevine, that George Walton was even screwing the dean's wife, Mrs. Curtis. She was forty-nine years old and had recently separated from the dean; George was the supposed reason.

"Bastards!" he bellowed to Denise, who was his constant companion these days; she spent most nights at his place, cooking for him, taking him on long walks in the evenings as he vented his frustrations at being treated so shabbily.

"There must be some fire where there is smoke, George," she calmly told him on one of their walks. "You've probably given the faculty cause for getting back at you."

He glowered at her but did not react immediately. He struggled for words.

"They are jealous. All they do is put in their time and look for a comfortable early retirement. None of them want to make a difference."

She had a look of pain in her face. "I understand, George. Giving of one's self is difficult. That's what makes you so ... so special."

Three months after the election, the discussion in class turned out to be on the use of personal power in politics. He had been careful to introduce the subject in such a way as to maintain a distance from his own experiences. During the lecture, he provided examples of former charismatic politicians who had used sex appeal to win votes.

"It's a viable device, and if used well, and subtly, can be tremendously powerful. Look at Castro, or even our own Trudeau—they had the vote of the opposite sex, because they were pop idols."

The mumbling audience quieted down and started paying attention. Several hands went up at that statement.

"Sir—" it was Fairley, a pimply A-student who spent all his time in the library between classes.

"Yes, Fairley?"

"Does it mean that those with no sexual talents are less favoured to run for political office?"

"That's not true. Each candidate brings a basket of talents; intellectual, professional, connections in the community, track record of accomplishments, honesty, integrity ... and ... sexual appeal. Not everyone has all these aspects, and some talents are more developed than others. But they all add up in their way."

Bobby Barlow, a jock on the football team, laughed and raised his hand. "Mr. Walton—are there any fringe benefits to being a politician with sex appeal?"

"I told you, Barlow—votes. For any others you will have to contact the politicians themselves."

"That's why I'm asking *you*, sir?" A guffaw broke out across the lecture room.

He began to sweat. He could feel their nosy, beady eyes drilling into him, looking for the slightest slip. He cursed inwardly for wading into these waters.

"My career was too short lived for that, Barlow." He tried to laugh it off, but realized he was sounding strained.

Then the brunette who frequently wore low cut halters that threw out her cleavage in ample measure, spoke up. Rosie Manini, who always sat in the front rows and bored holes into him, said innocently, "Was dating women easier when you were running in the election, sir?"

A louder guffaw in the room this time, and he grimaced. He stared at Rosie and swallowed. She was a young woman he would greatly liked to have bedded had she been around during his student days, but now being on the faculty end, he had restrained himself to lay off the student population for the faculty had provided much fodder for his sexual appetite. He suddenly felt diminished by this woman and her question.

"I won't answer this question, Rosie. It's personal."

"But we are talking about *personal* power, sir," chimed in Fairley.

"Do tell," piped out Bobby Barlow, and the rest of the class echoed the 'do tell' in a slow rumble that deafened him.

He took a breath and straightened himself. "I have never had an issue with dates, politics notwithstanding."

Then a male voice from the back jibed, "Even with Mrs. Curtis, sir?"

The class laughed instantly and then hushed as he glared at them, gripping the podium with bloodless fingers. He swallowed the obvious, "Who said that?" question as that would only draw attention to the rumour, even validate it.

He turned to the blackboard, stilted and pale. "Let's move on to discuss other aspects of personal power, shall we?"

He sat in the bar nursing his fourth scotch for the evening. He had found this watering hole, a home to bikers and truckers, just off the highway and a few miles away from the college, a welcome refuge, an anonymous hole where he could sit at the back and forget the day.

He needed Jimmy, not even Denise. Jimmy would understand the angst eating through him, the feeling that no one wanted him. He felt like he was climbing a mountain littered with human obstacles; men like his father and Greg Lawson, who were pushing him down, making him insignificant. That's why loose women were easier; they were warm and accommodating, easy to please with sex. Denise was different. She was looking for a stronger commitment, and that frightened him—another obstacle on the mountain. Something he was going to face sooner than later. He could not just let her go like the others, even though he was able to weave lovers in and around her without her knowing. Darn the leak with that Curtis woman—she couldn't keep her bloody mouth shut. Denise may suspect, but he had been clever to cover his tracks. Would that change if he married Denise? His lip curled in a smile. That would be a challenge worth exploring, wouldn't it? There weren't many challenges left.

He and Jimmy were alike in that way, remaining aloof and alone to the end, despite everyone who interfered with their lives. But where was that getting him? Drunk in a pokey bar with a bunch of smelly roadies.

Then that heavy feeling descended, like a cloak, obliterating any raised spirits he may have conjured with the alcohol. Should he have another scotch and lift himself above the cloak? How many drinks could he have? He had to drive home. A vicious cycle. The doctor had called it depression. Heck, everyone in this motherfucking country was depressed.

He got up and went to the payphone and called Jimmy. His friend wasn't home. He left a message. Frustrated he hung up and leaned against the instrument, the cloak now taking full possession.

Someone was tapping him on the shoulder. He looked through the haze in his eyes and saw the blond moustache, the bandana, the black leather jacket.

"You done with the phone?" The biker looked hurried.

"Fuck you!" It was nice getting it off on this piece of road kill.

The man laughed pityingly. "What? Watch your tongue, guy. Wanna get killed in here?"

Here was another obstacle looming at him—a big one. He swung at the biker's face, connecting on the man who looked surprised as the blow caught him square on the nose, bloodying him instantly and sending him staggering against the washroom door. A woman yelled, and the punched man straightened himself to plunge back into the fight. He hit the biker again but the man's charge carried them both back into the main bar, sprawling against tables, chairs, patrons, and into the midst of the man's pals who were nursing beers at the bar.

He picked himself up, feeling good, the blood pounding in his veins and driving the cloak away momentarily, only now he was surrounded by five other clones of his adversary.

"Go get him, boys," the bloody biker said, feeling his nose and walking toward the bar.

He was being picked up by several pairs of hands and carried out into the back lot, amidst garbage bags and alley piss.

"Give him the chain," one voice said.

"Nah. Let's carve him up a bit—leave him like a piece of art for his girlfriend to look at every day ... and puke."

They tossed him up in the air and he collided with the wall. He came back fighting, which took them by surprise. One punch landed in a soft belly, another in someone's throat. That's as far as he got, for a barrage of blows rained down on him: on the face, in the stomach, on the shins; someone even kept slapping his ears hard.

Somewhere in the pain, another cloak lapped at him, a cloud he wanted to embrace and sleep within. He heard the first biker yell, "Split! Cops!"

Motorcycles roared and added to the pounding in his head. He was left lying on a hard surface, and the smell of urine was strong in his nostrils—reviving him. He managed to put a hand under his body and push upwards. He was prone on the street. Then his hand gave way and he fell on the wet concrete again, awake only to his pain, immobile.

New voices arrived on the scene. "Get this guy a stretcher!" "Paramedics are on the way." "Looks like another drunk to me." "A brave one—or a very stupid one."

Jimmy arrived when they had got him inside the ambulance and were about to take off for the hospital.

"George—what the hell happened? Got here as soon as I could."

He tried to talk but his throat ached. Instead, he smiled weakly. "Thanks," he managed to croak, surprised at his ability to form a word.

Then the answers that he had been wrestling with all evening came to him in a rush. Fancy, it took a beating to get it out of him. He crooked his fingers at Jimmy.

Jimmy leaned over.

"Jimmy ... buddy ... "

"Yes, George?"

"I'm going to ask Denise ... to marry me."

He could see the flash of pain and disappointment in his friend's face. Understandable. But there was no other way.

"George, this is not the time—"

"No ... no ... it *is* the time. I've been ... dodging it, Jimmy."

"You are just feeling sorry for yourself right now, George."

"No, Jimmy—I am not stable on my own. I need her." There, he had said it. Now he was going to close his eyes and enjoy the ambulance ride. What a painful but fruitful revelation it had been.

***

Jan 21st 1976

Dear Mumsy,

Guess what? I am getting married! Yes, your daughter is "getting off your hands," as the old biddies in the Church used to say, and getting into the hands of another. George asked me to marry him—and I accepted!

Poor George, he had the most horrible accident recently. A gang of vicious bikers beat him up in a bar and he was hospitalized—broken ribs and nose, dislocated shoulder and some internal bleeding. He has had so much misfortune in the last little while; I must be his only bright spark.

I have spent these last three weeks at the hospital, and now he is in home care and mending quickly. I am in and out of his apartment helping him get to his feet. This is when I wish that we were living together so I could be on hand for him. But I know, Mother Dearest, I swore never to live with a man until I married him. I am still keeping my part of the bargain even though it is very hard to do so at present—I want you to know that.

As I wrote you earlier, he was sidelined by his party in favour of an older colleague who subsequently lost in the election. Just before he was attacked, George began having problems back at the school due to an ugly rumour floating around. Mind you, he is very attractive, and women look at him in a way that makes me mad, but to float a rumour that he was making out with the dean's estranged wife, was simply over the top.

Anyway, we shall overcome. And guess what—when I asked him if we could have the ceremony in Montreal, so that you could attend, he agreed. Isn't he sweet? Jimmy will be his best man of course, and I've asked Stella if she will be my maid of honour, and she agreed.

So there you are. We have set the wedding for next April, so you have plenty of time to prepare for it.

I like sending you these letters so much. They remind me of the years I spent in boarding school when the only way I could communicate with you was by letter. And there was so much I could say because I did not have to blush when saying it—you couldn't see my face. I am blushing now, actually.

George wants to start his own school. He is tired of the bureaucracy in the public education system, a system he loyally defended during his political campaign. He looks so vulnerable these days—a lot of his dreams seem to be flaming out. He says that from now on he is only looking after Number One. I don't think he will enter politics again, he is so bitter about how they treated him. I hope I can give him the encouragement and perspective he needs to make a fresh start.

I am going to bring him over to visit you—before the wedding—so you can see the man I am marrying.

The painting project is going well. I sent my first drafts over, and the board likes them. I even got my first advance. What bothers me is that this flurry of activity around the wedding, and looking after George, could make my work slide. As much as career and building up my art business is important, I have to honestly say that George is the most important thing in my life right now.

Anyway, Mother Dearest, wish me luck. Write soon.

Hugs and kisses.

Dee

***

Jimmy

With the greatest reluctance, I went to Montreal. I was giving away my best friend to the woman I loved. I was going to do it in a tuxedo, and with a smile on my face, for the cameras.

George and I had booked into the Delta downtown for the night before the ceremony. After the wedding Denise and he were going to Montebello for their honeymoon. I was going to head back by train to Toronto, lugging most of his non-honeymoon gear with me.

On the train to Montreal, he was in a frenzy of excitement, repeating over and over, between many beers, that this was the best thing for him to be doing. He was so excited that he kept misplacing his things on the journey; he left his Armani sun glasses in the washroom at the station, and we had to run back to get them, he left his credit card at the ticket office, and another frantic dash ensued to retrieve it, nearly missing our train in the process. I had to tally his personal belongings—tuxedo, honeymoon suitcase, overnight bag, camera, and make sure he carried them at every stage of the journey. I gazed out across the bleak countryside—trees denuded of leaves, cloudy dull sky—and tried to recall how my father would have been in circumstances when he maintained composure despite the turmoil raging inside him, a turmoil that ultimately killed him. I needed that exterior calm now, or else I might blow something too.

In the hotel, George smoked weed to calm down. Then he soaked himself in a bath for almost an hour and suggested we go out for dinner—just him and me.

We went to a Mexican restaurant, and he downed a few tequilas. It was a good warm-up from the cold streets outside.

"We are in Montreal, and you bring me to a cantina?" I said. I had been grumpy during the whole train ride.

"Variety, amigo!" His eyes were already glazed.

"Keep this up, and I'll be taking you to your wedding on a stretcher."

"No worries, brother. I will be all right tomorrow. You know the one thing that creeps me out, Jimmy?"

I waited in silence.

"You'll never guess," he shouted, blowing smoke from his cigarette into the noisy room, where mariachi music reverberated off the walls to the accompaniment of a roaring fireplace from the open kitchen. "It's her mother."

"Dee's mother?"

"Yeah—you'll meet her tomorrow. Eyes like a hawk—she sees right through me. Makes me sweat."

"That shouldn't faze you, if you've got nothing to hide."

"I'll always have something to hide, Jimmy. I'm just trying to minimise those things. I'm hoping Denise will keep me in check."

"You are a lucky man, George."

He hiccupped. "Yeah. Can't fuck this one up, Jimmy."

"You'd better not," I said. Now, why wasn't I convinced?

The church was dark and gloomy in the heart of Vieux-Montreal. Not quite old Notre Dame Cathedral but one of those offshoots lying in its shadow and down by the port. Denise's mother had worshipped here over the years, and it was close to her nursing home.

Snow still covered the ground outside as we entered the heavy wooden doors, dusted our patent leather shoes on the stone floor and walked up the nave to the altar rails. There was a limited seating area but the grandeur of the Gothic architecture radiated from the four pillared walls and stained glass windows surrounding it, testament to the glory of God being the focus of church-building in former times, the comfort of devotees being secondary. The two front rows were taken by people dressed up for a wedding: hats, suits, corsages, long gowns, mainly black.

"Glad we didn't do this in Toronto," George whispered to me as we walked up the aisle. He smiled at people as if he knew them for eons. "I didn't have to invite anyone."

"Including your girlfriends," I said acerbically.

"Shh!"

The smell of incense was thick by the altar as a priest in a white alb went about his duties of preparing the area— Eucharistic hosts, wine supply, candles, altar apparel, prayer missal—straightening objects that had been moved during the last service, replenishing others for the one to follow. He finally gave a nod of satisfaction and disappeared into a back room behind the altar. People in the pews behind us started to rise. George and I turned simultaneously.

"Denise is early," I whispered.

"It's not her—it's the mother."

"How do you know?"

"The wedding march is not playing yet."

"Ah."

The woman being wheeled by an attendant down the aisle was dressed in a black dress, with a pearl necklace and a frilled black hat barely covering her ash grey hair that hung to her shoulders. As she neared, the heavy makeup propping up lines and bags on her aging face became apparent. She had her head tilted to one side in what looked like an attempt to overhear something, then she swivelled her face at me and her light eyes bored right through, trying to focus. Her white-stockinged legs dangled listlessly over the wheelchair and her hands hung lifeless at her sides.

I realized then that this stroke-ridden woman could not write letters anymore, despite Denise's claims that she had an active correspondence going on with her mother. Perhaps Denise wrote to her mother *because* Dear Maman could not reply.

"I see what you mean," I murmured. "I hope Dee doesn't age like this."

"You're scaring me, Jimmy."

The attendant pushed the chair to the front pew and stopped, but Dee's mother signalled, with a nod of her head, to continue. The attendant inched the chair up to where we were standing. George took Mrs. Langevin's limp hand and held it tentatively. She leaned into him until their faces were almost touching. Not a word escaped between them, they just stared at each other for several seconds, with George wilting eventually. I'd never seen him back down in the staring department.

When Mrs. Langevin eventually let go, George looked pale. He straightened his jacket and cummerbund. Then she turned towards me, and her face broke out in a tender, tired smile.

I decided to ignore the previous exchange. "How do you do, Mrs. Langevin. Jeremy Spence. Glad to meet you."

The woman was still smiling at me, in marked contrast to her icy greeting of George, when I heard him whisper over my shoulder, "It's okay, Jimmy. Don't waste your breath—the old bird's deaf. The stroke."

The wedding march started somewhere, and the attendant, hurriedly moved Mrs. Langevin to the left pew in the front row. I looked behind me, and the priest who had been busy with his housekeeping duties had reappeared, wearing a green stole over his shoulders.

"She's here." George squeezed my hand, and his was icy cold.

Denise was walking up the aisle, an elderly uncle by her side. I let myself believe for that brief instant that she was walking towards me. That she was marrying me. How does one freeze a moment like that, a moment that I can still bring back to this day? For that one shining moment, she was coming to me, and my face broke out in the widest smile of acceptance that I may have ever displayed in my entire reticent life.

I sucked in the white dress, the veil flowing softly in her gentle wake despite the muggy air of the church, her features accentuated with subtle touches of make-up, unlike her mother's, the chain and cross lying upturned on the roll of her breasts, the bouquet in her hands symbolizing her life, and her body that she was offering this day and for evermore to *me*. But the magical illusion began to dissipate as she neared, for she was turning towards George, the look on her face: a mixture of longing and happiness, with a tinge of fear.

I hissed in his ear. "Don't fuck it up. I'll never forgive you."

Four—Into the Heartland of the Inca

Jimmy

The plane rattled and rolled on our way up to Cusco; this was the last flight for the day, later flights had been cancelled due to treacherous winds in the cordillera, we were told. Coming down, the huge puma-shaped foundation encircling the city was a formidable image. George called the head of the animal shape "Sexy Woman" although I tried to be respectful and tripped over the official name Saksaywaman many times.

The air was dry, and my temples started to throb the moment we stepped out of the aircraft doors. George tried to be nonchalant but he was panting by the time we wheeled our suitcases to the taxi stand. Fingers tingled and toes went numb during our ride.

We were greeted by a smiling receptionist at the downtown hotel, just off Cusco's Plaza de Armas, who seated us in the lobby and offered us a steaming pot of Coca tea, advising us to take it easy for the afternoon. The tea, rich in alkaloids and cocaine, was supposed to increase the blood oxygen supply, a combatant to altitude sickness. Our suitcases were carried up the stairs to the third floor by a nimble porter. There was no elevator.

Venturing into the sunlit narrow streets, pollution from the few vehicles that populated the town was exaggerated in the rarefied air. I had already developed a headache and found breathing difficult. We hung around the tourist shops ringing the plaza, changing money, buying postcards and looking at wood carvings of pumas, condors and Inca. Tourists walked the cobble-stoned plaza, taking pictures against the backdrop of the Gothic-Renaissance Cathedral built over a former Inca temple.

After a while, George cursed under his breath and suggested we grab a beer.

"Not the exact remedy required here," I reminded him.

"Oh, fuck this altitude shit! Beer works for me."

After a couple of beers, guzzled at a nearby hole-in-the-wall bar, George was in a worse state.

"You'd better get back to the hotel," I said.

"No," he gasped. "I need a distraction—the museum."

We took refuge in the Inca museum located off the plaza. The slow pace of our walking inside, along with the strong dose of Inca history, was welcoming to both of us. The detailed explanations of the exhibits in English and Spanish transported me easily back to the time of Pizarro.

"One wonders who was more barbaric," George said, when we took a break. "The Spaniards sacked the land, robbed all the gold and made everyone Catholic, but the Inca practiced incest, human sacrifice and polygamy—take your pick."

"The Spaniards did more damage. They wiped out the culture, or tried to," I pointed out. "Did you notice the photographs? Not a single Inca in his own regalia. Only Spaniards could parade around in Inca clothing, at least for the photographs."

"All colonizers do that. The lurking strength of the vanquished is frightening to the colonizer, and the power balance has to be restored. Cultural genocide is one method. Power is an insidious aphrodisiac."

We descended to the torture chamber exhibits in the basement. Waxwork scenes of various methods of torture employed by the Spaniards were on display—from finger smashing to the infamous "rack." A group of teenagers ran through the exhibits giggling and teasing each other, oblivious to the pain of their ancestors.

"I don't know why the Inquisition was imported here." I shook my head. "First the Spaniards converted the locals to Catholicism, and then tortured them for not practicing a religion they did not understand or identify with."

"It was another instrument of control, Jimmy. When you run out of controls, introduce another—an invaluable weapon of the conquistadors."

Our next stop was the catacombs—George's idea again; he seemed to want to see everything in Cusco in half a day. The catacombs comprised thousands of neatly arranged skulls in serially lined cells in the basement tunnel of the cathedral. The walls of the basement showed signs of structural damage from numerous earthquakes over the ages, and I felt that at any moment the whole place would collapse in another tremor and entomb us. The bones were arranged in such a manner that those belonging to the clergy were placed in airier rooms, while the commoners were crammed together in pokier cells at the end of the tunnel. Some sections could only be viewed under dim candlelight. The visit to the catacombs was a mistake for the close air inside quickly exacerbated our breathing problems. At one point, George looked pale and gripped my shoulder. I decided that it was time for us to find firmer ground and cut our visit short. George, surprisingly, did not protest this time.

Sitting outside in the sun, we were grateful for the air.

"I felt like death in there, Jimmy. It's a shame that once you're dead and reduced to a skeleton, everyone looks the same."

"Except that the clergy get better quarters," I said. We both laughed in relief.

"I wonder what happened to those two women we met in Lima. We should have seen them around the square—this is not a big town."

"Probably sleeping it off and trying to catch their breath. Perhaps that's what we should be doing, instead of packing it all in on the first day."

George grinned. "You know, Jimmy. You have not changed much. Never stepped out of the comfort zone. Except once, perhaps."

He was treading that dangerous area again, and I steered the conversation away. "I'm going back to the hotel. Wander around, if you must."

"No, no—hang on. I'll go with you. You must not take my digs personally. They come out involuntarily. Even after all these years."

***

George

That night the dreams came stronger, and he woke in a cold sweat. This time the dreams were filled with grinning skulls, taunting him for the useless life he had led. It was those blasted catacombs, he said to himself, staggering out of bed for a glass of water. He should never have gone there in the mental state he was in. Or was the dream something else, a message across the ages telling him that, try as he might to find parallels in history with his own derelict life, the only commonality was that he was one of those faceless skeletons of history destined for the tomb? No accounting was needed. And his end would be more painful for all the damage he had done to other souls along the way. He took deep breaths and tried to quell his panic.

In desperation, he staggered across to his bag, fished out the marijuana pouch and rolled himself a joint. He lay back in bed letting the sweetly sick smoke send him into a dull timeless place, populated only by the people he cared about—Denise, Jimmy, his mother—it was a select group. Towards dawn, he finally fell asleep.

***

Jimmy

A bus took us to the starting point of our hike the next afternoon—a short test for the longer one to come. After meandering through potato fields for half an hour we were dropped off at the settlement of Tipon, where we met our guide, Valdez, a short, thick set man with a pleasant smile that never left his face. He had the burnished skin and flat features of the local Quechua.

"Welcome to Peru," he bowed, securing the red bandana around his neck as if getting ready for some hard work. "Today, we take you on a little climb, just to see how your heart is—okay?"

Tipon held the cascading ceremonial pools of the Inca. Water symbolized the cycle of life. A spring inside the mountain flowed into a terraced pool above us, which split into two channels leading to another pool just below, and then into four channels and into a third pool lower down, flowing all the way down into the valley; the water finally drained into the Urubamba River, evaporated and rained down on the mountain to feed the spring and begin the cycle again. Valdez explained, in glowing terms, how Inca society had been strictly hierarchical even down to its fasting rituals—no food, spirits or sex—lasting one year for the poor, one month for the middle classes and one week for the rich.

"I know what you are about to say," I pre-empted George, who was lost in his absorption of the archaeological site.

"Oh that," he bestirred himself. "That I know. Nothing much has changed—for the rich. Or the poor. It's life, Jimmy. That's why I gave up politics."

"Perhaps you put too much of yourself into it."

"Uh huh, bloody disappointing. Shattered my illusions. Now I look after myself—kill what I can eat, and damn the rest."

Leaving Tipon, we traveled northwest to Ollantaytambo, famed for its terraces, and which was our "little climb" for the day. The giant face of a bearded man on the cliff-face opposite was striking. Valdez smiled as he narrated the legend: the commoner Ollanta who abducted the king Pachacutec's daughter, the imprisonment of the lovers in Cusco, their subsequent release and return to Ollantaytambo. Valdez's voice swelled with pride as he recounted the Inca story. It turned more sarcastic when he pointed to the face on the mountain. "Whose is that face, do you think?"

"Looks like Moses, with his long beard," I volunteered.

"It's the face of Tunupa, a messenger of the Inca god Viracocha. When Spaniards came, when Inca see Pizarro's beard, and all the white men's beards, they thought they were gods. So the Inca surrender and give up all the gold, because they do not want to make the gods angry."

"That story is in my book—my version," George said. "I don't think it was so easy for Pizarro, though. He got through on his wits. Nothing is easy in life."

We began our climb the terraces to the mountain facing the one bearing Tunupa's image. I started panting despite many weeks of training on the stair master at the gym. I looked behind me, George had his head down, and his breathing was heavy, but he kept pace with us. Fields of corn and potato lay spread around us, and the Urubamba flowed benignly along the valley below. Although the temperature was in the teens, I was starting to sweat. I stripped down to my tee-shirt.

"How are your hearts, senors?" Valdez, stick in hand, had paused midway and was looking down at us. "By tomorrow, when we start our main journey, you must be fit."

I took the last few steps towards him and had to pause until I caught my breath. When I got to the summit, I waited until my breathing evened out before replying. "I've never been so out of shape in my life." George hadn't even made it to the top yet.

Valdez grinned as his hat blew off his head and dangled on its string around his neck. "Many foreigners like you, don't realize the magic of the Inca trail. It is a holy journey. Your personal journey. Tomorrow, when we walk, I will not talk, except to show you some interesting sights. Otherwise you will walk alone. With your thoughts. It is the best way."

When we made our way down, George was sitting on an outcrop of rock, his camera hanging from his neck. He looked pale.

I was concerned. "You think you will be ready tomorrow?"

"I was looking out at the drop below us and wondered how easy it would be to step off the ledge and end it all. To end 'the slings and arrows of outrageous fortune that flesh is heir to' eh, buddy?"

"This is not the time for Shakespeare. It's time to find out whether you are in condition or not."

He removed his cap and placed it on his knee, looking across at the other mountain with the giant face on it. His head was plastered with sweat. "Of course I will be ready tomorrow. I'm no quitter, Jimmy. It was just a thought, that's all."

There was a tear trickling down his cheek, and I realized it was more than the altitude accounting for his condition.

He rose, dusted himself and started down with us.

"You know, Jimmy—Denise treated me like Viracocha, a god. But I behaved like Pizarro."

"You really haven't forgotten her, have you?"

"Have you?" He left the question in the air as we resumed our descent and struggled down the steep steps back to the bus.

We spent the night in a smaller hotel in a village just outside Cusco, closer to the starting point of our trek to Machu Picchu the following morning. The property was a rectangle of rooms surrounding a lush flower garden. At the village night market, George and I bought ourselves Inca hiking sticks, stout shoulder height supports with red and green cloth handles.

"Now we can climb any mountain, Jimmy," George said, buoyed by the sudden lift the sticks gave to our strides. We ate a hearty meal of Papa Rellana, Arros con Pollo and Lomo Saltado, laced with corn beer. I broke my resolve and imbibed the beer; I was feeling mellow. Surprisingly, George was reticent through dinner, guzzling the beer, eating little, ignoring the Lomo Saltado completely; even the strolling entertainers playing "El Condor Pasa" did not lift his spirits. He retired to his room soon after dinner.

I had just lain down when I felt a vicious gripe in the stomach. I panicked. This was what I had been dreading—diarrhoea. I had been warned before leaving Toronto: when it comes, it comes quickly. And it had come, despite my precautions of not eating fresh salads or drinking tap water. Perhaps it was the Lomo Saltado we ate at dinner—the salted meat had looked a bit raw, but I had put it down to the Quechua style of cooking.

After three visits to the washroom and three Imodium caplets, I was ready to collapse, and stepped out into the garden for fresh air. It was pitch dark outside; the fragrance of the flowers, as the cool wind blew on them, assailed my senses; that and the sweet sickly smell of marijuana coming from George's room next door.

And as my bowels were breaking down on me, I was reminded of another haemorrhage ...

Five—Aborted Missions

15th August 1976

Dear Mum,

    I'm in the dumps this week. I made a shattering discovery and have to admit that you were right. But it's too soon for things to get this way. I'm not unattractive am I? I haven't put on any weight since the wedding, although I now crave going on a chocolate binge after what I discovered this week.

    George and I were invited to a professor friend, Bob's, cottage on Georgian Bay. The first four days were wonderful: boating, lying on the sundeck, cocktails in the evening, a barbecue that never seemed to be switched off. Bob's wife Shirley is about ten years older than me, and they have no children. Bob is nearing early retirement age and is thinking of opening a private teaching academy in the lake district for rich people's children. George is very interested in the idea. He is also interested in buying ourselves a cottage in the area. He's got it all worked out. My next commission should net me about ten thousand, and with a loan from George's college pension fund, we could scrape together the deposit. Frankly, I am not opposed to the idea ... if ... well, let me continue.

    George golfed every day, and Bob and Shirley who are avid golfers, accompanied him. Given my inability to hit a still object without flailing at it several times, I quit after the first day as I did not want to slow the others down. There was plenty to do on the water. The colours from the dock changed at different times of the day, giving me lots of ideas for new portraits while working on my tan. I sketched furiously and experimented with different combinations of paint on my palate to try and capture those hues.

On the fourth day, Bob got an emergency call from his financiers and headed back into the city and was gone until the end of the week. George continued to golf with Shirley.

The day before Bob returned, George and Shirley were late returning from the golf course as a thunderstorm intervened. George called me from the club house to say that they had stopped on the eighth hole and were set to resume play as soon as the marshal declared it okay to get back on the course. When they were not back at 6 p.m. (they'd been eight hours on the course, and the rain had ended four hours ago, mind you), I drove over to the club to see what was happening. The club house manager confirmed that rain had stopped play, but that all the golfers *had* got back on as soon as the downpour ended and should have finished their rounds at least an hour ago. The marshal arrived, and on my enquiry, checked and said that the "husband and wife" duo of the Waltons had requested a rain-check and driven away while it was still raining.

I reminded him, rather snippily, that *I* was the wife, at which point he apologised and walked away, and I knew he was sniggering.

When I returned to the cottage, George and Shirley were back, drinking cocktails on the deck. Shirley had her leg thrown over the deck chair, offering George a grandstand view of her underwear—if she was wearing any, that is—in the most casual manner I have seen of her since we'd arrived at the cottage. I looked at them from inside the house before going out on the deck. Why are humans so blatant in the signals they send each other? I saw right then, and for the rest of the evening, even though I did my best to play dumb, that their relationship had grown from one of guest and hostess to something more intimate.

When I asked what had happened, George said that the rain had continued without stopping, and it had become boring to just sit around, and they had set out to look for cottages in the area that were up for sale.

"Well, you could have come and taken me, couldn't you?" I said icily. "Aren't we buying this cottage together?"

"Sorry, honey," George said. "There were two showings in Haliburton closing around 3 o'clock, and I didn't want us to waste time by backtracking to the house to get you. Anyway, you needn't have bothered—they are out of our price range."

He didn't explain what the heck they had been doing from 3 p.m. until now.

Mum, you know, I'll be the first to admit that I had been blind to George's misdemeanours, before we married. I have kidded myself that I could make an honest man out of him. I felt George was more a wounded soul who needed someone like me to keep him in line. Unless I have facts, am I supposed to doubt my husband? The man I gave my oath to? But jealousy can be a powerful killer of trust and it has left me quite confused.

I don't want any "I told you so's"—just some sympathy if you respond, which I know you can't do.

I am reaching for the cookie jar as I drop this letter in the envelope ...

Dee

***

Jimmy

I saw the trouble George and Denise's marriage was in on the night he came to my bachelor apartment, four months after their wedding. His hair had grown over his shoulders and was unkempt; the tee shirt he wore was torn under the armpits. He looked like he had been drinking.

He walked right into the apartment and started pacing in the living room, ignoring me.

"We fought," he said finally, after I had been standing there for five minutes.

"Who?"

"Denise and I. I have to leave her."

"Yeah, right." Inside, my heart leapt. With joy, I think.

"She sees a woman in every corner I am in."

"And is there?"

He stopped his pacing and looked squarely at me. "No." Then after a pause, "only in a few."

"You are cheating on your wife and you expect her to act normal?"

"You know me, Jimmy. I never could cut it with one woman. After I married Denise, I kept things...discreet."

"The Party didn't think so."

"That was different. They wanted me out."

"She stood by you during your crisis, George."

He looked around. "Got any scotch? I'll kill for a drink."

I shook my head. "I don't stock that stuff, except on an occasion. Sorry."

"It's the routine that's killing me, Jimmy. Time to be together—to go to church, to visit friends, to entertain them at home, to go grocery shopping together, house-cleaning together, gardening together—this togetherness of married life is suffocating. And I thought she was a great challenge. Not anymore."

"I'd find your married life refreshing."

"Can you take care of her for a few days? I've gotta go out of town. A deal I am working on with Bob that could see me to a happy retirement. Denise and you get along. She has nothing but high regard for you." There was a look of envy in his face and yet a naive sense of trust in me.

"I'll look in on her." I said. "Stay off the women. I heard about your deal with Bob—remember, he's no businessman, just a teacher like us. But stay off the women."

"I'll try."

I think he was willing himself to be honest when he said it.

I stayed away for an interminable four days. Then I called his home and got Denise on the line.

"Oh Jeremy, I'm so glad you called." She sounded anxious but relieved to hear from me. I had always been the sounding board whenever the man we mutually loved was in his altered states.

"How's George?"

"He's not home. He went away to Georgian Bay. Business, he said."

"When is he coming back?"

"I don't know. I am so muddled these days. About everything."

Thereafter followed my visits to her, to chat and share in her pain, while my great friend was on his "walkabout." What began as one visit turned into many, as George would disappear for periods on end.

He had been in a similar weed-induced state when he came to see me that day with his new girlfriend, an assistant professor who had signed on at the beginning of that school year. She was a couple of years younger than Denise, blond, with a body that compelled one to look at her, large eyes that were glazed with marijuana.

"We are going away for the weekend, Jimmy." George announced, a carefree look on his face. "Stopped by to tell you on our way out of town."

"Enjoy!" was all I could manage. My feelings were a mixture of rage at his brazenness and joy for the weekend I would have free to spend with Denise.

"You will look in on her, will you?" George said, a trace of anxiousness creeping into his voice.

The assistant professor giggled. "He's solicitous, isn't he?"

"Watch your driving," I said and slammed the door on them.

There was a tapping at my door about five minutes later. I waited awhile before opening it. I knew he would be standing there. He was; behind him I saw the assistant professor by the elevator, out of earshot.

"It's not as you think, Jimmy. The real world's a bit fucked up for me. I hope you understand."

I slammed the door in his face again. This time, without a word.

***

George

She was a wild one. He'd noticed her when she was a student, a bright one. She usually lingered after classes, waiting to see him, pummelling him with intelligent questions, but always having that, "What's next, sir?" look on her face.

When she took up teaching and remained at the college, he'd hoped half-heartedly that she'd settle down and find a boyfriend. But she asked to help shadow him on some of his classes. He was her role model, she said. When they debriefed afterwards in the cafeteria, she touched his thigh under the table as she sucked on her coke with a straw, eyes down on the notes, leg pressed against him. He was excited. One day, he slid his hand below the table and stuck it between her legs, wondering how far she'd let him go. Her legs parted, there was no underwear, and he felt prickly short hairs; she continued to suck on her straw and then turned her face to him, the innocence was gone, the look now said, "What's next, my man?"

He withdrew his hand in a rush, his excitement making breathing difficult.

"Come out with me to Wasaga this weekend," he said.

"Where will we be staying?" she countered.

"I'll find a place. A good one."

"I'm late for my next class," she said and picked up her notes, the diligent look back on her face. "Pick me up Friday evening."

After she left, he pushed his chair back. That had been so easy. And he had resisted her for so long. He shrugged. Better late than never, they said.

Yes, there had always been affairs with faculty, but they were married, older than him and looking for fun, like Mrs. Brown, those many years ago. He had become an expert at spotting them; they worked late, had lots of stored energy, were dismissive of marriage whenever he brought it up in conversation to test the waters; they also touched a lot or liked being touched. And they would be discreet for they had as much to lose as him. And then there were the single mothers; they were more difficult as they got clingy and emotional and tried to place him inside the hole that was in their lives. Yes, he could peg his women out well.

Heidi was only twenty-three, a different breed altogether, barely out of her student days. He could get into trouble with her. But there was the freshness of her skin, the innocence of her face as she let down the adult guard she walked around in—virgin country—well, as virgin as they came these days.

Denise intruded on his thoughts and he tried to put her out of his mind. Denise had been like that in the beginning—fresh, naïve, talented, beautiful even if you got past her tendency to dress like a hippie. A vast unconquered continent—Denise. But wrested now and controlled and no longer attractive. Attractions don't last—nothing lasts.

That Friday evening, after he left Jimmy's apartment, Heidi began snorting the white stuff before they hit Barrie. That had surprised him.

"Slow down," he said. "We've got to get to the cottage looking civilized."

She sniffed, smiling, a blank look on her face, which told him that she must have taken another hit before he picked her up. "You're old fashioned, Georgie?" she said, cloyingly.

"I'll stick with weed," he replied. "*After* we get there."

She was hyper and incoherent by the time they got to Wasaga Beach. He began looking for the address of the cottage he'd rented for the weekend, wondering why he had bothered to bring her.

"You are a fucking amateur, aren't you?" he said. "Think you know how to play in the big leagues?"

She threw both arms around him, nearly sending him off the road. "Be nice to me Georgie. You are my role model."

"You nervous?"

"I was. But I am not now."

When he finally found the place, she was alternating between shakes and snores. He was starting to get worried.

He carried her out of the car. Barbecues spewed smoke in neighbouring cottages, and people were gathered around. A little boy pointed at the two of them staggering into their darkened cottage. "Look—they are drunk," he heard the little inquisitive creature say aloud to the adults who were paying attention to their beers. A man operating the barbecue shouted at the kid to "mind his business and not disturb the neighbours."

He laid her out on the bed. He emptied the contents of the car: a bottle of scotch, beers, tinned food, steaks, burgers, frozen vegetables, milk, and her favourite, candy and fruit loop cereals. He grabbed a beer and walked out onto the back deck overlooking the lake and wondered what an idiot he had been. But this was the thrill of the chase he reconciled with himself after the third beer.

What the hell, he might as well get his money's worth, he told himself taking a long drag from a freshly-rolled weed cigarette. The party next door was dying down, and people were drifting off to cottages in the neighbourhood. The barbecue operator was cleaning his utensils.

He waved at some of the partygoers as they went by—no sense in making enemies. He wished he'd gotten something to eat from them, he was famished. He opened a can of soup, drank it from the container and wiped it off with a slice of bread.

He went back indoors, swimming in that lusty, languid state of mind brought on by the marijuana, watching the young woman ignominiously piled on the bed, coming down from her high, her dress up over her thighs which raised his lust another notch. He began to strip her. When they were both naked, he fantasized hearing peals of delight coming from her as he entered her. His father's stern face suddenly flashed in front of him. "Eighty-five per cent is not good enough!" *Fuck!* His mounting erection softened. "Get away from me you bastard—I am good!"

His shouting must have woken her, for she looked frightened at his naked figure standing over her with his face twisted in rage.

"George!" There was alarm taking hold of her face as the cobwebs of drug and sleep continued to fall away. She started to inch away from him.

She was getting away from him! Panic gripped him. He'd come too far to give up this pursuit. He grabbed her arms and forced her down on the bed, pinning her. He took a pillow and placed it over her mouth. He had the hardest erection—it almost hurt—and then he tore right into her. She was tight, and he felt big and powerful as she thrashed under him. He continued thrusting, holding onto this magical sense of power that overwhelmed him. This was worth all the manoeuvring it had taken to get here for the weekend. He was almost at his peak when she managed to get a leg under him and kick out, a thrust that separated them just as he came, shooting into the air.

"No!" he yelled, thwarted, released yet not satiated. She rolled away from him and landed on the floor. But he was spent now and had no desire to go after her. All he wanted to do was sleep. He slumped back on the bed and floated into a peaceful place.

When he next opened his eyes, he did not know how long he had been in that drowsy state. His heart froze. She was gone!

He staggered to the front door. The half-empty bottle of scotch on the kitchen counter glared back at him accusingly. The car was still in the driveway. He ran to the back and stepped onto the deck. He could make her out, a shadowy figure, unsteady on her feet, heading downhill through the trees towards the lake. In the moonlight glittering through the trees, she was still naked.

He jumped off the porch and felt his ankle twist upon hitting ground. He hopped through the pain, following her, falling down a couple of times before arriving at the tiny pier. She had managed to get into the single row-boat and unhitch its mooring. Standing unsteadily in the middle of the vessel, she applied the oars.

"Heidi! Come back! I'm sorry." Of course he was not sorry, he was bloody mad! He'd show her when he had her safe and sound on shore. He stepped off the pier hoping to swim after her before she got too far out. He dived into the water and began a steady crawl. The land dropped off immediately into deeper water. She was pulling with harder strokes and outpacing him. He was out of breath; marijuana, sex and approaching middle age didn't help beat the boat, and the younger woman, stoned though she may be, was getting ahead. After awhile the boat got absorbed into darkness as it entered the middle of the lake, away from the lights of the cottages lining the shores. He cut his stroke and tried to listen for the sound of oars peddling, but the water was rough in the centre and he couldn't distinguish any unusual sound.

Then he heard it: a sharp cry that was cut off immediately. He started off in that direction. There it was again: a woman's muffled scream. He swam faster, arms aching, lungs bursting, desperation in his heart, saying, "Please don't let this happen."

His hand, while in mid-stroke, struck something and he was up against the hull of the boat. It was turned upside down. Then he heard the woman's plea again, plaintive this time, yards away; then it dissolved in a gurgle. He lunged in the direction of the sound until he estimated he was at the point where it had vanished. Gulping air, he dove below the surface and immediately hit a body. The naked flesh, the line of belly—it was enough. He scooped her up and pushed up to the surface. They broke water, and he gasped for air. He grabbed her by the hair and pulled them both towards the capsized boat. He hugged the boat for a long time; her body lay limp beside him.

Then his panic returned. *She's dead.* He heaved with all his might and managed to turn the boat right side up. He went underwater again, placed his head between Heidi's legs and pushed upwards, getting her head and upper body over and into the boat. His heart was busting at this point and he had to rest with Heidi half in, half out, and the boat tilting towards the capsize position again. He swam under the boat to the other side and pulled down on it to steady her. He grabbed her hair again and pulled her completely into the boat. After another short rest to settle his cramping muscles, he hauled himself into the now weighted boat.

It had been a long time since he had learned CPR as a star on the school swimming team, but he applied it now with panic. The kiss of life never tasted so tasteless and desperate compared to the ones he had imagined placing on her tonight. She responded by gurgling dirty lake water laced with the contents of dinner back into his mouth. He spat, nearly puking, and continued his resuscitation, brutally pressing on her lungs when earlier in the day he had imagined stroking her to the heights of passion; she responded with coughs and returning signs of life that to him right now were sweeter than sounds heralding the greatest orgasm.

He only relaxed when he had established that she was not going to die. She lay groaning on her side. He took stock of their surroundings; the oars were gone, they must have fallen overboard with her. They were marooned in the middle of the lake, stark naked. A shiver coursed through him, and he let out his relief by throwing his head back and laughing. "Up the creek without a fucking paddle—I couldn't describe it better. Jimmy, if you could see me now, this is to die for!"

His hysterical outburst was cut short by a sound of a motor heading his way. The sailor of the other vessel must have heard his swearing. "Hey there! Need any help?" A searchlight shone on him, and he shielded his eyes. A guffaw from the other boat, "Having a bit of fun, eh?"

"Cut the light, will you?" he called back. "Our boat capsized."

"Depends on what you were doing in it," came the reply. The voice sounded familiar. "You the folks the ones that arrived in the rental cottage today? I recognized you. Glad I heard your missus yelling when I was walking the dog. Thought I'd come check it out."

"Thanks."

The searchlight left him and played over Heidi's body, a little longer than necessary.

Something whizzed past him and fell into the boat. "Take the rope. I'll tow you back to shore," said the amused voice in the rescue vessel. The light still remained on Heidi. She stirred and raised a hand to her eyes. Then the light went out. "Sorry, ma'am—just wanted to make sure you were all right." A chuckle, sexual in nature. The motor boat revved its engine and pulled out, tugging the row boat in its wake.

He slumped into the darkness that enveloped him, glad for the brief respite before they hit shore and had to answer questions.

Mercifully, his neighbour, and it was the man who had been operating the barbecue next door, did not speak until they got to within jumping off distance of their pier. When they were safely on land, he tossed a couple of blankets over saying he would collect them in the morning, retrieved the tow-rope and backed his boat out for the short ride to his own dock.

"Stay warm. No more skinny-dipping tonight, eh?" The neighbour chuckled as he sailed away.

Needles of pain shot from his foot with every step as he half-dragged, half carried Heidi uphill towards the house. He wrestled her onto the bed, threw his blanket on top of hers to keep her warm. He staggered into the living room and fell on the couch, exhausted. But sleep wouldn't come due to the pain in his ankle and the myriad thoughts that played through him as he wondered what the morning would bring.

The following day she woke at two in the afternoon. She didn't remember much of the previous evening and he did not elaborate. Going on a weekend with him had given her a panic attack, she admitted. She hadn't meant to create such a mess, but the drugs and alcohol had quite overcome her. To his relief, she did not mention the sex.

He fed her soup and let her rest on the couch. His ankle was still swollen, but he took himself off to a nearby golf course and played nine holes with the help of a motorised cart. He wanted to stay away from her.

That night, she drank scotch and *wanted* sex. She was drunk, brave and silly. He obliged her. But it wasn't like the night before when he had taken her by force and conquered her. Now she was just another easy woman looking to get laid, a mildly amusing and pleasurable pastime for the bored.

"Gosh—you go on forever!" she said curling up in his arms, sweating after she had come, twice.

She woke him at 3 o'clock again, but he knew she was faking it, pretending to be insatiable. Halfway during sex, she dozed. So did he.

The next morning he woke her at 10 o'clock. He said he had to get back to the city urgently; his wife needed him to run some errands.

"Your wife? I thought she was out of town visiting relatives?" Heidi looked confused and annoyed. He had wrecked her beauty sleep and her returning confidence.

"She returned home early," he replied, picking up his already packed suitcase.

"And you just pack and go when she taps her fingers? Just like that?"

"Yes," he said calmly, walking out of the bedroom. She threw a pillow after him, but it hit the wall and landed on the floor.

After he dropped her off at her apartment, following a silent ride back home, he sat in his car for a long time. He certainly would not be seeing her again, but there would be other conquests like this in future. There had to be. A smile played on his face as he gunned the engine and eased back into the slow moving Sunday traffic on Yonge Street, heading home to Denise from another one of his "business trips."

***

Jimmy

It was the end of summer and the closing of many cottages on the lake. George was celebrating his birthday. Bob and Shirley were in Italy and had lent their cottage to George for the celebration. I was invited. I had stayed away despite his many previous invitations; partly because the still newly-married couple needed space I guessed, and mainly because my frequent visits to Denise were reawakening painful feelings inside me.

When I parked my modest Toyota Corolla, it rubbed shoulders with a Mercedes and a Cadillac. A parking lot had been cut into the woods and a gravel pathway led uphill to the cottage, or mansion, I would say, overlooking the lake. I wondered how Bob, a teacher like us, could afford it—Shirley's family money, I discovered. The heavy, polished pine wooded exterior was a huge improvement from cottages of yore. Stained glass double doors led me inside to noise and revelry.

It was one of those Indian summer days, unseasonably hot, and although it was five in the afternoon, the revellers had already had a lot to drink. Two uniformed waiters circulated with bites while everyone showed more interest in the booze and was paying attention to George behind the bar dolling out drinks.

A drunk, red-haired woman in a bathing suit bumped into me. Her tanned flesh was cold and soft, as if she'd been in the water all day. "Hey, you're overdressed. Want a sip?" She stuck a glass in my face, spilling beer on my shirt. A short, bald man brushed through and pushed her away, with a "Gotta leave honey, the kids, remember?"

"Fuck the kids," she said.

The couple disappeared into the crush. I was up at the bar, and George was throwing me a beer in the bottle, which I grabbed before it hit another woman on the head.

"Happy birthday!" I shouted out, and received the thumbs up from George before he turned around to serve another guest. I took my beer and retreated to the far corner of the room. I pinched a sausage roll from a passing waiter, and he smiled like I had fulfilled his purpose for coming out today. A stereo blared Led Zeppelin, and a couple—the woman was too young to be a wife or girlfriend—ascended to the upper floor, holding hands and slobbering over each other. I recognized the man; he was a senior faculty member at the college, one of George's buddies, a man I did not like.

I looked out the French windows into the garden that ran down to the lake. A volley ball net was erected on one side, and a rowdy game was in progress—more party-goers who were falling down more than hitting the ball. A couple of paddle boats were hauling people to and from the lake on rides; these were the quiet ones or the ones who'd had too much to drink and wanted someone else to do the driving. A barbecue belched fumes at the other end of the garden, and some guests were busily crowded around, grabbing the latest round of steaks coming off the grill.

I stepped outdoors; the smell of burning meat was preferable to the loud music. I caught sight of Denise sitting on a deck chair, talking to an older lady. Seeing me, she excused herself, rose and came over. Her hair was cut very short, like it had been chopped by a careless barber. Her smile was tired. "Hello Jimmy, nice of you to come." She took my hand, and I could see that she was glad for my company; she looked lonely in this crowd, just as I was.

"Quite a party," I said.

"George has many business connections in the area now. Plus the faculty."

"Yes, I noticed. Some of them do not act their age."

She gave me a knowing smile and kicked at the stones on the path as we strolled down to the water. A speedboat raced by hauling a water skier. As the boat passed, the skier lost control and splashed down into the water, and the boat cut its engine. Denise laughed. "My amusement for the day," she said.

"Sorry I've stayed away this month. How are things?"

"Still can't get back to my painting. It's been like that since we returned from the honeymoon."

"I'm shocked. Why?"

"It's tough being a married woman. George's lifestyle has many demands."

"And distractions."

"I guess I cannot get my head into it. I have three more paintings to do on my contract before November. Not sure how I will get to it."

The skier was back on her skis, and the boat roared back to life hauling her slowly this time. A paddle boat pulled into the private dock of the cottage and disgorged its occupant who ran back to the house shouting, "I need another drink!"

"You need to be happy," I said. "That will stimulate your creativity."

"Happiness is relative, isn't it?"

"You were happier when I first met you. Before you married him."

"Being with George, when he is around, makes me happy. But when he is not around—which is most times now—makes me very lonely. He is an 'in-your-face' person as you know, and vulnerable under his brash exterior. I guess that's why I fell for him in the first place."

"But you aren't happy now, are you? Even with him being a few hundred yards away with all his buddies." I didn't want her to avoid my question any longer.

"I'm not happy when I am not working. Painting has been my life. I miss it terribly."

"Why don't you just mark off some time and get back to it?"

"Without the happiness factor? I just can't get back in that frame by pretending."

"Can George not see your predicament? He loves your work."

"I don't want to stop him and his plans at the moment. He has big things in front of him. Perhaps there will be time later."

The older lady came back with a plate of barbecued food and offered it to us. I helped myself to an ear of corn. Denise excused herself and walked back with the woman to a group of new arrivals who had just stepped out through the French windows. I strolled back to the house, deposited my empty beer bottle on a picnic table and slipped past the new arrivals into the cooler indoors. I had decided it was time to head home. I had shown my face, at least. A giant cake was being rolled out from the kitchen, and guests were calling for George. He was not serving drinks behind the bar any more, however his senior faculty buddy who had gone upstairs with the younger woman had taken George's place. I looked around and saw George descending the stairs buttoning his shirt, a smug look on his face. *Pizarro descends to his subjects.* Behind him, the tousled younger woman came out of one of the upper bedrooms, adjusted her bra straps and followed George to the cake cutting ceremony.

I left.

"He's sleeping around," Denise said, applying a daub of paint on the canvas.

The apartment was littered with paintings again, some on the floor, others on any piece of available space; on the dining table, on the couch, leaning against the bookcase. I moved some assorted books off a stool and sat down.

I had "come to see her" as George had asked me. After the party at the lake, I had resumed my visits, whenever he was not around. I wasn't holding back anymore and found any occasion when he was away to visit. Seeing the paintings gave my heart a lift.

I couldn't take my eyes off her, and in the confines of this room, with her personality radiating off the paintings as well as off her body, her presence was overwhelming. Paint, canvas and Denise complemented each other. That was how I had seen her the first time we met.

"He always slept around," I said. "That's George. I warned you before you married."

"And I thought you were the jilted suitor."

"That too."

Then she threw down her brush, her body convulsing, tears brimming in her eyes. "What's with you men? The chase?"

I got off my stool and went to her. My hands were clammy and my heart beat irregularly as I held her, still conscious of the fact that she was another man's wife.

"Hold me properly, Jimmy," she said collapsing deeper into my arms, her hands clutching my shoulders from behind. Her need was stoking a fire in me and I submitted to it, holding her tighter.

When our lips found each other's we had given up caution and propriety; our hands explored each other's bodies hungrily, lips grinding greedily.

We knocked aside the canvas under construction; it fell to the floor tipping her box of paints, spreading colour on the floor, over which our bodies descended, locked in embrace, seeking, penetrating, shutting out the world, even for a few minutes, for we knew that was all we had. Her yearning body was pulling me in, holding me, as if I were an elusive scrap of paper that might blow away in the wind at any moment.

When we had spent ourselves, we lay in each other's arms, smelling the simmering heat of each other; the clock ticking on the mantelpiece was the only sign of the passing moment. Our clothes were littered on the floor, soaking up the paint.

"I never thought you had so much passion," she said, clearing a lock of hair from her face.

"Me neither. I guess you bring it out in me."

She rolled over and stroked my chest. "I've never been held like that in a long time, Jimmy. Thank you. George stopped holding me, after I became his wife."

"The conquest was over."

"Am I a conquest to you too, Jimmy?"

"I've desired you from the moment I laid eyes on you."

"Why? Because I was George's?"

"I desired you *before* I knew you were George's."

"Then why did you not come after me? It's nice to be needed."

I remained silent. Yes, why had I not pursued her and given George a run for his money? "Deep down I had given up, even before I started," I admitted. "Besides, I gave him my word. And if I broke it, I still knew I would lose, especially when it came to feelings. George wears his on his sleeve. Women fall for that stuff."

She rose from the floor, her naked body glistening with sweat. She gathered our paint streaked clothes and rearranged them on the half finished canvas. "Perhaps, I'll finally have my post-modern art piece after all."

Against the background of a pastel garden scene, that had been the original theme, were my paint smeared shirt and pants intertwined with her bra and panties. "Shall I call it 'Infidelity'? Or 'Lust'?"

I sat up, reaching for her once more, like a drunken sailor reaching for his bottle. "How about 'Unrequited Love'?"

She threw her head back and laughed, and fell back into my arms. The canvas and its soiled contents fell to the floor again, dispersing into different forms.

"I haven't figured what sin I have committed," she said, rolling on top of me and arousing me once more. "But for now, I don't want this to end."

"Me neither," I said, thrusting upward and into her.

***

An extract from *Conquistador*—a novel by George Walton

They were camped in the Rimac valley, a day's march from Ciudad de Los Reyes, on their way to finally emancipate Cusco from the besieging Inca. In the haze behind them rose the walls of Los Reyes, the City of the Kings, fast becoming the colonial centre of Peru, which one day would be renamed Lima. Many in Spain had heard of the riches of this continent and were settling in his capital, fuelling commerce and trade.

*Francisco sat outside his tent as the sun went over the Andes, nursing
his saddle-weary feet, looking admiringly upon his troops who were
pitching camp for the night, reinforcements that had finally arrived from
Panama; five hundred men, including two hundred and thirty cavalry
with fresh horses, and sufficient guns and ammunition to rout those
savages once and for all.*

*"A horseman, Your Excellency," Espinosa, his second-in
command, announced, hurrying up the hill. Watch fires were being lit
around the camp perimeter as a horse broke through the ring.*

*The dusty horseman and his frothing horse drew up in a cloud
of dust in front of the governor's tent. The horseman looked like he was
passed caring about protocol and lay hunched in the saddle, dejected.
Then he jerked to attention, realizing that he had miraculously arrived
at his destination. Francisco held his breath; the man had the colours of
Alvarado's troop, the advance brigade that should be nearing Cusco by
now and awaiting the governor's arrival to launch the final attack.*

*"Speak up, man!" Francisco stood and straightened, ignoring
the stiffness in his legs.*

*"General Alvarado...has been taken prisoner, Your
Excellency." The man managed to say before crumpling to the ground.*

*Francisco grabbed the fallen horseman by the lapels of his coat
and hauled him off the dust. "Taken prisoner? By Manco? Five
hundred men? Impossible!"*

*The man cringed. "No, Your Excellency, by Don Diego de
Almagro."*

"What? Almagro is on his way to Chile, you fool."

*"No, Your Excellency. He turned back because of the bad
weather and returned to Cusco. And he defeated the Inca surrounding
the city, taking them by surprise. He has taken your brother, Hernando,
prisoner. Now Don Diego has control of the Inca capital. We got word
of these developments, and General Alvarado prepared to attack. But
Don Diego surprised us too. He split his force between the bridge and the
ford and attacked us on two fronts. General Alvarado is now a prisoner.
Only two of us managed to escape the battle on the bridge. My partner
died along the way."*

*Almagro! Once his friend, now his greatest threat. Even
Manco, if that savage was still alive, paled by comparison. What good*

would his five hundred men do if Alvarado's five hundred had failed? Perhaps he was losing the confidence he'd had when he took on Atahualpa and his hordes. That had been only six years ago. Was he getting old?

"At sunup, we return to Los Reyes," he announced.

"But, Excellency...?" The dismay was palpable in Espinosa's face.

"We will not win this battle by force. We will win by stealth," he concluded, and stepped back into his tent to hide his disappointment and plot his revenge.

***

Jimmy

I had bought tickets to the concert; the TSO was having a Mendelssohn evening, and Denise loved the composer's creations. George was out of town that weekend. I had reserved a table at Biagio's Restaurant, a family affair that had hit the big time, thanks to being featured in *Toronto Life.*

I called her that afternoon to make sure she would be ready by 6 p.m. Denise was bouncy, happy to be going out with me. She had bought a red dress, she told me.

I rushed through my last class, handed off assignments flippantly and left work at 3 o'clock so that I could get a haircut, take a close shave and have a shower before the evening ahead of me.

A light snow was falling when I arrived at her apartment. I was whistling when I rang the doorbell. My whistle faded when George opened the door. I was relieved I had not brought flowers with me that day.

"George! What are you doing here?" I tried to hide my disappointment. Behind his grinning frame I saw Denise laying the table. She was not wearing the red dress, but a tee shirt and jeans.

"Hah! I should ask that of you, my friend. But come in, come in—it's always nice to see you."

I stepped inside. A garment bag lay sprawled by my feet.

"Got through the work early. Bureaucrats! No one works on the weekend."

"I thought you'd be used to them by now." This was unreal, this was not happening—Denise was laying three places for dinner.

"Dee told me you'd be dropping by. Care for some dinner with us?"

"Why ... sure." What else could I say?

"But first, a drink." George said, rubbing his hands together. "What's yours?"

"Wine, I guess. Red."

"You have to graduate to scotch someday, old man," he said and went off into the kitchen.

I tried to catch Denise's attention as she lingered at the dining table, but she looked up at me, tears in her eyes, and shook her head. Then she turned and went off into the kitchen.

I sat on the leather couch; three days ago we had been making vigorous love on it. Somehow it felt soiled to me. I moved over to the CD player. I scanned the music selection—then realized I could not play any, as these were the songs we had talked for hours over and made love to. I felt trapped. Why was George suddenly so interested in Denise again? Because I was showing her more than the usual interest?

"Red wine—Californian Merlot." I spun around to see George with hand outstretched, the wine sloshing in the glass and over the sides. "Pardon the clumsiness, old pal."

I took a tissue and wiped the dripping glass, a few drops fell on the beige carpet.

George took a healthy swig from his glass of scotch, wriggled his mouth, gulped, took a smaller gulp and threw himself on the couch with a satisfied sigh. "Ah, it's good to be back home."

I looked at my watch. I guess there was going to be an empty table at Biagio's tonight. I could kiss goodbye to the concert too.

"Going somewhere tonight, Jimmy?" George was observing me over the rim of his glass, a slow smile playing on his lips.

"I dropped in to see Denise. You asked me to, remember?"

"You are a good pal, Jimmy."

Denise came out and announced that dinner would be ready in five minutes. The telephone rang, and George got up to answer it. I took the break to offer help and followed her into the kitchen.

"Does he know?" I whispered to her by the stove.

"I don't know," her voice was resigned. She took the pizza out of the oven. "He caught me by surprise by showing up an hour ago."

George walked into the kitchen.

"Can you help me with the salad, Jimmy," Denise said and brushed past into the dining room.

George twirled his glass, looking after her, a satisfied look on his face. "What a girl, eh? Turns out a dinner at such short notice. I must keep her on her toes, eh, Jimmy?"

"You are a lucky man, George."

But he was reaching for the bottle of scotch. "Let's have another before dinner," he said, chuckling.

"It's an instrument of control, Jimmy. When you run out of controls, introduce another—an invaluable weapon of the conquistadors." If I had heard that line from George years earlier, I may have handled things differently.

Soon after his fling with the assistant professor, George came to see me one day, in the middle of the first snowstorm of the season. He had taken a shave, had his hair cut and was dressed in laundered clothes under his thick winter coat.

"I'm turning a new leaf, Jimmy," he announced. "The private school project is off. I'm going to build an extension to the house, put in an extra room. Add a deck. That will keep me occupied at home during the summer holidays."

"Does Denise know about all this?"

"No. I can't talk to her. She found out about Heidi— the prof. Don't know how she did. I was discreet. Denise won't talk to me now."

"Serve you damn right."

"I know, I know—it's all my fault. Running away from reality. That's what I have been doing."

"And what do you need from me?"

"I want you to talk to her. Explain that I mean it this time. I want to give her a baby, settle down. I know that's what she has been expecting."

"Is that who you are going to build the new room for?"

"Yeah." The hope in his eyes was pathetic. But my gregarious friend was now a wimp sitting in my living room, entreating me to help him yet another time and intercede with the woman I loved.

"I've lost credibility trying to sing your praises. You never hold up your end of the bargain. Are you sure you can handle the 'routine?'"

"I will this time. You've gotta believe me." What was harder to accept was the look on his face implying that he had indeed turned the corner.

But there was another confession I wanted to wring out of him. "What's with this Shirley woman?"

His face blanched.

"How ... how did you know?"

"Let's say that your discretion is not working anymore, George."

He looked beaten, head swaying from side to side, swearing under his breath.

"That was my pay-off to Bob. He's impotent. I was supposed to keep her from straying."

"So you can add gigolo to your many talents?"

"You don't understand, Jimmy. It was all part of the deal. Bob got to exercise control over me by offering me a stake in his school venture, which is funded by her money. In return, I serviced his wife. She controlled him, he controlled me and I controlled her—it worked!"

"You're a bastard."

"How else could I start up in business? I don't have that kind of money. But Shirley is a tiresome old bitch at times."

"So you take off with the Heidis of this world."

"Well, there you have it. Are you happy that you have made me grovel?"

"And you want to give Denise a baby and bind her deeper into your insidious web of sexual liaisons?"

"No, I've given that all up. I called it off with Bob today. He's an idiot. Besides, I need my freedom. The baby will give me a focus, Jimmy. Please, you've gotta believe me."

He had his hands together wringing them, pleading. He was such a show-off. I secretly envied his unabashed ability to let it all hang out whenever it suited him.

I went over to the window and stared out; heavy snowflakes were coming down, burying our sins, his and mine.

It had been a similar day just last week when I had risen from making love to Denise and looked at the rain falling outside. The only difference then had been that George was out of town, again, and I was looking out of *my* bedroom window.

Our love making had been mechanical this time, not the frenzied passion of the last three months, after our guards had been let down that first time. We had settled back on our respective corners of the bed, the spectre of George hovering like a ghost between us, increasing in admonishment the more we indulged our desires.

"Do you think this was a mistake? Us?" she asked. I turned to her. Her unbraided blond hair was spread in waves over the pillow; luminous blue eyes filled with tears. She pulled the covers over her, not in time for me to admire her firm and contoured body; nor the lush patch between her legs where I had drunk until my heart nearly burst. When she returned to George I would fall into the deepest despair of longing for someone that I could never have, and stew in the guilt for betraying my friend.

"If you leave him, it will not be a mistake."

"And he would never forgive you."

I felt like Judas. I turned away. Her next words chilled me. "We have to end this, before he finds out."

I rolled over to her side of the bed and grabbed her hand. "No. I will not let you go. He cannot take everything I have always wanted. I want you."

"Because, I am George's wife? Sometimes I think you men only think of one-upmanship, of conquering the other's territory."

I pressed my lips to hers desperately. But she was unresponsive. "There is something else, I need to tell you," she said.

"I love you," I replied.

"No you don't love me, Jeremy. You want me as your possession, you don't love me. There is something I want to tell you ... "

I rose and walked away and started to put on my clothes.

"I've been so distracted, I wasn't careful. I missed my last period ... "

I spun around. "George ... ?"

"No—you. He has not been around much."

"All the more reason for you to leave him. If you don't tell him, I will."

"No you will do nothing of the kind. We have to find another way. I can pretend the baby is his."

"And what about me, Dee? You will go back to George and pretend that this never happened?"

"You will always be in my heart, Jeremy. You know that. We came together for a reason. You have helped me reconcile with George, in my mind. He is not the only one who cheats. Most men and women do, even the good ones like us."

"You want to go back to George? After all his whoring?"

"Yes, it's the only way. My mother stuck by my father, even when he played around and left us. She regrets to this day that she did not do more to hold on to him. Then she had her stroke, and there was no going back."

Now, as I turned away from the living room window, I casually asked George, "Is Denise already pregnant for you to be making these plans?"

"No but she will, when you help us patch up," George said. The hope in his eyes was reaching out and hitting me at my core.

"I'll see what I can do," I said.

I invited them to dinner soon after George entreated me to intercede with Denise on his behalf. I cooked for them: honey-glazed lamb chops, herbed potatoes and an authentic lettuce-free Greek salad. I also had two bottles of Denise's favourite Chardonnay in the fridge. I had set my timers and sequenced the cooking so that everything would turn out perfect—and it did.

After polishing off the food and wine (Denise did not drink the wine, feigning a new diet she was on, so George and I finished off the two bottles), I brought out the piece de resistance, Crème Brule, which I had specially ordered from a French patisserie downtown as I did not want to spoil the moment by trying to make it myself and screw it up. Denise's eyes watered because this is what I had always brought to her from the patisserie whenever I had visited her alone these months. I rose and pulled out a bottle of ice wine that I had been hiding; after all, why not go all out? I proposed a toast, and Denise scooped a chunk of the crème Brule into her mouth.

"To the two of you!" I said.

"Hear, hear!" said George, raising his glass too quickly.

Denise swallowed and chinked an empty glass with her husband's overflowing one, looking dreamily into his eyes.

"I know both of you have been through a lot lately." I continued like a silly idiot. This was my rehearsed speech. "I hope you lead a very happy life from now on. Put the past behind you and all that."

"I'll make your life very happy from now on, sweetheart," George said. He burped and continued. "You are just the right woman for me."

"Touché!" Denise said, eyes watering.

Then I heard myself saying. "And don't ever ask me to carry this burden for you again," I know the tears were pouring down my face.

I recall them staring anxiously at me, both for different reasons. *Don't let the cat out*—they were both trying to say in their different ways.

"What a fucking charade," I said. "A travesty!"

"What do you mean?" George was coming out of his alcohol-induced soporific state. Denise had panic written all over her face.

"What do I mean?" I was snarling, for I had completely lost it. My father had said to let it all out, don't keep it in. "You abandon your wife, fuck around all over town, and now you come back when it's convenient and take the only woman I ever loved away from me? When the hell will you stop leeching off me, George?"

"Jimmy—you ... Denise ... ?"

"George, darling, I think we should be going. Jimmy has been under a lot of strain lately. We should not have bothered him with planning this dinner for us." Denise was rising, her eyes imploring me to stop. Finally I had them both where I wanted them; I was tired of being the doormat.

"You ... you slut!" I shouted back at her. "Go fuck him tonight, so he couldn't tell whose child you are carrying. Go on, take him. Get out of here."

George stumbled upright from the table, knocking the bottle of ice wine and spilling its contents into the Crème Brule. A glass rolled off the table and crashed on the floor.

Then, bolstered with courage that I translated into physical effort, I took a swing at George. I should have known that I was pushing my luck there. He stepped aside neatly and clobbered me on the temple. I crashed into the side table and brought the whole thing down on the floor.

Denise began screaming and pulling on George who had also lost it by now and was reaching down to give me more punishment for sleeping with his wife. I grabbed his leg and tugged, trying to bring him down to the floor from which I could not get up at that moment. I felt weighed down by an invisible force.

Finally, I managed a massive pull, and George and Denise both came crashing down on me. It was great getting him down to my level and banging my fist into his handsome face, releasing my frustration, although I think I was receiving more blows back from him.

Then we were apart, standing in our corners, bruised, bloody and cooling down from the emotions that had overcome us. Denise was in the middle, her blouse torn, arms outstretched, trying to keep us apart. But my eyes were riveted on the trickle of blood that had started to flow down her legs, staining her nylons. *My God, we hit her too!* Denise followed our eyes and gripped her stomach. George and I both rushed forward to grab her as she sobbed and went down on her knees into the pool of blood, as if trying to gather it up and force it back into her.

Six—New Conquest

Jimmy

The trail began through flat country. Mountains beckoned in the distance, so did the rain cloud. We had to go up and down two mountains, the first one—Dead Woman's Pass—being the tallest, at nearly fourteen thousand feet above sea level. During the first couple of hours, we passed villages and fields, some sprung up around volcanic rocks that had rolled down the mountains during earthquakes. The threat of imminent extinction hung in the air, but the attitude of shrugging off disaster and carrying on with a smile held true in the faces of the locals who waved us past.

My stomach had settled after leaving Cusco; I felt weak and was glad for the flat terrain. I was also reassured that we had opted for four Quechua men to carry our tents and cookware for us. They nimbly skipped ahead, along the ancient stones of the trail, and Valdez advised us that we would next see them at the camp that night where our tents would be made, and dinner simmering.

After a brief stop for a sandwich lunch, we began the climb. We were only traveling four miles that day but it felt like forty. The steps that made up the trail from this point were broken and uneven, and steep and narrow in places.

The rain started to come down midway. At first it was refreshing from the sweat of the trek, but as we ascended, it turned cold.

George fell behind, and Valdez kept pace with him, bringing up the rear, and I was on my own for most of this section of the climb.

I pulled on a sweater that got quickly soaked, threw on a poncho and increased my pace. The light started to diminish at the halfway point. Turning around, I discovered that I was alone on the trail; only the steps heading steeply down indicated where I had come from. I heard faint voices below; Valdez and George were somewhere out of sight. When I stopped, the voices amplified. Satisfied, I continued.

My muscles began to cramp. Raising a leg on to the next stone step became difficult, then impossible. I started to panic. Should I turn back? My water bottle was long empty; besides the Diamox took it all out anyway in the frequent passing of urine. But just like the night before, I wanted to keep going. The sheer rush of adrenaline, the fact that I was doing something I had never attempted before, and the fact that George, who was in worse condition than me, was *behind*, was motive enough to keep moving, despite the freezing limbs and groans that were, by now, unshakeable companions on the journey.

I had a sudden burst of anxiety, not for me, but for George. He was never going to make it this far in his condition. Marijuana was no antidote to altitude sickness. I began to slow down, the cramps in my legs had spread to my upper body and every step was now a struggle. Under my sweater, poncho and the two other layers of clothes, I was sweating in this cold, damp Andean climate. The voices behind me got louder. I caught sight of Valdez with his hands widely gesticulating, perhaps spinning another Inca story, fabricated or real, we tourists would never know. But it was George I was focused on; he had his head down, buttressed against the strong wind that had started down the mountain.

Every time he faltered, he strained with renewed effort to keep going.

"The camp is not far," Valdez called out, quickening his step. "We have to move faster before we get pollo—how do you say—chicken, no?" He was grinning as he passed me. "Vamanos, amigos!"

I held back until George drew near. "How's it going?" I wanted to hold him, give him what strength was still left in my body. For once, he did not look so indestructible.

"I've got such a fucking headache ... " he mumbled and lurched passed me, his backpack bumping and nearly toppling me off the narrow steps.

"Gotta vamanos," he had fallen into a drone, head down, plodding on. "You heard da man—keep going ... one foot...in front of the other ... Fucking hell ... it hurts so much..Vamanos amigos ... vamanos ... "

We lapsed into a chant, and it was deliriously exhilarating. We were beyond tiredness. Somewhere ahead was a camp with four Inca descendants waiting for us with a hot meal, and we were not going to be chicken-shit gringos about to pollo out. "Gotta vamanos ... gotta vamanos ... " Making our hiking sticks strike the stones to the beat of our chanting had suddenly become the most immediate challenge.

Just when we saw the blue tents over the tree line, and the smell of cooking wafted down to us, George began throwing up; clumps of yellow bile adding to the smoke from the campfire, spewing by me and floating down the mountain in the wind. He staggered up two more steps and fell forward in a heap. I reached for him and held him in my arms.

"Sorry, old buddy. Didn't mean to be rude." His bloodshot eyes were trying to look humorous, but he was whacked. He was also burning up under his clothes.

"Hang on to me." I unhitched our backpacks and managed to haul him up on his feet again, slung one of his arms over my shoulder, and we staggered the rest of the way. The men were running down to meet us as we rounded the bend into view of the camp.

"Bring the backpacks," I gasped. "I've got George."

Valdez looked worried after we had cleaned up as best as we could with water from the cooking pots, and laid George down inside his sleeping bag in the main tent. "He has the altitude sickness."

"Then we need to get him to a doctor." I had forgotten my own creaking bones.

Valdez looked dubious. "Senor, it is one day walking back and two days walking forward, and nothing in between. You decide."

"We go back then."

"No fucking way!" came the impassioned voice from inside the tent.

Valdez shrugged. "You heard? Perhaps once he sleeps tonight—if he does not die—he will be better tomorrow. We will give him lots of Coca tea. But no alcohol and marijuana, okay? Make sure you take that all away from him. Not even cigarettes."

George groaned through the night, sticking his head out through the tent flaps many times to empty his guts. The tent smelled of vomit. Towards dawn, he began snoring deeply, and I fell into a dream-filled doze.

My dreams were of George dressed as a Spanish conquistador and me as an Inca chief in Spanish clothes, colonizing parts of South America. We had divided the continent between us, taking countries at random. At last, we faced each other in Machu Picchu—there were no more colonies to take, just each other's. The Puma head on top of Saksaywaman had been replaced by a naked Denise—sexy woman, as she was called. We circled each other for the final duel, him spewing vomit at me, and me shitting in his face. I awoke in a rush, a cry in my throat. George was snoring, but his breathing was regular, and I did not want to disturb him even though I could hear the porters taking down the tents and getting ready for the continuation of our hike.

Rain clouds were turning black overhead when George finally woke at mid-morning. The porters were packed and ready and playing cards, while Valdez blew tunes on his flute, and I paced biting my nails. George stretched as he walked out of the tent and announced, "I feel like shit, but I think the worst is over. What are we waiting for? Let's vamanos!"

We continued our climb to a peak that looked like a giant female breast—Dead Woman's Pass. It was deathly cold, and we were walking *inside* the rain cloud. We paused at the crest to take pictures next to a sign that gave us our elevation—we were at the highest point of the climb. Now it would be downhill for the next three hours, and I soon discovered that going down could be equally punishing on the knees as climbing up. Mangy llama, grazing on sparse outcrops of vegetation, watched us descend. Pausing to take pictures of the stray animals gave us a chance to relax muscles and joints.

Then the rain came down again—gushing torrents, unlike the steady drizzle of the previous day. Muddy water flowed down the broken stones ahead, threatening an ankle-shattering slip at every step. Our hiking sticks were of immense support at this juncture. The porters had disappeared down below, and Valdez was in front this time. Either he couldn't care whether we lived or died, or he had gained confidence in our abilities by now.

My boots squelched water and had gone out of shape. Clothes clung to bodies, and I gave up trying to find any protection from the elements. This was a test for the "waterproof" marks on my watch and camera.

"This is great!" George said, looking up at the heavens. "It's raining guinea pigs and llamas, as they say. We are in fucking Purgatory."

"I'd say—Hell," I grumbled, trudging on miserably.

"No, that's still to come."

An hour into the rain, and there were no signs of a let up. I pulled George into a shoulder in the rock that offered partial shelter. "Let's sit it out."

"Valdez will panic if he doesn't see us following him."

"Serve him right for bringing us out in this shitty weather."

George fished under his poncho and brought out a hip flask. "Here, this will warm you up."

"I thought you were not supposed to have any more alcohol?" I was, however, grateful for the brandy scouring my throat and warming my belly at that moment.

"Emergency supplies," George winked. Despite the rain he seemed to be making a speedy recovery from his altitude sickness. Besides, we were in descent and perhaps this had something to do with it.

"You know, Jimmy, I always looked on you to be my protector—right from our Scarborough days."

"It's been a huge responsibility."

"I was glad you were there for me yesterday. I thought I was not going to make it."

"You didn't look like you were about to quit."

"I've quit too many times before, Jimmy. This was a special trip—to undo all the wrong things I've done."

I was anxious to get moving again, partly because I did not want to lose our guides, and partly because George had touched a nerve that made me uncomfortable.

We walked in wet silence—two full hours in the rain. Valdez met us at the bottom where the trail started winding upwards again. "Amigos, you took your time. Good! Enjoying the weather? Now we climb again—smaller mountain—and we camp just south of the summit."

We were too wet to complain. Like meek lambs heading to the abattoir, we followed on muscles that had now become miraculously compliant from the cold, rain and continuous exercise.

Trouble awaited us when we arrived at the campsite. The fog had descended and daylight was fading fast. The rain had eased, but the world was wet. We were walking through piles of mud. The campsite was partway down the second mountain inside an indentation on its face. Being sheltered by the overhang, it was relatively dry; I could understand Valdez's desire to camp there. However, a solitary foreign grey tent, larger than any of ours, was already erected in the centre, and our porters were arguing among themselves, standing around it. Valdez quickly interpreted, after getting the facts from his crew. "Some tourists have already taken our site. There is not enough room to pitch all our tents. We have to find another site."

George roared into life. "Hold on. Not after all this walking. Go tell them to fuck off. We had reserved this site. Squatters are simply not allowed."

He stomped off towards the tent that had its flaps closed.

"Hey there! Anyone home?"

There was a rustling inside.

"They closed the tent and refused to talk to my men," Valdez explained to me, shaking his head. I was curious, despite my fatigue. The tent wobbled, as if its contents were about to spill out of the opening, with George standing opposite, hands on his hips. Then the flap opened, a blond woman stuck her head out and said, "Well, if it isn't our intrepid explorers!"

George stepped back as if punched, then rebounded quickly, smiling widely, "Well, well, well ... look who's here! We've been traveling all over Peru to find you, Ali."

The second woman stuck her head out and instantly recognized our guide. "Valdez!"

"Miss Beatrice!" exclaimed Valdez. "Ah, how fortunate! I thought you were not coming until next week."

"But we sent you a note from Lake Titikaka saying we were coming this week."

He shrugged and blushed. "Ah, so the postal system, it's not the best in my country."

I decided to step in on the more practical matter while our respective party members were 'bonding'. "Ahem ... ladies and gentlemen ... I think we have a small problem to settle regarding the accommodations."

But the enterprising George had already solved that one.

"No problem, we can settle this quickly," he chimed. Then turning to the women, he bowed. "Allow me to formally introduce ourselves. I am George Walton, at your service. This is my trusted friend, Jimmy Spence."

Ali smiled at his gallantry. "I am Ali, but you already know my name. And this is *my* trusted companion, Bea."

We shook hands all around. Then I turned to George. "I'm still waiting for your solution to our camping arrangements."

George drew in his breath and puffed out his chest. "If you will all allow me, here is my proposal. We are only short of space for one tent. Jimmy, so let's not pitch ours. You can sleep with Valdez, the porters can have theirs, and I am prepared to share with these adventurous ladies." He bowed with a flourish, then looking up quickly, winked at the women, "Strictly above board, I assure you. Besides, I only snore moderately, I am told."

The two women looked at each other. Bea seemed hesitant, while Ali smiled broadly. "Sure. That sounds more fun than pitching our tent in the middle of nowhere tonight in this rain. Come on, Bea—besides you can now work out the details with Valdez here."

So, it was settled.

Ali and Bea were invited to have dinner with us at the campfire that the porters got going as soon as our sleeping arrangements were finalized.

The women had changed out of their wet hiking clothes; a pursuit they had been engaged in when we had arrived at the camp, hence the buttoned down flaps of their tent. George and I huddled by the fire, trying to warm up as best as we could, for our fresh clothes were still in knapsacks, and the rules for undressing had not been established yet. The potato soup was relishing, so was the guinea pig stew.

Ali entertained us with stories of their trek, and George launched animatedly into the conversation. Bea gave them wry glances and looked at me periodically as if for understanding.

"We were well past Dead Woman's Pass when the rain hit us," Ali said. She took out her digital camera and played back shots she had taken on the pass. "She must have been guiding us spiritually on our way. I could feel the other-worldness of the place."

George laughed heartily. "One dead woman was enough for that legend, eh? Besides, I don't think the old gal was likely to share her reputation with you."

"Well, we did not have the luxury of porters," Bea said. "We were hauling everything ourselves."

George reddened despite the cold. "It was still pretty tough going. The rain followed us for longer—four solid hours. The porters were long gone and were of no help."

"I'm grateful for the hot meal," Ali said, slurping her soup. "Bea, this is the way to travel in future, porters and all."

"How does Valdez figure with you folks?" I asked cautiously. "Was he supposed to escort you next week?"

"Heavens, no," said Ali, looking across at her friend. "Perhaps I'd better let Bea tell you about it."

"I don't particularly want to talk about it right now," Bea said.

"Oh, come on!" George urged. "You are among friends, after all."

Bea flushed in the firelight. I noticed by now that she always kept the unscarred side of her face towards her audience, a pose that gave her the appearance of someone hard of hearing in one ear. I felt warmth overcome me when I gazed on her—it was her vulnerability. She also had the same hunger for privacy and was inhibited like me. Who said that like-poles repel?

She struggled for the right words. "It's just that it has taken so long to get this far, one obstacle after another. I don't want to talk loosely about it any more. I'm superstitious. Excuse me, I am going to get some fresh air." She rose and walked out into the night.

After dinner, George and I took turns using the women's tent to change into our dry clothes. Valdez and his men began erecting the other tents.

I lingered inside the women's tent. Wet clothes were piled in a corner; an extra sleeping bag had been squeezed into the centre for George—talk about a thorn between two roses. Despite the damp and the mud squelching beneath the canvas floor, there was a feminine warmth, a faint aroma of talcum powder and perfume; wet bras and panties hung from a string drawn across the roof. I envied George again—always the chosen one.

Darkness had fallen when I emerged from the tent into the stark light of Petromax lamps around the campfire area. The women and George were standing on the edge of the camp, talking; an occasional burst of laughter from Ali to an anecdote from George. Even Bea had rejoined the conversation. I walked over to Valdez's tent where my sleeping bag had already been laid out. The smell of tobacco, sweat and raw meat was strong as I entered. The insides were well used, the canvas walls were dirty, the white sheet on Valdez's bag had long gone brown, and muddy water oozed from a crack in the canvas floor. Frogs croaked outside.

I stepped out of the fetid tent. I did not know how I would sleep tonight, fitfully at best. I was exhausted; the days of physical exertion were starting to take their toll on me. And there was another whole day of trekking ahead. I walked past the campsite, descended a few steps down the trail and sat on a rock. I wanted to be away from everyone for awhile.

George irritated me. Just as I was beginning to accept and forgive him for the past, he had reverted to his old self.

Sicker and older he may be, but give him the scent of a woman, and he was off again: charming, seducing, impressing.

I heard a step behind me, and a short figure approached. "Senor?"

It was Valdez, smoking a cigar. He sat on a rock opposite me and let out a slow groan. He muttered something in Spanish.

"I thought you were used to these trips," I said.

"Every year it gets more difficult, senor. But this is the only work I know."

"I'm glad I'm not the only one feeling like I've been on a Spanish torture rack."

"You have had good time for reflection, senor?" Valdez placed his cigar on the rock beside him.

"Bad memories ... " I mumbled.

"Ah ... yes. They also come when one is reflecting. I think of my wife many times when I am on the trail."

"What about her?" I squatted next to him. The rain had gone but the ground would remain wet until the morning.

"She died, senor—giving birth to my fifth child, a girl."

"I'm sorry to hear that."

"Now I look after them. My mother, and my sister and her family help sometimes."

"Do they miss you?"

"I miss them. My oldest son is also training to be a guide. The real money for people like me is in the tourist business."

"What's Bea doing here?"

Valdez was quiet for awhile. He picked up his cigar and dragged on it. "She is going to adopt my sister's son."

"I see. Do you want that to happen?"

"It is best, senor. The children, particularly my sister's son, they have not much future here. In Canada, they will be okay, no?"

"I suppose so. But I didn't see Bea wearing a wedding band. Is she going to be a single parent?"

"My sister is also a single parent to my nephew. You see, the boy's father was a Spaniard tourist, a treacherous bastard. He promised her the moon, gave her a child and ran back to Spain. My sister's present husband, he's Quechua and has three grown children of his own. He is not a very good man. He does not like this boy, my nephew, because the child is a mestizo. Maybe that's why Miss Bea likes to take him."

"We all have sad stories," I said, listening to the laughter from the women's tent, hoping they would quiet down soon. The damp and the smell of Valdez's tent would be bad enough; the sound that carried through the thin walls of the tents would be another to contend with.

Valdez looked over at the tents. "Sometimes, when I am on the trail, the women tourists want to sleep with me. They need to have sex, because they are in the middle of nowhere and feel no restrictions."

"You're out of luck this time, my friend." I said.

Valdez laughed. "It seems like that. But what about you? There are two women in there. Your friend has them both."

"He can have them."

"Sometimes when I look at you and Senor George, I think of the conquistadors who fought over our country. Only you are fighting over women."

"We played Conquistadors and Indians as children. But I'm not fighting anymore."

He must have sensed my embarrassment for he followed immediately with, "Pardon senor, forgive me. I get carried away. Perhaps it is better that we also go to sleep, no? If we set off early tomorrow, we can stop in my village to show Miss Beatrice the child. Then we can still make it to the last campsite before sunset."

I did not say anything but nodded. I rose and headed back to the camp. Valdez followed me. The smell inside his tent was still strong but its sting was gone.

"Tomorrow, senor, we will pass the seven valleys that surround Machu Picchu., mostly going downhill."

"I'd better rest my knees then. Downhill is worse than uphill."

"Yes senor—sometimes things that look the easiest, are the hardest."

"And Valdez," I said, as I pulled the covers over me. "I don't sleep that easily with women. Maybe that is my problem."

"Si, senor. Sorry to have mentioned it."

I woke several times that night. Valdez snored rhythmically. Even the voices from the women's tent had ceased; they had increased around midnight and then subsided. Around two a.m., I saw a flashlight emerge, traipse the campground and go into the woods towards the makeshift lavatory. I heard whispers, grunts and snores; someone farted; the sound of crickets got louder as the land dried. The smell inside the tent did not bother me after a while; I must have absorbed the comforting mustiness.

I had a nightmare towards dawn: George was hopping from sleeping bag to sleeping bag, going at it with Ali first, then rolling over to Bea. The women were in a state of ecstasy, totally submissive to what George could dole out in this barren piece of nowhere on the side of a mountain. Then George rolled both women into his bag in the centre and began a threesome; all the while, grinning at me as if to say, "Gotcha this time, sucker!" I woke up after that and listened to the crickets, augmented by bird calls. Sleep was out of the question anymore.

The sun was bright the next morning, blue skies, and the river winding below us was clear. Valdez was already humming and heating the sooty kettle that would generate Coca tea and porridge for us. The air was brisk. The steaming mug of tea with green Coca leaves floating in it was welcome as we stumbled out of our tents.

George looked rested. Ali was talking animatedly to Bea who appeared even more withdrawn.

When he saw me, George said, "We are going to take a short detour. To Valdez's village."

I nodded. "I know the story."

"Good, that's settled then." George looked at the women as if there was no need for further discussion on the topic.

On cue, Valdez announced, "Today, we go downhill, close to the Amazon jungle. It will be hot, and as you say ... sticky. We will reach my village by noon. We will have lunch there, but must leave by three o'clock the latest if we are to reach the public camp by sundown. Many people come from all over to this camp. There is even a disco for later tonight. But we have to rise at four o'clock tomorrow and walk the last one hour to Machu Picchu to arrive before the sunrise— it is the most magical time to see the ancient city. Okay?"

"Sounds like a plan, amigo," George said. "Let's rip!"

When we broke camp, Ali and George headed off in front, setting a brisk pace behind the porters who were already skipping downhill with our equipment. Bea followed them closely, wrapped in thought. I kept a few paces back, and Valdez, whistling "El Condor Pasa" (the tune had by now assumed national anthem status in my mind), brought up the rear.

We were descending a thousand feet into tropical leaf cover, and the temperature was sweltering by ten o'clock. The women stripped down to their singlets. We were covered in sweat. The heat, the women's bare arms, their bodies pressing against flimsy fabric, the sound of Ali's voice, all evoked a long buried longing in me. I quickened my pace and caught up with Bea.

"I don't mean to pry, but Valdez told me about your adoption plans."

She shrugged. "I guess it has to come out some time."

"Are you single ... married ... divorced?"

She smiled, and her serious expression slipped for the first time. She looked like a little girl putting on a grown-up act.

"Nobody asked me. So I guess I am single. And you?"

"Single. And too old to do anything about it."

She laughed. "Some days I think that way too."

"Taking on a kid will be life changing."

"I'm too old to have one myself. I can't be bothered looking for a husband anymore. I've had my share of losers in the past."

"Was the adoption process difficult? I've heard horror stories ... "

"There have been a lot of roadblocks. The authorities frowned on my single status. Therefore, Ali co-signed the application."

From then on, talking with her became easy. She did not engage in idle chatter and thought through her answers before replying. I discovered that she and Ali worked in a technology firm in Kitchener.

"Ali is in charge of sales. I'm 'back office,' making sure the systems run. She needs me all the time."

"Just like George and me. Only I haven't looked after him in twenty years."

"Oh, a reunion then?"

"You could say that."

"Ali is the perfectionist. She's already reading manuals on how to raise the perfect child. I'd rather raise a healthy one."

When we came through a break in the undergrowth, Valdez stopped to point out a flag protruding between two mountain peaks in the distance. "That is Machu Picchu," he said. "You see these mountains surrounding? Well, when Spaniards came, they went around and missed Machu Picchu. But people in Machu Picchu think Spaniards coming, so they leave everything and run away. What a shame. Three hundred years later, Hiram Bingham finds the city covered in jungle.

The Inca had no faith in their gods and their protection, and the Spaniards had no faith in their compass."

We continued downhill and were under rainforest cover for awhile. I was glad for the shade. George and Ali had disappeared ahead. Bea and I talked about books. She was surprisingly literary for a techie. We liked the same authors—Gallant, Greene and Rushdie—authors who were exiles from their own lands, loners.

"But they weren't losers." Bea said.

"Have you ever lost anything. Or anyone?"

"My parents. They died in a car crash. Dad had a heart attack on the highway while driving. Took Mom with him across four lanes of traffic. He never made it. I am the only one who escaped as I was in the back seat." She unconsciously fingered her scar.

"I'm sorry."

We walked in silence for awhile. Beads of perspiration trickled down her face. A rain cloud hung overhead, threatening with moist heat instead of a downpour. I gave her my water bottle as she'd already run through hers. In this humidity, her proximity was making me desire her. It had been such a long time since I had been with a woman; there had been only a couple of dead-ending relationships since Denise. The quickening of the pulse, the desire for flesh, for womanly scent and warmth, was overpowering. I walked ahead of her for awhile. *Shit, I just met her the night before.* George had slept closer to her last night. But then he had always slept closer and more intimately with the women I had desired.

"I lost someone, once," I said. We were arriving at a village. Smoke rose over the trees, and the path widened and intersected with a broader road. A car rattled by with three Quechua children shouting and waving at us through the windows. I felt the solitude we had been immersed in over the last three days start to dissipate; soon we would be among people again. I wanted to remain in this cocoon I had built with Bea, a woman I hardly knew, yet someone I could share my secrets with.

She paused and looked at me, as if not wanting to head into the public space until I unravelled the secret I had just let her into. "Yes?"

We were interrupted by Valdez, coming up on us from behind. "Amigos—my village! Come, let's vamanos!"

"Later," I said to Bea.

But the spell was broken; she was already rushing off after Valdez, saying, "Take me straight to Tamaya—right away! I don't want to miss a minute."

The rain was starting to come down again.

When we got to the village, George and Ali had not arrived.

***

George

She excited him. It didn't happen as frequently now, and the toll of the last few days had weakened him considerably. But somewhere in his gonads, desire that had propelled his life on many a wayward track was still working. It pleased and exhilarated him. After the work the doctors had done on him recently, he had harboured doubts that he would ever be himself again.

He watched her breasts press against the skinny she had stripped down to, patches of sweat under her arms and in the middle of her back. She had swept her hair into a bun, and the back of her neck glistened. Every time he neared her he could smell her heat; faint traces of deodorant and perfume mixed with the animal musk of her body. He had brushed against her on narrow stretches of the trail, and she had easily glided toe to toe with him without pulling away.

Physically, she resembled an older version of Denise: the walk, the toss of her head, the way her eyes lit up at new stimuli. But there was also something different: the harder, business-like demeanour of a person who was used to getting what she wanted.

"I would not have done this trip in this way if not for Bea. Give me my five-star hotel at the end of any trek, any time."

"Ah, but then you would miss the essence of the land," he said. He took her hand and steered her across rough patches of the trail, and she let him.

When the sun was at its zenith, they approached a village. They merged onto a broader road. Ali stopped and pointed to a waterfall about five hundred yards off the track, downhill on their right. "I'd give anything for a dip under that." She was already heading off the path towards the increasing sound of falling water.

He went after her, smiling. "Why don't we?"

"You think we might hold up the others?"

"If we were supposed to arrive by noon, then that must be Valdez's village we skirted. We can have a quick dip and be back there before they start out again."

"Good. That's what I suspected. I don't have any swim gear."

"That shouldn't stop us, should it?"

She laughed and accelerated her pace.

They pushed through thick undergrowth to get downhill. Progress was difficult, but within a hundred feet of the waterfall the steepness eased. He looked back up to where they had branched off and swore under his breath. It was going to be a tougher haul getting back, but he was too embroiled in the chase to turn back now. He ducked instinctively when he saw Jimmy and Bea pass overhead, deep in conversation, followed a few steps behind by the whistling Valdez. Had any of them looked to their right, they would have seen Ali rushing downhill to the water, thrusting aside foliage and sending a minor avalanche of pebbles in front of her. But no one looked, and soon they were alone.

The water fell from twenty feet above onto a flat stone surface, then gushed across the finely eroded plateau and crashed against more rocks to flow down into the river ten feet below them, rolling in the direction of the village.

Ali threw her knapsack down and quickly wriggled out of her shorts. Then she looked at him with a mischievous smile. "Would you be embarrassed if I took the rest of my clothes off?"

He smiled. "Try me."

She flipped off her top and rolled down her panties slowly, looking at him as she did it. He stared at her unravelling naked body, wild and natural as the surroundings.

"I haven't visited my aesthetician since I hit the trail," she said. "Does it bother you?"

Her bold earthiness only drove him crazier. "Not at all."

She stepped on the stone and entered the water, shivering slightly as its strong blast hit her. Acclimatizing quickly, she opened her arms and stared up at the sky, relaxing—a nymph. She seemed to be offering herself to him, inviting him to share in her sensual pleasure. He felt the familiar stirring in his groin and the quickening of his breath. He was getting an erection, a rarity these days. *Damn those fucking doctors!*

He threw his stick and knapsack down next to hers and ran under the falling water with his clothes on. Soon they were laughing under the overhang of life-reviving water that pushed them down with its weight and washed away sweat, weariness—and as he quickly realized—his unexpected awakening of desire.

"Go on, take your clothes off. It's more fun," she teased, thrusting her breasts at him wantonly then retreating quickly with a sly chuckle.

"This is my chance to get my clothes washed," he lied, mesmerised by her body and disappointed in his; wanting to grab her, hoping that would reignite his damp squib.

"Well, I've had my shower," she said after awhile, feigning a sudden lack of interest and stepping out of the water.

He grabbed her and pulled her towards him, crushing his lips on hers, feeling the icy coolness of her flesh, the warmth in her mouth, the swell of her body pressed against him as the water engulfed them once more. Her tongue danced inside his mouth, aggressive, taking, insisting; reawakening that smouldering fire in his belly. This was the urge that had been his constant life companion, one that suppressed rationality and unleashed lust.

Holding her to him, he staggered out of the waterfall into the sunshine, across the stone and onto the grass verge. They rolled on the ground, with stones, sand, grass and detritus sticking to their wet bodies. Locked in a long kiss, her legs undulated under him, thrusting upwards, her hand unbuckling his belt, ripping his fly open, grabbing him, discovering his moment of truth.

"Padre, padre—tourista! Hacer el capullo!" The shout rang out from above.

Ali swore, "Oh shit," and broke away, reaching for her shorts. A car had pulled over by the edge of the road, and three children were hooting and pointing at them through the window.

He shielded her as she quickly put her clothes on.

"Bloody peasants!" he muttered under his breath. "Vamos!" he yelled up at them.

A man got out of the driver's side of the car; he was chewing something and let go a stream of spittle before speaking, but the wind blew his voice out of earshot. The man's wide grin and the hand on his crotch did not need translation, however.

"Let's go!" Ali had her clothes partially on. She grabbed his hand, pulling him downhill. "Let's follow the river to the village. I don't want to face those people."

They struck out through the underbrush, branches swinging in their faces, nicking skin. Bamboo reeds dominated this area and some had prickly ends that pierced and cut. The ground squelched with mud, and frogs croaked within reach. The river bank felt like a giant bog about to cave in and swallow them.

He stopped and pulled her towards him. "We've got to head back up to the trail."

She swung back, anger in her eyes. "Are you chicken too?"

He held firm, his grip tightening on her arm. "There is no path ahead. You'll be wading in mud or in the river soon. You don't know how deep it could get. Those peasants will leave once they lose interest."

"No, they won't," she said, wrenching her hand free and striking off into the brush.

As if in confirmation of his surmise, he heard the car start up and pass overhead. He went down on his haunches. He was feeling tired and disappointed. He heard her footsteps clomping ahead, then a sliding sound and a splash.

He was on his feet instantly, moving towards her and away from the river where he knew the ground would be firmer.

He heard her muted swearing to his right as he drew near. He parted bamboo reeds with his hiking stick and saw her, up to her waist in mud and sinking with every jerk of her body.

"Ali. I'm over here. Don't move—you're in quicksand."

Her face froze in horror.

He took out his pocket knife and cut a bamboo shoot. Ripping a strand of cloth from his shirt, he lashed the bamboo to his hiking stick. Then he extended it over the mud to within Ali's grasp.

"Hold on. We are going to ease you out."

She grabbed the stick, the anger and frustration on her face changing to gratitude.

"Lie flat. I am going to pull you some ways. The ground is firmer where I came from. Let me know when you feel you can stand up."

He pulled hard and retraced his steps. His chest began to pound but he kept going. It was like a tug-o-war: for every two steps of progress he lost one the moment he stopped to catch his breath.

Ali screamed. "This fucking mud is in my mouth and hair!"

He laughed, sucking in air. "Don't worry, we'll take a shower back at the waterfall. With our clothes on this time."

After about five minutes of pulling, losing ground, and pulling again, he heard her sigh. "I think I am safe now."

It was his turn to sit. Lights swirled in front of his eyes. He felt like he was blacking out.

Then she was pulling on his hand. "George, you okay?" She was muddy brown from the neck down. A faint memory of Denise flashed by: the caring wife who always took him in when he was too stoned or drunk to care. He held onto her hand greedily.

They sat there for awhile, soaking up energy from each other, silent, until the sun moved behind the trees.

He rose and waited for his light headedness to ease. "Time for showers."

They showered under the waterfall, standing separate, clothed, immersed in their thoughts. When they put on fresh dry clothes from their knapsacks, they did so backing on to each other.

He was drenched in sweat and panting profusely again by the time they got back on the trail. Ali seemed to fare better than him and was her old self in no time.

"I'm sorry it didn't work out," he said, hobbling on his stick, another bone in his body somewhere refusing to co-operate. It was tough apologizing to a woman.

"It's my fault," she said. "It's harder for a guy to perform under those circumstances. Thanks for coming back for me."

"There is always later," he said, hope springing momentarily in his breast.

She looked askance at him, that mischievous smile returning to her face. "I like an optimistic man."

He chewed on those words all the way into the village.

Seven—The Lost Conquest

Jimmy

I was surprised to meet her at the airport in Toronto. It was
five years after they had moved to Vancouver. I had put
them out of my mind as best as I could.

Fragments of their life had trickled in during the
intervening years: George opening up an ESL school to
educate the wealthy but language-deficient hordes pouring in
from Hong Kong and the Far East; a second home in the
Rockies. There were no bytes on children, or on Denise.

And yet, here she was in the departure lounge, head
burrowed in a paperback, wearing reading glasses. I might
have missed her had I not been looking closely for a seat in
the lounge. Someone vacated theirs just then, two rows away
and opposite from her. I grabbed it, rested my heavy shoulder
bag on the floor, sat down and observed her. Her shoulders
were stooped; she had put on some weight; the hair was cut
short with its straggly ends brushing her baggy grey sweat
shirt. It was her face that was the most revealing every time
she removed her glasses and glanced up from her book
towards the departure gate: disappointed and tired eyes, wan
skin without make-up, and the drawn features of aging.

We were on the same flight it appeared. The plane was continuing to Vancouver after my stop in Calgary. Where was she going?

When boarding was announced, I inched up to her. "Denise," I called out, my heart beating.

She must have not heard me in the crush of people rushing for the gate. Then, as if some inner voice commanded her, she turned and looked in my direction. A faint smile crossed her face. She began heading my way, upstream through the milling passengers, her carry-on bags squeezed on either side as if they could be pulled out of her arms at any moment.

"Jimmy? It's so nice to see you." She smiled that genuine open vulnerable smile I was so accustomed to in the old days. Only this time, the crow's feet at the edges of her eyes were something new.

"I'm going to Calgary," I blurted out, but she placed a finger on my mouth and said, "Shh—let me just look at you. Like I did the first time I sketched you."

We stood there for a long time, looking at each other while the lounge emptied. We were in a cocoon that neither of us wanted to break. I recalled that first night at the exhibition when I was contented to stare at her while the lights went out around us.

The bag on her right shoulder started to rumble on its own, and I heard a muffled bark. She broke her gaze and slipped the bag off her shoulder. It was partially unzipped, and from inside she pulled out a sleepy golden retriever pup.

"You have a dog?" I said stupidly, coming to my senses and instantly wanting to break the embarrassing spell that had enveloped us in this public space.

"I'd just got Jasper and couldn't leave him home with George." She petted the dog, kissed it on the snout and gently placed it back in the bag.

"Are you going back to Vancouver, then?"

"I was. Until I saw you."

They were calling our names at the departure desk.

"We'd better hurry and board," I said.

She held back. "What are you doing in Calgary, Jimmy?"

"Conference. One of those boring academic ones."

"Where are you staying?"

I told her, my excitement mounting. *This is not happening.*

Announcements from the departure desk were becoming more threatening—something about offloading our bags if we were not on board.

"I have no bags—just what's on me." She laughed.

"We should board," I urged.

"Let's," she giggled and traipsed off in front of me, bags swinging, hips swaying with a lightness I hadn't seen before.

There were a few empty seats at the rear of the aircraft, and we asked a helpful crew member if we could sit together.

Jasper surfaced once more before take-off; Denise fed him a liquid, and he slipped quietly to sleep. We were silent until the plane levelled. When the drinks cart came out, I ordered a coke for myself. I was surprised when Denise ordered a double scotch. It was 10.30 a.m. She let the drink course through her, savouring it, occasionally sniffling, as if holding back tears.

We made small talk. This was her first visit east since their move to Vancouver. Her first stop had been Montreal, to see her mother in the nursing home; then on to Toronto to visit her student haunts. George's business was doing well, but it was hard work. They didn't see much of each other when they were working. She managed to get away for a few days each winter to ski around their chalet in the Rockies. George and Denise never took holidays together because the school had to operate three hundred sixty-five days a year to support their lifestyle. Their apartness suited them for it kept unpleasant questions from surfacing.

Downing her drink in a quick gulp, she got to the point. "I'd like to get off with you in Calgary, Jimmy. I'll be quiet. So will Jasper."

I looked at her. Of course, I wanted her with me in Calgary, but this was all too sudden.

"What about George?"

"I'll call him when we land and let him know that I stopped off a few days at the chalet—it's a couple of hours out of the city in the foothills."

I took a deep breath. "You've figured this all out."

"Yes, that's why I came to Toronto. I needed to get away. I'm going nowhere with my life. Meeting you is the sign I was praying for. Besides, an unpaid employee like me is owed a few extra days off."

"Are you painting?"

"I'm the administrative manager at the ESL school, George's general dogs-body. Painting is not part of the job description."

"Yet, Vancouver has such beautiful landscapes."

"It's harder being there. Amidst all that beauty. It drills home what I miss. Anyway, I am not sure I can paint anymore, either."

"You will always be a painter—it's in your genes."

"My hands are getting arthritic. It's all the typing. Even these couple of weeks off in Toronto hasn't helped."

"When did you take to drinking?"

"When you live with George, you drink. It rubs off on you."

The meal service began. It was still in the days when you got free food on airlines. Denise ordered another double scotch.

"Don't worry, Jimmy. This is my last one. I need to sleep. I've stayed up most of the last week in Toronto. Thinking."

"You should have told me you were in town. I could have kept you company."

"No. I needed to be alone. And then, God sent you to me. Don't you see, Jimmy? Meeting like this is not a coincidence."

"Next you'll be telling me about synchronicity and all that crap that women your age are grabbing at to give their lives some meaning."

"My life was dead-ending, until I saw you." Her words sent shivers down my spine.

She played with her food but ate nothing. Then she downed the second drink and settled back in her seat. "Knowing you are here will put me to sleep."

She was asleep even before the trays were taken away. Her hand gripped mine, tightly at first, then it relaxed, as if reassured that I was not going away. I didn't eat my food either, but ordered a beer before they closed the bar service. I had plenty to think about.

We checked in as Mr. and Mrs. Jeremy Spence. It felt great signing the hotel register. I was the sole participant from my school at this conference, so I did not worry too much about being noticed with Denise, although I did not want to push it—the academic world was a small and incestuous one.

Denise left a voice message at the school for George, saying she would be out of contact for awhile as the phone at the chalet was not working.

"He might call to check," I said.

"He wouldn't bother. Probably curse me under his breath for leaving him with extra work. He might also be wondering if I will stumble on any more of his sins due to my unscheduled arrival at the chalet. Not that it fazes him anymore."

"He hasn't lost his edge, has he?"

"No, it's sharpened. I'm immune to the number of strange pieces of underwear I find where George has been and gone."

I resisted taking her in my arms the moment we were in our room together. Perhaps it was the years between us, blanks that needed to be filled. I switched on the TV while she took a shower.

The rental car got us out of the bustling city, where the construction from the recent oil boom was stifling. We crossed the Bow River and the last of the skyscrapers, then ran along a flat highway with vast panoramas on either side leading us towards the distantly rising majesty of the Rockies. Just short of the town of Kananaskis, Denise asked me to take a side road that led down to the river. We followed the water along a dirt road for about five miles and started climbing. The air was bracing despite this being late September but the skies were blue and snow melt already lined the river banks in places. Another sharp turn onto a narrower road and we had plunged into a pine forest, still climbing.

"Pull over and stop," she instructed, and I did, steering the vehicle into a patch of grass overrun with many tire tracks.

"We walk from here," she said, springing out of the car. We donned sweaters. She took my hand and hurried me down a walkway to a wooden house sitting in a clearing in the pines.

"Your cottage," I said.

"George's cottage," she corrected me. "His dream hideout."

A wooden staircase led to a stoop that ran around on three sides. The jawbone of a horse hung on the threshold of the unlocked front door. Inside, a well-stocked bar faced us; pictures of buffalo and the Calgary Stampede adorned the wooden walls, and the rustic furniture was in disarray. Two bookcases supported the bar like bookends. There were unwashed glasses on the counter, and the room smelt of alcohol and tobacco smoke. Ashtrays lined a side table, un-emptied; many cigarette butts had lipstick smudges on them. My sense of order was shaken.

"Quite a party in here recently," I commented.

"George must have been missing me," Denise said sarcastically.

I began tidying up instinctively.

"This bothers you, doesn't it?" she said.

"How he lives with this ... with this mess ... beats me."

"Before I come to ski up here, alone, I hire the lady in the village to clean up."

Within minutes we had established some kind of order. I helped myself to a beer. Denise had caught my bug and was now bent on scrubbing out every bit of the party from existence.

When she was satisfied, she brushed back her hair, straightened up and walked over to the telephone that was sitting on a pile of cushions on the khaki sofa. She yanked the cord out.

"Now, my story corroborates. I won't even bother with the bedrooms upstairs. Come—let me show you the best part of this place."

She led me out the back of the house, down a steep rocky hill to the river, which had narrowed to a stream. A canoe leaned on its side on the bank. Jasper, barking behind us, ran and leaped inside the boat.

We pushed the canoe into the water and jumped in. She took the oars and skillfully rowed us along the stream for ten minutes. As we rounded a bend, the stream widened into a lake, surrounded by mountains so large the clouds cut them in half.

The ripples from our canoe rolled across the still lake, breaking up the cloud formations mirrored in it.

"This is why I like to come here," she said, letting go the oars, closing her eyes and inhaling the cold air. Her head leaned back to rest in my lap.

"Fantastic!" I said.

Our voices carried and echoed off the protecting mountains. We were alone. I could not believe that I had been transported to this magic world with the only woman I had ever loved and given up for lost, when I had set out on a rainy drive for Pearson Airport earlier this morning with only the prospect of listening to a bunch of bored academics reading papers that supposedly provided relevance to their wasted lives.

We circled the lake a few times, paddling, stopping, letting the canoe drift, letting silence do our talking. Jasper jumped out and swam around in places, and upon a single command from Denise, headed back towards the boat and looked pathetically up at us to be helped back in. The only unpleasant part of the ride was when Jasper shook himself dry inside the boat. Denise laughed at my discomfort.

"Upsets your equilibrium, doesn't he?" she asked. Her eyes were alight. Gone was that tired expression I had seen earlier today.

I laughed too, letting go. "Jasper's making me damp and cold—and ruining an otherwise perfect day."

She cradled the dog and sat him down in the middle of the canoe. "There, I'll keep him quiet for you."

"Thank you."

Then I kissed her. How could I hold back? The mountains, the lake, the cold, the air—this was a moment given to us by God, and it could disappear in a flash. She clung to me, returning my kisses.

"Denise, where have you been all these years?"

"Doing my duty. And finding myself."

I wanted her then and there. But she took the oars again and rowed us back, along another route, slightly longer, and soon we were running downstream towards the house.

The sun was setting when we beached the boat. Jasper took off towards the house. I held her on the shore, my kisses more insistent. She pulled away. "Not here, Jimmy. Not in this house. Take me back to the hotel."

We spent four nights back in that hotel; four wondrous nights when we would emerge from one bout of lovemaking, rest, as if trying to make sense of it all, and then plunge back into another. I barely attended the conference sessions, finding the slightest excuse to duck out and dive back into bed with Denise. I felt I was owed after all the years of drought and denial. It was also my way of paying George back for taking her away from me.

"I want you to come and live with me, Dee," I said on our last night together. I had been building up to that moment; now I felt good saying those words.

"I was going back to Vancouver to tell George that I was leaving him. But at the time I did not know where I was going. I just knew I needed to get away."

"I'll make you a home, Dee. A friend of mine has a cottage up for sale in the Kawarthas. It's not quite like the Rockies, but it's on a lake. If you join me, it will give me the incentive to buy it."

She was silent for a long time. Neon lights flashing through the window played on her naked skin. "I don't fully know what I want just yet, Jimmy. I only know I wanted to get away from George."

"But you like the quiet on a lake, in a canoe. And you could paint again."

"You have more confidence in me than I have."

"You need a strong man behind you. A steadfast one. I am steadfast to the point of boredom."

She laughed as she rolled over and embraced me. I felt the stirring in my loins and entered her again. We rocked together, pre-occupied this time. Then she eased off me. "I just want you to hold me, Jimmy," she said. My euphoria clouded the desperation of her embrace. We stayed like that for a long time, until I dozed off, foolishly secure that everything was going to be all right.

Even today, I vividly remember snatches of our life together at the cottage in the Kawarthas. Or, at least, I remember the parts I want to remember, or that cannot be erased.

The property was more run down than I had expected, hence the low price. My friend had not used it in the last few years since he had transferred to Halifax. I had to knock down and replace the washroom, and redo the plumbing. The back deck that looked out onto the lake had many broken timbers. I took a month's sabbatical in the spring and spent it repairing the cottage. I wanted it to be in pristine condition when Denise arrived in the summer, a date she had hinted at.

She too had a surprise waiting for her when we parted in Calgary. Her mother suffered another stroke. It made Denise's leaving George easier; she went to Montreal to care for her mother during the winter. Her mother did not survive and passed away in February. I went to Montreal to be with her. George did not show up—the school had to be kept running.

Denise looked beautiful even in her black mourning clothes. We spent very little time on that visit. She said that she was saying goodbye to too many people and wanted to spend that time to herself. I respected her wishes and left after the funeral. I got to take her hand at the ceremony and hold her when she finally broke down and cried on my shoulder as they lowered the coffin into the grave.

Before I left she told me that she had written to George, letting him know she wasn't coming back to him. She was going to stay in Montreal until I fixed up the cottage. So far, George hadn't responded.

Denise and I kept up our mail correspondence after I returned to Toronto. I gave her descriptions of my work on the cottage, and she talked about the journals and photographs her mother had left behind, most of which she had never seen in all the days they had lived together. Her mother had been a very private person.

The last strip of wallpaper went on the washroom wall at the end of March Break, and with the weather getting warmer, I turned to the deck outside. This was hard work: pulling apart the rotted two-by-fours and putting in new ones after ensuring the supports were strong enough. One support had to be replaced and the whole structure sagged while I was getting the new one in place. I wasn't much of a carpenter, and I sweated, wondering whether I had taken on too much. But I seemed to be second guessing a lot—Denise still hadn't confirmed *when* she was coming to live with me, yet I carried on in fervent hope that it would be soon. Had she even agreed to live with me? I went back over all our conversations and letters and started to get muddled.

I spent lonely and restless nights at the cottage. There was no phone line to communicate with Denise, even my car phone signal was weak, and I would wait anxiously for dawn to run down to a public phone booth in Peterborough and talk with her.

On those nights, I dreamed of what life would be: canoe rides in the lake, long walks through the woods, cross country skiing with her in the winter, watching her paint— portraits of me mostly, in different poses, bringing out the hidden facets of my personality that only she knew how to reveal. I blotted out the ninety-minute commutes I would have to take to the college, each way from the cottage—this was a sacrifice I was willing to make for her.

I sent her a telegram when the last two-by-four was in place, describing the view of the lake, asking her what colour she would like the deck painted in. I did not get a reply that day. The next morning I suddenly got that sinking feeling that she was not coming after all, that I had built this castle in the air and was now left marooned yet again. I got in my car and sped to Peterborough, hunting for a phone.

When I finally got her at her cousin's house in Montreal, where she had been staying these past three months, she had just returned from a church service for her mother.

"I finished the deck," I said, panic in my voice.

"Yes, I got your telegram."

"You are coming, aren't you?"

There was silence on the line. I could almost hear her sigh.

"Paint it dusty rose," she said.

"Yes, I will. It's still raining. I'll do it in June, when it's drier."

"Tell me when you have done it. I'd like to see it."

"You are coming then, Dee?"

"In June, after you paint the deck."

I can't remember what I did next. Probably dropped the phone and staggered outside for air. That's why there are only a few moments I remember of our life together in the Kawarthas.

The phone rang for the first time. I had just installed it in the cottage the weekend before Denise arrived. Who the hell could have got my number so quickly? Or wanted to?

It was George. The line crackled.

"Jimmy—you bastard! Now I have to call you a wife stealer," Something crashed on the other side. He must have been drinking.

"She left of her own volition, George."

"And into your open arms. If you hadn't been around, she never would have left."

"If you had treated her better, she would have stayed."

"Dammit, I treated her well! Gave her a dream lifestyle in Vancouver; a houseboat, a chalet in Kananaskis. Even after she fucked around with you and almost had your baby."

"You did not give her your companionship and your love, George. That's what she needed the most."

"Fuck all that! That's for the romance books. Trust me, you will never please her. She is a depressed woman."

"Two depressed people cannot live together, George."

"Oh, fuck off ... !" He uttered a few more colourful words.

"I don't have to listen to your crap any more, George. I am going to hang up. It was nice talking to you after all these years."

"Good luck, bro. Much happiness with her. That's what I called to wish you about. I guess I got emotional."

The line went dead.

I did a pirouette in front of the phone. For once I had beaten him. But why did it feel like I wanted to get as drunk as him and blot out my victory?

When she walked in the door of the cottage the first time, I realized I had gone overboard. She took one look at the new paintings on the wall and dropped her bag, wide eyed. I had carefully researched, paid a lot of money and bought paintings of scenes of Kananaskis from local painters to give her a semblance of what she had left behind, to make her feel at home.

"What have you done?" she asked, a look of horror frozen on her face. Even Jasper, now a fully grown dog, barked questioningly.

"Well, this place is not exactly Kananaskis."

"I don't want the past, Jimmy. I've come to a new future, tacky though this place may be."

Ouch! Tacky? After all my hard work.

I apologized and took down the pictures. She had been on a flight, she had left her husband, lost her mother; she was entitled to be irritable. After I ran her a hot bath, and she had soaked in it for half an hour, she went to bed immediately.

There are other scenes that I remember; driving through clogged highways to get home in time for a candlelit supper with Denise. I did the cooking of course, and tried to outdo myself on the menus. Now that I had someone to cook for, this became an obsession. Occasionally she would wrest control from me and prepare a simple meal: a salad, a roast, potatoes and gravy, a vegetable dish or a pie. They were gestures to be grateful for. No one had welcomed me to a home-cooked meal in my adult years. I felt guilty, but I let her get on with it. But she just sat there in silence, eating small morsels, asking me how my day had been. I had no difficulty in recounting life in a community college, replete with its petty jealousies, politics and unruly student populations. When I asked her how she had been filling the hours, her usual reply was, "Oh, this and that," which seemed to be a combination of reading, taking walks, and eventually drifting back to her painting. She never joined any of the Kawartha arts groups that I urged her to engage with. Jasper was her only companion in those days when I was away at school.

One night when I got home, she and Jasper were missing. I got out the flashlight and went looking for her down the familiar hiking trails around the cottage. After half an hour of searching I began to panic and returned home, wondering whether I should call the police. I found her silently stroking Jasper on the deck, as if she had never left.

"Where have you been?" The exasperation in my voice was evident even to me.

"For a walk. Is that a problem?"

"You could have gotten lost."

"Oh, come on. I am a big girl."

"This is the first time you've been out this late. It's not your pattern."

"Pattern, pattern—what's with you, Jimmy? Do you always have to have a pattern?"

I flushed. I had not expected this hostility. I bit my tongue and remained silent.

"If it's any consolation to you, I went by the lake to try and capture the colours at sunset."

"And did you?"

"It was a blank—one big, black hole."

"But it was great outside today."

"The black hole was not by the water, you idiot. It was in my head."

A couple of weeks later, Jasper died at the cottage. The poor creature jumped off the boat one day, and a neighbour's whizzing powerboat sliced him in half. Denise went into deep mourning after that, refusing to step out of the house for weeks after the accident.

I compensated by taking time off to spend with her during this period of loss, but she kept mostly to her room. After some arm twisting on my part, she pulled out her paints and sat on the deck, but did no painting. I experimented with the barbecue and tried my hand at new recipes while she sat out on the deck; after a few days she began painting again. She painted many portraits of Jasper. I got a little fed up because at one point there were fifteen acrylics of the animal in the living room. I gently suggested she try something else. And she tried.

I say "tried," because one day she got up, took her pallet and threw it into the lake and stormed down the driveway. In a panic, I looked at what she was painting— there were splotches of colour on the paper—no forms I could identify. She had never been an abstract painter. I wondered...and feared.

She returned after about an hour, sufficiently calmed down. I had finished vacuuming the house and had opened a bottle of wine, just in case. I poured her a glass. She did not touch it and sat clenching and unclenching her hands.

"There's no use, Jimmy," she said finally. "I can't do it anymore. The images won't come."

There was the *other* image that is also vivid in my mind. It was six months after she had arrived at the cottage, and late fall rains were beating down outside. I awoke to see her by the window in her nightgown. I rose and went over, putting my arms around her. "Bad dream?"

Outside the lake was brewing into froth, with an occasional wave hitting the dock and sending the paddle boat bobbing up and down, threatening to break it free of its mooring.

"My mother was right," she said, putting her arms around her body and shivering. "You can't leave your man, after you invest too much of yourself in him."

"I'm not expecting any returns on investment from you, Dee."

"It's not you I'm talking about. Mum never divorced my father, despite all the physical abuse he piled on her during their marriage. She remained Mrs. Langevin until she died. George has taken out too much for me to find myself again."

"You need time, honey."

"I can't stand the days alone in this cottage, while you are at work. And with Jasper dying, there are too many bad memories hovering around."

"Why don't we get a place in the city then? And come out here on weekends only? You could get a job in the city."

"You put all your money into this cottage, Jimmy. I don't want to put you out again. I feel so guilty."

I recall memories of our life in the city, after I finally convinced her that moving back to Toronto was for the best. It helped with my long commutes too. The flaw in our plan however, was that it took her a long time to find work; librarian, art teacher, decorator—the kind of jobs that Denise could aspire to—were not there for the asking. My finances began draining away on the mortgage for the cottage plus the rent for the one-bedroom apartment in the city. I tried not to show it, but my demeanour must have been one of impatience, even pre-occupation. I put it down to the fact that our honeymoon stage was over and we were now traversing the drudgery of coupledom. I was convinced that I still wanted to live with her, despite the fact that, like her Catholic mother, she had no plans to divorce George.

And what of love, that powerful desire I had experienced in the hotel in Calgary? It had turned into pity now. I wanted to protect her, for she rarely raised desire in me anymore. A depressed woman was how George had described her. Perhaps he was right.

One day, she came home late. For once, she was ebullient, despite the late hour. "I've got a job," she said.

"That's great, honey." I put away the exam papers I was marking.

"The hourly pay is crap, but the tips are great."

My heart sank. "Waitressing?"

"Better. I'm a hostess."

"Which restaurant?"

"It's a gentlemans' club, Jimmy. I don't want you to ever set foot in it."

"Why, Dee? Why that kind of place? Why not a library or a bookstore, or even volunteer work until you land something good?"

"I will not live off you, Jimmy. I learned that lesson with George. Besides, it was one of his old political contacts who introduced me to the club manager."

I bit my lip. "George—that son of a bitch! Even in his absence he influences you through his agents."

"I told you, my mother was right. It's hard to get the man out of your bloodstream."

"And I can never enter yours."

She took off her jacket, tossed it on the sofa and walked into the bedroom.

It was a downhill journey after that. I rarely saw her during the week. She would be gone by 8 p.m. and slink back past 4 a.m. I got used to the nocturnal sounds when she woke me up coming into the apartment: the drop of boots in the hall, the creak of the hanger in the cloak closet, the tap opening and the splash of water in a glass, sometimes the chink of cutlery, a sigh of slaked thirst, a burp of satiated hunger, the washroom light coming on under the closed bedroom door, the sounds of ablutions, then the weight on the bed as she slipped beneath the sheets. Despite the washing and brushing, she could not hide the smell of cigarette smoke that exuded from her. I pretended to be asleep, trying to convince myself that our relationship could still work out, that one day she would get a proper job and all this would be behind us.

A year into that job, she gave up looking for work elsewhere. She was too exhausted in the daytime to go job hunting. The apartment remained cluttered with empty pizza boxes, popcorn wrappers and beer cans. I was constantly picking up after her when I got home while she was in the washroom getting ready for "work." No more candlelit suppers, although I always cooked dinner for her and left something in the fridge for when she would come back in the small hours of the morning. There were no more visits to the cottage, for she had to work weekends too. I sold the cottage, and overnight, with two incomes and no mortgage, we had plenty of money. But we seemed to have paid for this material uplift with our happiness.

Then the night sounds of her arrival home took on additional rhythms. The dropped shoe was accompanied by a lurch and a crash into the furniture, a muted curse at first, then a louder one, and more furniture crashing. The ablutions went on interminably, and sometimes I wondered whether she had drowned herself in the bath. When she finally stumbled into bed, the smell of cigarette smoke on the bed-sheets was accompanied by the stubborn reek of alcohol from her pores which the water had failed to wash away.

***

Dear Jimmy,

By the time you get this letter, I will be on a train somewhere along the St. Lawrence, having left Toronto for good. Please don't come after me or try to find me.

I am finally taking a step I should have taken a long time ago, before I married George. I thought I took that step when I left him, but I fell back into the trap of obliging others when I came to live with you. I do not mean to be rude or unkind, but I just exchanged one form of servitude for another.

You were very kind and took me in when I was vulnerable and lost. You tried, valiantly, to give me a home. And you were faithful, which is something George never was and never could be.

But another person in your life takes up space and energy. And it's hard when you have lost most of it already.

This past year at the club has not only robbed me of my strength, it has also robbed me of my soul. Pandering to middle-aged men like George every night, watching them cavort with women half their age, has not shed my husband and his depraved life from me in the least. Instead of running away from him, I've run back to him by proxy.

Oh yes, we have been through the argument of why I continued to work in that place. I wanted financial independence, and it overrode all other considerations. I could never live off you, or off any other man's largesse, not after the servitude under George. But I created another prison for myself as a result of moving in with you.

Last week I received a letter from my aunt's estate trustee. My dear aunt (my mother's sister who married wealth in Quebec City) has left a little nest egg for me, her sister's little wastrel daughter as she calls me, in her will (snarky lady, eh?). This is the last chance for me to make it on my own, to reclaim my life and find myself. I have to leave both you and George to do that.

Please do not take this the wrong way. You are a truly wonderful man, even though limited in your ability to express your feelings. Sometimes I think the only time I knew you, was when we were illicit lovers, not during the last two years we spent together.

You really need to stop trying to organize the lives of those around you, and let us pick ourselves up once in a way. Let the woman in your life cook and clean occasionally if she wants to—she needs it for her physical, mental and emotional growth. And for her sense of freedom. You gained a domesticated pet in me, while I lost one in Jasper.

I will write to you when I am settled and when I feel I can re-open a dialogue with you. I know I have hurt you with this move. I also know that hurt people, hurt others. In my present state, I am not good for any man. That is also why I have to be away from you.

Shane Joseph

All the best with your life. You do have a very settled one, one that some of us are envious of. Don't give it away, or trade it off for any woman.

With all my love!

Dee.

**

An extract from *Conquistador*—a novel by George Walton

Hernando Pizarro descended into the cells from the plaza. The smell of urine and shit was rank as he went deeper—these places were never cleaned. What was the use? The inmates never stayed long.

His torchlight flickered against the damp walls; water dripped somewhere, and the moans of indistinguishable human clumps inside the cells followed him as he made his way to the end block with the two guards. They saluted and opened the metal door for him. Stepping inside, the humid staleness hit sharply; and another smell too, that of a dying animal.

Marshal Don Diego de Almagro, lay on a straw pallet. Stricken with an incurable disease before the final battle for Cusco, he had been unable to stop the carnage that Hernando and his troops had wreaked upon his men.

"Have you come to spare my life?" Almagro rasped.

"I have left it in the hands of the governor. I await word from him."

"The Pizarros do not fight by the rules. I pardoned you and let you go in exchange for leaving me in peace in Cusco, and this is how you repaid me?"

"I was acting on orders of my brother—"

"—who broke our truce, the moment I released you, and attacked Cusco. Orgonez warned me not to trust you, and I did not listen. Poor Orgonez, killed while handing over his sword in surrender."

"Your son, Diego, will have safe passage from Cusco to Los Reyes."

"Thank God! And Lerma?"

Hernando shrugged. "An unfortunate incident in the infirmary. A soldier he had wounded in battle broke protocol and stabbed him to death."

Almagro slumped back in his pallet. "Oh, you unfortunate men. Both my lieutenants, Orgonez and Lerma, murdered in captivity. Tell your brother that he may yet save face if he releases me and treats my son Diego with respect."

Hernando looked down on the dying man. Almagro's words worried him, for the marshal was extremely popular and respected by the troops and the Inca surrounding Cusco. Hernando did not want to initiate anything to upset the balance of power. Like Pontius Pilate, he had deferred to his Herod, Francisco Pizarro, now governor of all the lands of Peru after this final battle of Las Salinas outside Cusco.

"I will have you moved to better quarters shortly. This place stinks," Hernando said. He was dismayed to see this dying man clinging to the glimmer of hope that he may yet be released, even though his body was rapidly betraying him.

Hernando stepped out of the cell and made his way quickly to the surface. When he returned to his rooms, the secretary brought him a message. "From His Excellency, sire."

Hernando grabbed the parchment and ripped off the seal. His brother's loyal secretary Picador's, neat script leapt at him. "Deal with the prisoner, conclusively. — Francisco."

Hernando sat on his chair and laid his head on the worn backrest. He wanted to believe that it was Picador who had written this note on his own initiative, for the trusted retainer often wrote on behalf of his master and reproduced Francisco's signature when the governor was too busy. But Hernando recognized the flecks on the sides of the signature on this damnable document; they could only have been made by the governor himself—Francisco's secret signal of authenticity known only between the Pizarro brothers.

"Deal with the prisoner, conclusively."

That night two figures crept into the cell block; the guards had been called off duty. One was a friar who administered the sacrament to the puzzled prisoner. The other, a hooded figure who had held back during the priest's ministrations, then stepped forward, slipped the garrotte over the unresisting prisoner and sent him into eternity.

Eight—Battle Lines

Jimmy

We followed the path of the car into the village; a collection of uncompleted adobe structures, with blackened tiled roofs, lined the road that ran through it and into the mountain.

"Come, my house is at the end," Valdez urged Bea and me, quickening his step to lead the way.

Quechua women in ochre blankets stared after us from doorways. A couple of bold ones rushed out and tried to sell us alpaca sweaters and Inca crosses as we went by; Valdez shooed them away with an embarrassed smile, saying there will be time "later."

In a sandy plaza shaded by a tall gum tree, a group of young men were playing a game of toss: metal discs being thrown into a bucket fifteen feet away. They stopped their game and invited us to join, wide smiles on their faces.

Valdez turned around, grinning. "After lunch perhaps you will join our local 'curling club,' eh, senor?"

The road narrowed, and the houses bordering it on the right were situated on terraces descending the mountain. The car that had passed us earlier was parked next to a flight of stone steps carved into the precipice. We descended the steps to the first house; its second floor was unroofed and littered with clothes drying on a fraying telephone cords. An old refrigerator stuck out of a corner and sacks of potato lined one wall. We descended another flight of steeper steps to the main floor of the house.

The smell of cooking was strong, and Valdez said, "Ah, my sister is making the lunch."

The living room, furnished sparsely with broken chairs, ran the length of the house and was dark and cold, its walls dirty; the floor was cemented, and a crucifix hung on the far wall. Dingier rooms ran off the living room. We headed in the direction of the food aroma, into an unpaved courtyard at the rear. In the centre of the yard, several pots were being heated over an open wood stove. There was a hole in the ground next to it from which smoke and the strong smell of roasting meat emanated. A stout young woman cleaned her hands on a rag and turned towards us, smiling.

"This is my sister, Naira," Valdez said. The young woman bowed and smiled several times. She led us back into the house and into one of the smaller rooms.

The only light in the room came from a small dusty window with wooden slats on the outside, half drawn even at this time of the day. A camp bed filled most of the room, the rest of the furniture consisted of a small table and a child's chair. The room was musty. A little boy of about four, who had been sleeping, wakened and huddled against the wall, pulling a blanket against him.

Naira spoke to him gently in Quechua and pointed to Bea and myself. Valdez translated.

"This is Tamaya—Tommy, as the tourists call him."

Bea knelt beside him. "Hello Tommy. I've come a long way to meet you."

"Sutiymi Tamaya," the boy said slowly, letting the blanket down gently.

"He is telling you his name. He only speaks Quechua. He learns English—mainly bad words—from the tourists."

Bea laughed. Her face glowed. "We can fix that when he comes to Canada. Why is he in bed at this time of the day?"

Valdez cleared his throat and gestured to his sister. She took the blanket off the kid, carried him off the bed and stood him on the floor. The boy stood lopsided, one leg, heavily scarred, dragged at an angle, while the other held his weight.

Bea gasped. "What happened?"

"An accident, senorita," Valdez said. "Please let us go outside to the courtyard, we can talk there."

We returned to the courtyard, Bea and Naira holding the boy on either side as he limped slowly. A table was being laid at the far end, and two women had taken over the cooking in Naira's absence.

Valdez brought out plastic chairs and shouted to the women for chicha, cola and aqua minerale.

I was glad for the corn beer, but Bea declined, a worried frown on her face, her gaze focused totally on Tommy. The boy sat on a chair next to her and gave her furtive looks and the occasional shy smile. Suddenly he burst out in English, "I am Peru!"

Bea suppressed a chuckle. "He speaks English. And not all his words are bad."

Valdez inhaled deeply to begin his story when there was an interruption: a rather fresh looking George and Ali, dressed in clothes they hadn't been wearing when they started out on the trek, entered the courtyard.

"Well, well ... look who's here," I said, glad for this diversion. Suddenly there seemed to be new stories in need of recounting.

"We got lost," Ali blurted out.

"And found a waterfall," added George.

"We get the picture," I said.

"This is Tommy," Bea said, introducing the child to the newcomers.

"My God! What's happened to his leg?" Ali exclaimed. Even in his sitting position the mangled left leg dangled uselessly off the chair.

"We are about to find out."

Valdez offered his new guests refreshments. Then he took a deep breath once more.

"Senors and senoritas, Tamaya means 'in the centre' in Quechua. We named him so because his father is Spanish and his mother, my sister, is Quechua. His middle name is Peru. That's what he has learned to say to tourists because he gets better tips. Why these names? Because he represents what was done to this country for many centuries.

"My sister became an outcast in the village after she gave birth to this child. Tamaya's father was a tourist passing through. You see, my sister was helping me during that season with the tour guiding because I had hurt my foot. Last year, we arranged and married her off to Manuel from the next village, whose wife had died. Manuel has three sons and is double my sister's age. He took much dislike to this child from the day he arrived to live here; that is why we want to have Tamaya adopted."

"I've heard that history before. What happened to his leg?" Bea was having difficulty curbing her impatience.

"Ah yes, an unfortunate accident." Valdez took a deep draft of his chicha. "Manuel, he drinks much, because he grows the potatoes—hard work. He wants ... what do you say ... the comfort ... when he comes home. A year ago, he came home and saw Naira teaching Tamaya to play the flute. She had forgotten to take the meat off the fire,and it was overcooked. Manuel went into a rage and threw the cooking pot at her. It missed and hit the child. Our village doctor could not help much ... I am sorry we could not explain this in our letters to you."

"Son-of-a-bitch!" George swore, putting his beer down.

"But it's too late to fix this now," Ali said. "The child is permanently disfigured."

"Not yet!" Bea said. "Let's see what the doctors have to say in Canada."

Valdez beamed. "Ah senorita, you make me and my sister very happy. We thought you would change your mind."

"A child is a gift from God, Valdez," Bea said, embracing Tamaya tightly to her. The child responded without resistance, putting his arms around her.

Naira took Bea's hand and kissed it.

"Bea," Ali interrupted. "Bea, we need to talk. There are some practical considerations here ... " But she was interrupted by further new arrivals.

A grizzled man dressed in a sweater and muddy jeans, a cigarette hanging from the side of his mouth, walked in, followed by three teenage boys. At the sight of them, Tamaya froze and hugged Bea tighter.

"Son-of-a-bitch!" George swore again and exchanged glances with Ali.

The man paused to stare at Ali, his eyes devouring her. Valdez interrupted and spoke to him gruffly in Quechua. The man replied and nodded towards the food table, then waved to his boys. They strolled to the open pan, ladled food onto plates and went outside again.

"Manuel and his sons. They have been working since dawn in the fields. Now they are hungry."

"And they are rude," Ali said.

"Ah, but come." Valdez gestured. "Now that we have only the pleasant company—we will have lunch."

We were introduced to Pachamanca: lamb and pork mixed in a tamale prepared in a sack in the hole in the ground; and papa a la huancaina: potatoes served in a spicy sauce, with olives, lettuce and egg as accompaniments. Homemade corn bread made up the rest of the meal. More beer was served. It was a glorious repast and took the edge off the morning's activities. Ali gave us an account of going to find a waterfall and landing in quicksand instead, and how George had gallantly come to her rescue. The child sat in a chair close to his mother and picked at his food, studying us quietly. He only smiled at Bea.

After lunch we dispersed in several directions until we were to regroup for our departure at three o'clock. The women of the village had set up several tables on the main street to display their wares: sweaters, blankets, trinkets and paintings. Ali and Bea browsed, and George went to watch the game of toss. I followed George.

George became animated watching the game. "This is like the horseshoe toss I had in my backyard at the cottage. I got good at it when we had company around. Made some money on it too."

The ill-mannered Manuel was leaning on a chair behind the bucket, smoking. His sons were playing in the game with some of the other men. Occasionally he roused himself to hurl advice or curses at them.

Spotting Valdez, George called him over. "Hey Valdez, I want to play this game. But only with that guy Manuel over there. Can that be arranged?"

Valdez looked crestfallen. "Senor, Manuel is the expert here. No one in the village plays with him anymore, because he only plays for money."

"Good. I need an expert."

Valdez went over and spoke to Manuel. Manuel looked over at George and returned to smoking his cigarette and to shouting at his sons. Then, as a shrugging Valdez turned to head back in our direction, Manuel spoke. The two men exchanged animated words for a few minutes. Valdez walked away, swearing under his breath.

"What'd he say?" George asked.

"Senor, this is not good. He wants to wager for your camera."

"Great. What is he putting up in return?"

"Two Quechua blankets and a bag of potatoes."

"Tell him the blankets are fine, but I'll think up something in lieu of the potatoes."

"You are going to lose another camera, George." I said. "Not sure I want to hang around watching this."

Valdez returned after conferring with Manuel. "He said it is okay. You do not have to think too hard as he is going to win anyway. Senor, I hope you can give him a good beating."

"I will."

"You can start as soon as this game is over."

I picked up my knapsack. "I think I'm going for a walk. I can't bear the sight of you losing."

"No confidence in me, eh, Jimmy boy? That was always your problem. Here, hang onto this, just in case you are right."

George slipped the camera's digital chip into my hand.

"That's the only important piece, as far as I am concerned," he said. Turning to Valdez, he brandished his hiking stick, "Lead on, amigo. Let's go into battle."

I passed the portable flea market again and went down the stone steps to the next terraced level and walked downhill from there. I peeked into a house as I went by and there were about two dozen guinea pigs running around in the bare living room. A kid stuck his head out, grabbed one of the creatures by the tail and asked me if I wanted to buy. I shook my head and walked on. Maybe it was the heavy meal inducing drowsiness, but I was feeling overwhelmed again by the trek of the last few days.

They say your life flashes in front of you at the moment of death. I had been reliving my life, at least the significant events in it, ever since coming to Peru. Looking out across the valley at the mountains hemming us in on all sides, I wondered whether this place did that to people. Valdez had talked about a personal journey of discovery. The Inca trail was doing that to me. Did it mean that death was close at hand? Whose?

Voices speaking in English spilled over the road above and reached my ears. Ali and Bea were arguing. I cocked an ear.

"But you promised, Ali. You put your name on that paper."

"You don't know what you're getting into. You're over your head on this one. You haven't been a mother to a normal child. A crippled child is ten times more complicated."

"We can work it out. There is good care back home."

"I'm sorry, Bea. I cannot go through with this."

"You're too bloody scared, that's why."

"Let's go on to Machu Picchu and take a few days to think this over. You'll see my point of view, eventually."

A roar of voices came from the direction of the plaza, and Ali quickly cut in. "It sounds like George's game is warming up. I've got to see this. Come along."

"Suit yourself. I'm going back to see Tamaya."

I was already up and moving. George's game had raised my curiosity too.

When I arrived at the plaza, the crowd was cheering. Manuel stood by the bucket into which the discs were supposed to land, hands on his hips, looking satisfied. A few discs lay in the dirt around the target, the stray shots. On a chair next to the bucket sat two multi-coloured blankets upon which reposed George's camera. I found Ali and Valdez on the fringe of the crowd.

"Senor George has to put this throw into the bucket to win. His last one," Valdez said, wiping his brow with his bandana.

George was passing the disc from hand to hand, measuring the distance with his eye, sweating profusely, yet smiling. He stopped, stood erect, paced up and down for a minute as if recalling something, then took up his throwing position again.

The crowd hushed as he crouched and swung his arm back in an arc—once, twice, three times—letting go on the fourth swing. The disc sailed through the air, hit the side of the bucket and fell inside, tipping the bucket on its side without spilling its contents.

"Senor George—he wins!" Valdez yelled, and the crowd's roar drowned out his next words.

Manuel looked incredulous, then he spat on the ground. Valdez broke away and ran towards the two contestants who were walking towards each other. George had his hiking stick in his hands. He turned to our guide.

"Valdez, give the blankets to our fair ladies. And tell this guy I have decided what I want in lieu of the bag of potatoes."

"What senor?"

"I want this piece of shit to promise me that he will never ever strike his wife or his children, particularly little Tommy, again. And if he doesn't keep his promise, I will fly down here and kick his ass. You got that?"

Valdez translated, and Manuel's eyes widened as the message sank in.

Manuel waved his fist in front of George's face, spat, and began to walk away.

That's when George hit him. The hiking stick swung like a baton, making an arc through the air and hitting Manuel across the back. The man screamed, fell involuntarily to his knees, and screamed again. Members of the crowd, who were beginning to disperse with the ending of the contest, turned back to look.

"Go on, promise me, you useless fucker!" George yelled, the stick raised to strike again. Manuel cowered.

Valdez jumped in the middle. "Senor, senor ... please—he will promise!"

George struck again, driving Manuel into the dirt. "I didn't hear it." The sound of the blow was like the beating of a carpet in spring.

Valdez screamed something to Manuel, and the latter screamed back, breaking into sobs.

"Okay, okay, senor, he promises now."

George stepped away and retrieved his camera. A few people in the crowd sniggered, and I realized that they were sniggering at the fallen toss champion, the man from the other village, the wife and child-beater.

As Manuel picked himself up and hobbled off, George stepped over to Ali and me. "That was the best part of the game."

"I wish I'd placed a side bet on you, George. Well done!" I said and meant it. "You'd better watch your back from now on."

"Oh, I wouldn't bother. That is how the conquistadors kept order—with brute force. The locals recognize it. It still runs in their genes."

At 3.30, as the rest of the party were packing their gear in the square, I went to fetch Bea from Naira's house.

I found her in the back courtyard, playing with the boy. Naira and some local women were cleaning up after the lunch they had put on for us. Bea was throwing a ball to Tamaya, and he threw it back, laughing, excited with every catch and throw. I could see that she was aiming the ball carefully, so the boy would not have to lunge or run for it. She lost her aim once, and he lurched away in pursuit of the ball, dragging his foot behind him, determined to impress his benefactor; he tripped and fell headlong in the sand. None of the other women in the yard paid any attention—this seemed normal. Bea jumped and ran over to Tamaya, scooping him up in her arms and holding him to her breast, stroking his head. The boy whimpered. They looked like two scarred animals that the rest of humanity had discarded.

For a moment I imagined Dee in this situation, if she'd had the baby, our baby. A lump came into my throat, and I tried to dispel the image.

"Bea, we have to go," I said, guilty for being the one to break up the developing bond between this woman and child.

"Is it 3.30 so soon?" she called over her shoulder. "Time flies when you are having a party."

"It sure does," I said. "The others are waiting."

"I have to go," she told the boy. "But I will be back soon."

He sensed the impending departure, the loss of so brief a respite, and tugged at her hand, reluctant to let go. There were tears in her eyes.

"Oh Jimmy, this is so difficult."

Naira came over, addressing the boy sternly. He let go immediately, and like a little puppy with its tail between its legs—only it was his crippled leg—he started back towards the house. Naira followed him, speaking loudly in Quechua.

"Tamaya, I will be back," Bea repeated. The boy paused at the doorway, looked at her, finger in his mouth, then sighing, turned and went indoors.

"Come along." I unconsciously put my arm over her shoulder and steered her towards our rendezvous point.

Nine—The Fall of the Conquistador

20th May 1985

D ear Maman,
How I miss writing you these letters. They were my means of coming to terms with things. And then you died, and I couldn't write to you anymore. Today, I feel so burdened that I must write again, even if I am not able to mail it. I hope you are reading this letter over my shoulder.

These five years in Montreal have had their ups and downs. I finally put my paints away, resigned that I could not do it anymore. I tried my hand at poetry—sent off dozens of anguished poems to magazines. When one editor had the courtesy to reply to me and commiserate with my misery, that's when I realized that I was writing for purgation not for art.

Your friends have been kind and have adopted me into their circle. The annual arts and crafts show is one I look forward to and volunteer time at. Aunt Clara's bequest is generous. That and my part-time caregiver's job at the seniors' centre are more than enough to meet my needs. Yet, I remain alone.

This crushing sense of loneliness is the hardest to get away from. I've stopped looking at myself in the mirror. My clothes are two sizes bigger and getting tighter. There are some things I can control and others I dare not, or else I might have a nervous breakdown. Curling up on the couch and watching the soaps with a bag of chips is not something I am willing to trade off, nor are my tots of scotch in the evening.

I went for my check-up last week, and the doctor was quite alarmed. She said that my sugar was high, I was overweight, my blood-pressure was also high, and that I needed to get a specialist's view on the menstrual bleeding that has become irregular and heavy these last few months. She was stern in her comments. She said, "Denise, if you create a swamp, the mosquitoes will come."

Me, a swamp? More a wasteland. I went to a lecture at McGill the other day on Spanish conquests in the new world. This was one of George's favourite subjects. I dragged myself through the pouring rain. They were featuring Peru and the Inca kingdom. I had to leave halfway. I developed a lump in my throat as the lecturer talked about the atrocities, the inquisitions, the human sacrifice, the polygamy, rape, incest— all those masking the great advances in astronomy and mathematics that the Inca made, or the gold that the Spaniards bought back home. He showed us pictures of some of the cruelty—quite a contrast to the harmonious yet realistic scenes I tried to portray in my paintings. I went home and cried. Then I finished what was left in the bottle of Scotch and went to bed.

I feel like the ravaged land of the Inca myself, letting two conquerors, first self-indulgent George, then quiet and controlling Jimmy, have their way with me. Five years later, I am still trying to emerge from their shadow, and have now given up trying. I am what I am, or what they made me.

I never told you this before, but now that you are dead, I can. Do you know what George told me after we had made love on our wedding night? I think I told you about the wedding night itself, and what a great love-maker he was. After we had made love, he rolled away from me and was quiet for a long time. I knew he wasn't sleeping. When I snuggled up to him, he said, "Dee, I made a lot of promises to you today in church, but I can't keep the one of fidelity. I know myself enough. I'll keep all the others."

Were these the words of a cheater or of an honest man? Most husbands just don't tell their spouses but cheat on them anyway. When I heard him utter those words however, I felt the ground give way under me. I knew that I would have to try very hard to keep him to myself. In the end, I lost—not too long after the wedding. I think I wrote to you about that woman Shirley (at least, she is the first I knew of).

Was I acting like a conquistador too—trying to control and keep George to myself, when all he desired was freedom? Perhaps he would have loved me better if I had not been so jealous, and in my jealousy, despised him in the end.

I haven't connected with either George or Jimmy these last five years, other than via the odd letter and I think it's best that I don't. They just bring out bad memories and I have enough of those to deal with anyway. Oh yes, the doctor also said that I suffer from depression and wants me to go on anti-depressants. Those medications are largely hit and miss and I can't be bothered—people will have to accept me as I am. The only time I can forget myself is when I am tending to someone else whose need is greater—at the seniors centre, for instance. But when I return home, wham, it hits me!

So there you have me, Mum—a rather sour, frumpy daughter who hates her existence. It's like the life force went out of me when I lost the baby. Maybe, losing the baby was the price I had to pay for adultery. As much as George and Jimmy hurt me in a way, I guess I hurt them too.

Anyway, it's nice writing this letter to you, even if you are dead. At least I can still write, although I can never paint again. I still pull out those old portraits from time to time and look at them.

Goodbye Mother, in the end, you were my only friend.

Dee.

***

Jimmy

The camp in Huinay Huayna was a row of tents of assorted colours and shapes; trekkers descended from surrounding trails into this last rest stop before the final push into Machu Picchu. There was a hostel-bar and cold showers for rent at five sol per person. Despite the rain falling outside, I wanted to clean myself from three days of dust, mud and exhaustion, and lapped up every drop of the ice cold drip that poured out of an ancient spout, water from the surrounding mountains collected and flushed down into these stalls, a far cry from the ancient Inca bath terraces. I felt the sweat drain from me like thick oil, and my skin tingled under the cold water. Outside, draped in a towel, the air really bit, but I was feeling in control again. The humid downpour had passed, and a rainbow hovered over the camp.

"I'm bunking with Ali tonight," George announced casually when I returned to our tent. He winked at me as he unpacked a towel and stripped down to his boxers to head for the showers.

"I am not sleeping with Valdez anymore," I replied.

"You don't have to. How's Bea coming along?"

"Fine. But we haven't become sleeping buddies yet."

"Then it's time you did."

I nearly lost it, and my voice rose. "What the hell's got into you, George? I'll go sleep in the hostel then."

The women in the nearby tent must have overheard my raised voice, for Bea stuck her head out. Her hair was wet and frizzy over her shoulders. "Jeremy, it's okay. Ali and I have talked. You can share my tent. For sleeping only, okay?" The question on her face was sincere. My anger abated upon seeing her. She also looked like she wanted to be away from Ali at that moment.

"Okay. Thanks." I said. She ducked her head back inside before either of us could say something foolish.

"See?" George was smiling. "She likes you. You are fretting for nothing, old man. Guys our age should be lucky when women like that come on to us."

On the way into Huinay Huayna, Ali had walked ahead with George. They must have had plenty of time to work out their sleeping arrangements en-route. Bea had been quiet all the way on this last stretch, and I respected her privacy knowing the mental turmoil she must have been in.

I shook my head. "Sex is a sport for you, George—an athletic exercise. Ali's at least fifteen years younger than you. Doesn't it bother you that you may not hit her top ten on the performance scale?"

For the first time I saw him hesitate, and that look of smugness fell off him for a moment. "It bothers me like hell, Jimmy. But I subscribe to that sage who said, 'feel the fear and do it anyway.'"

"You're the type who doesn't quit when the going's good. One day you will be like a male version of Norma Desmond of Sunset Boulevard." I left the tent and went for a walk. The air between us had become oppressive.

There was an ancient amphitheatre on the edge of the camp, lending character and significance to Huinay Huayna. The magic of the moment was enhanced by the rainbow that was half inside and half outside the ancient ruin. I walked down the broken stone steps, overgrown with grass and weeds, into the core of the amphitheatre and into the heart of the rainbow. This trip had indeed released many memories, no doubt—but there was the final episode that still lingered and needed to be set free. I needed to get that out of me now...

***

George

He got out of the taxi, a block away from the cemetery, feeling naked and exposed. He had left the safe confines of the school: marking papers, preparing lectures, processing applications, occasionally bedding a willing student or colleague—activities that put him in control of his life. And now, with the new "life enrichment" courses underway, taking time away had been even more difficult.

Out here, where the air was colder, wetter, francophone, he was in a foreign place. The walk to the cemetery was hard. He shrugged off that feeling of middle age catching up. *Damn it, I'm still good.* That was why he needed constant acknowledgement from younger women of his manliness, his intellectual acuity and his sexual prowess. He didn't need this slowness of step that made breathing difficult. *It's guilt that's slowing me down!*

He paused before the gates. There were several funerals in process in different areas of the cemetery, and he scanned the crowds for a recognizable face. He made out Jimmy immediately, dressed in a dark suit, head bowed, sombre, standing next to the priest who was shuffling the pages of his breviary and conducting the ceremony; a smattering of heavy suited mourners, mostly women in veils, stood by the gravesite. He felt awkward with his bright blue shirt, top button undone, covered with a light grey leather jacket. *Heck, I live in Vancouver!*

He paused behind the gathering and leaned against a giant gravestone dedicated to some business person with a long Quebecois name—so Catholic, this whole thing! This scene only heightened his guilt, and he used the gravestone for cover as much as for support. Denise had descended more into her Catholic roots here in Montreal, especially after the uterine cancer was first diagnosed, already at stage four.

Her illness had exposed him to his mortality and panicked him, and sparked the flurry of medical tests he'd submitted himself to; finally, even letting the doctors into his colon. Some of the results he liked, some he didn't. *I'm still good,* he reassured himself.

At one point he had wanted to sell everything and head down here to be with her. But he wasn't sure how she would react to that. After all, she was still Mrs. George Walton, stubbornly refusing a divorce, like her mother before her. But they had been living apart from each other for seven years, and a lot had changed in their lives in-between—Jimmy for instance. But Jimmy had always been there, it was hard to imagine life without him.

But he also knew that his impulses to sell and flee were only that—impulses. His self-preservation instincts had held him back. Denise represented his failures. He patted himself on the back for facing up to them at least this once.

The priest finished his prayer and Jimmy stepped forward and threw a clump of earth into the open grave, followed by the others. *Old reliable Jimmy—the bedrock of our lives, both Denise's and mine.*

***

Jimmy

When I stepped back, dusting the muddy wet earth from my fingers, I saw George leaning against a gravestone several feet away from Dee's grave. Despite my anger at this whole sorry business, I was relieved to see him, the only known face amidst a bunch of strangers. I inched my way passed the crush of Dee's new-found friends—artists, tree-huggers, feminists and cancer-survivors—all eager to cover her up with earth like I had done, and headed straight for George. His smile looked fixed, but I could sense his brain doing cartwheels, wondering what to say to me after all these years.

I extended my soiled hand to him, and he flinched, as if parts of Denise lay in it already. He didn't take my hand, instead he laughed nervously. "Didn't think you'd see me, did you?"

"No. Didn't think you'd have the balls to show up."

"You still look good, Jimmy—trim and fit."

"I guess I hide my bleeding heart well."

"We hide *our* bleeding hearts."

"I've had no one to console me at nights while the disease ate through her."

He remained silent at that, out of words for a change. Then he tried another tack. "Mercifully, it didn't last long. Hers was the type they call the 'silent killer'."

"Have you stopped to think that every time your cheating prick went into her, you were poisoning her with your toxins? And with those of your lovers."

"Hey—slow down!" He stepped back. "That's kind of radical, isn't it?"

"Have you, George?" I had taken him by his collar and was shaking him. I heard hushed voices around me; people were staring. But I was among strangers, and who gave a damn? I know I was being irrational, but today was an occasion to let go.

"Slow down, Jimmy," he was pleading now. I had been expecting a fight. He must have softened over the years.

I pushed him hard. He bounced against the gravestone and fell to his knees. I instinctively went into crouch position, conditioned by the number of times we had fought as boys. This time I was going to win. Strangely, he did not respond, but got back up, dusting his peach coloured pants, an apologetic yet charming smile aimed at the onlookers.

"Jimmy, let's get out of here. How about a drink?"

My anger ebbed, and I felt foolish. I wanted to get out too. I had wanted to get out since arriving in Montreal that morning after driving through the night.

"Let's find a bar," I said.

"That's more like it!" He smiled. It was vintage George. "Didn't know you were a seasoned drinker."

"Today is an appropriate occasion." I started walking towards the gate. George bowed politely at the mourners—he was still the widowed husband, desirous of their sympathies. He uttered a few words in French to gain favour and followed me out.

In a little café, a block away, we ordered a bottle of wine and baguettes.

He told me about the school, how he was expanding it. He had introduced new courses in history, both Canadian and colonial, in addition to business subjects. He had a bench of contract teachers on staff, skilled in the various disciplines. He was thinking of taking the school to private investors as he couldn't cope with the growth possibilities.

"New immigrants are lapping up this stuff like crazy. They even want to know about their own countries, information that was hidden from them before they came to Canada."

"Are your staff unionized?"

"Hell, no. I can't afford union wages. Besides, they stop working once they join the unions—we know that, Jimmy. I was able to run in an election while working at the college in Toronto in the old days."

"I remember how agitated you used to get about the unions losing power in the schools. You campaigned on that platform."

"That was a long time ago Jimmy. I have evolved from an enlightened capitalist to a pure capitalist now."

I had come to the end of my second glass of wine, and the memory of what we had just left behind in the cemetery washed over me. Talking to George had only been a temporary reprieve.

"She died alone, George."

"She had a lot of friends here."

"She didn't have us."

"Maybe she didn't want us. Did you ever visit her?"

"No. She was still coming to terms with our separation," I said.

"She never came to terms with mine. But she would write. That was safe."

"Yeah. We spent a lot of time on letter-writing too."

He hefted a pile of letters from the inside of his jacket, sealed in plastic wrap. "I found these when I went to

Dee's apartment to clear her things out earlier today. Letters to her mother over the years, probably retrieved after the old lady passed away. There were some written even after her mother had died, and they had no postmarks, probably never mailed. I did not find any letters or replies from Mrs. Langevin to Dee."

I read the letters. I cried and drank more wine. He cried too and drank more wine.

"You can keep some of them letters," he said. "She was much a part of you as she was of me."

"Thanks. I won't refuse." I scooped a handful of the yellowing papers into my coat pocket.

We ordered another bottle. It was great being with him. In the end, he was George, my old buddy.

"You still feeling like beating me up?"

I grinned sheepishly. "No. I got carried away in the cemetery."

"You remember those old times back in Scarborough?"

"I still drive by the old neighbourhood sometimes."

"I wish I could go back," he said, looking out the window. "I can't, Jimmy. Too much water under the bridge, as they say. I like exploring new horizons. Ever travel?"

"Done a bit of the Caribbean and Europe."

"I'm teaching a class on colonial history. Went to Indonesia last year to study the Dutch occupation. I am planning to go to Macau next year to check out the Portuguese. I wonder what Peru would be like?"

"You pick odd places for a holiday."

"It's not a holiday for me, Jimmy. It's a quest. Like nothing else."

"Not even like chasing women?"

"Not even."

"How's that coming along then?"

"What, the quest?"

"No. Chasing women. I heard it's going out of style. Men are becoming more gender-sensitive these days."

He poured another glass of wine. "It doesn't get easy. But I like the challenge."

"When did it start for you, George? This desire to dominate, to chase? I know it's a male thing, but with you it's on steroids, always has been."

"I try not to figure it out. I found out my father was just the same, although he kept it concealed from us. It's in my genes, I guess. I tried to get Denise to understand it. How do you change nature? It's like my compulsion to understand colonial domination. Maybe the key lies in history."

"Your dad, never thought you could measure up. Remember? Maybe that's what started it."

He downed his drink and knitted his brows in anger "Yeah. And yours was so damned remote, no wonder you're such a cold fish."

"It was different with Dee. If you two had divorced, I would have married her."

"Yeah? But she wasn't happy with you either. Too orderly. No passion."

Suddenly I wanted to hit him again. Instead, I asked, "Did she write you all that?"

"I didn't need letters to figure it out."

He was about to order another bottle when I stopped him. "I have an early start tomorrow. It's a long drive back to Toronto. Are you sticking around?"

"I have to. After all, I am still the official husband. Want to stay and help?"

I drained my glass and stood up. "No. For once I'll let you clean up your mess. Drop me a note now and again. Or come for a visit." I tossed my card on the table for him. I didn't see him again for twenty years, until we met in Lima. That seemed to have been as long as it took him to summon the courage to journey to Peru.

Now, standing inside the rainbow in Huinay Huayna, I felt released from them both. Maybe it was the long trek, seeing George again and getting a few things off my chest, getting out from under his shadow, releasing the memories that had been locked inside, or simply this wonderful rainbow that was enveloping me. Letting go—I had done that at Dee's funeral and in the bar afterwards. I wanted to let go now, permanently. Let go of all the restraints that had bound my life from as far back as I could remember. I shouted into the rainbow, and my voice was loud in the amphitheatre. My natural reticence made me stop involuntarily and look around. *Stop being a coward. You always looked around, scared to tread on others' toes.* I let out another blast, a roaring "Ahhhhh," and this time it felt really good.

I heard a sound behind me and was embarrassed to see Bea descending the steps, heading in my direction. Had she heard me?

"It's magical, isn't it?" She was dressed in a red sweater and her wet hair had been pulled back in a pony tail. She was wearing shorts and sandals despite the descending chill, and for the first time I saw her well proportioned legs. I wondered why she covered her assets most of the time. If she had heard me shouting in the wind, she did not show it.

"We are going to the disco," she said. "Want to come along? Ali likes to party. Frankly, the way I feel right now, I could get drunk."

"Why not?" *Why not? No holding back, remember?*

"I didn't mean to embarrass you when I talked about sharing the tent tonight," she said.

"You saved me from beating up George. Or spending a night in a stinky rest house."

"George was well behaved last night. He told us lots of stories. Told us about you too. You are his best friend."

"We are more like each other's nemesis."

"Sort of like Ali and me."

"She doesn't waste time acquiring men."

"Or in disposing them. She's run through three husbands already. George looks like he is anxious to be acquired."

I wanted to ask her about Tamaya and what she planned to do about the child, but I was not supposed to have overheard her conversation with Ali in the village. So I remained silent.

She sat down on the stones. Her legs were pinched with cold, and she hugged them to her. "You were going to tell me something yesterday. Do you still want to talk?"

"Now is not a good time. Talking would spoil the magic of the rainbow."

"It's starting to fade already. Night is coming."

"We'd better get back. Valdez told me these ancient ruins are haunted. Ghosts of sacrificial victims."

She rose, dusted off her shorts and unconsciously extended her hand to mine, which I took. "Let's go to the party then, shall we?" I said.

***

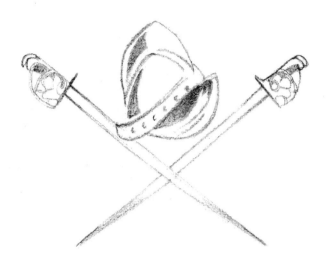

An extract from *Conquistador*—a novel by George Walton

Francisco Pizarro dressed for dinner as the cathedral bells across the square rang the noon hour. From his second room window he saw the crowds from the morning mass spill out of the giant doors: men in their silken woolen capes and plumed hats with their darker Peruvian wives in rainbow coloured gowns and gaudy jewellery.

He should feel good today. Peru was all his at last. The Inca were finally subjugated, reduced to isolated pockets of marauders who hid out in the mountains, and the elder Almagro was out of the way. Yes, he should feel good. But...

Figures moved in the window of the house next to the cathedral, young Diego Almagro's house. Out of courtesy—or was it guilt?—he had allowed his old colleague's son to live freely in Los Reyes. And now the "men of Chile" were plotting to kill him, it was rumoured.

He had not gone to mass this morning on the advice of his secretary, Picador, who had heard of the conspiracy. The fat fool had himself to blame for deliberately provoking the opposition by distributing inflammatory notes to the Almagro faction. Francisco had therefore decided to remain indoors with trusted friends today: his half-brother Alcantara, Judge Valasquez, the bishop and Picador, all who were assembled in the dining room for a quiet meal.

He decided not to wear his gold medallion and chain for this occasion. Throughout his reign as Governor of Peru he had dressed simply: a white shirt, dark jacket and breeches, and a black cloak. Gold was for acquisition, like a woman, not for display, he mused, as he ran his hands over the oversized medallion that he wore only for ceremonies. But he hadn't treated his women well, especially the local ones. He suddenly dropped the golden chain into its box as if it had burned him; last night's dream flittered before him, one that had been returning with increased frequency...an event that had occurred some years earlier, now darkening and sharpening with every reoccurrence...a premonition, perhaps...?

He hadn't caused the barbarism on that occasion; it had been Manco's fault during the Inca wars. If those savages hadn't murdered the slave bearing his gifts to the Inca prince, he wouldn't have had to teach them a lesson. But why did he have to choose her, the ice princess, his former lover; strip her naked, tie her to a tree in the square and have her beaten with rods? Of course, to teach the enemy a lesson and instill discipline, without which this place would be ungovernable. She was chosen to serve as the surest example of his dominance over the Inca kingdom. Or...was she chosen because of his fear of her? For it was not the incident that bothered him, but the look on her face: eyes piercing him, unflinching, never begging for mercy. He had finally ordered his men to shoot her with arrows. But even with her dying breath, she had never wilted. She was Inca, she was of this land he had conquered. But if he were to interpret her unrelenting stare, had he really conquered anything?

He caught his reflection in the mirror: tall, hair greying, a slight paunch in the belly; and below that—the embarrassment. He never let women into his bed now unless they were of the docile kind who kept their mouths shut afterwards. Still, he was in supreme command, while others, like his dear friends Almagro and Padre Luce, had fallen by the way. He felt particularly sad for the elder Almagro who had been his constant companion, an orphan like him who had risen above his station and had always been at hand when needed. He regretted sending that final letter to Hernando, but it had been necessary for his own survival.

Tearing himself away from the mirror, Francisco went to dinner. Conspiracy, be damned. They would not touch him!

"A toast to your health, Your Excellency," Valasquez was raising a goblet when he entered the dining room. A page handed him another, brimming with wine, and the men in the room raised their drinks in honour of their host.

"Sit down," he ordered. Pages went around serving fruit to begin the meal.

"The conspirators must be in a quandary because you did not show up for mass as expected," Picador said and stuffed a handful of grapes into his mouth. The juice trickled down his jowls.

"You have nothing to fear, Excellency," Valasquez said, stifling a belch, "as long as I hold the rod of justice in my hands." The judge held up his wooden staff that he carried everywhere with him.

"And as long as conspirators also go to confession," the bishop squeaked, "their secrets are safe with us."

Francisco took a long draw from his wine and felt the liquid warm its way down into his belly.

Just then a shout broke out in the outer courtyard. "Death to the tyrant!"

Alcantara jumped up and ran to the window. "Dios mio! They are coming. Who left the gate open?"

"But...but—" Picador was trembling, unable to complete his sentence, spittle mixed with grape juice spilling out of his mouth.

"Madre Dios!" the bishop exclaimed while the judge hoisted his rod as it were a sword of protection.

"Death to the tyrant!" rang outside, louder. The conspirators had reached the inner courtyard.

Francisco leapt into action, the familiar adrenaline flooding his body. These were moments when his mind cleared. "Chavez!" His chamberlain came scurrying. "Bar the door to the ante chamber.

Alcantara—help me with my armour. The rest, leave immediately and fetch reinforcements."

The others began filing out of the rear door that led to the garden, from where they could flee to safety, but only if they left now and if no attackers were lurking at the back of the house. *Valasquez's* rod of justice trailed behind him like a frightened tail as the rear door closed behind the guests. Only Francisco and *Alacantara* were left in the dining room, buckling on their cuirasses, with *Chavez* trying to bolt the other door.

"You have grown too fat, my brother." Alacantara grinned; he had pulled on his own armour and was wrestling to fasten Francisco's.

"I will lose my fat today. We will get lots of exercise." He grinned back, drawing in his belly.

He turned towards where the shouting was amplifying and swore. *Chaves* was still peering out of the open dining room door into the ante chamber, his curiosity having got the better of him. *"Bar that damned door, you idiot!"*

Too late, the door crashed inward, sending *Chavez* sprawling. Men in dark cloaks rushed in, like ravens of death. Rada, the tall cavalier, *Almagro's* loyal servant, was in the vanguard. *Chavez* rose only to receive a sword through the heart and sink back on the floor like a gored pig.

Alcantara left the dangling armour on Francisco and took his sword to the assassins. Francisco ripped the encumbering metal from his body and flung it into a corner; he wrenched his cloak off his shoulder and wrapped it around his left forearm. He tapped his sword on the stone floor. Now, he would deal with these miscreants.

When he saw *Alcantara* reeling from several sword blows to the head and legs, he knew this was going to be the toughest fight of his life. Last night's dream flashed before him again.

Francisco rushed the intruders. He slashed left, right, left again, and two men fell to the ground. He would fight them like a puma, he would show them who was in charge.

Left, right, sparks from metal, grunts from men, blood flying in the air, two more stumbling away holding mangled limbs, and then Rada shoved a man in his path. He got his sword into position, in time, *impaling the man on it. Too late he realized that he had embedded his weapon too deep and could not get it out in time.*

A glint of steel to the right, and he felt the searing fire of Rada's dagger plunge into his throat.

Coughing blood and gasping for air, he staggered back. Then they were all stabbing him, and his sword arm was flailing but his weapon hung to it like a limp phallus. It was over.

The mighty Pizarro fell to the floor shouting "Jesu!" to a God he had never honoured but had expected much reward from. His blood-suffused lips hit the cold stones and lay pressed upon them like a man kissing a woman in the heat of passion; it was as if, even in death, he was trying to lay claim to the land he had vanquished but that in turn had consumed him.

A roar went up from the assassins. "The tyrant is dead!"

***

Jimmy

The disco was a shack at the back of the guest house. The only solid piece of construction was the wooden bar at one corner around which most of the room's inhabitants had gathered. A crumbly, battered amplifier system belted out disco music; a few couples, mostly western tourists, were dancing in the centre.

The only drinks were chicha, pisco and spirits. Valdez arrived looking relaxed and suggested we order Cuy—guinea pig—a Peruvian delicacy. Buoyed by the booze, we did, and very soon four whole pitted and roasted guinea pigs, minus their outer skin, were staring back at us from our plates.

"How marvellous," said Ali. She tried dismembering the carcass, her eyes alight with excitement.

"I'm eating it, as is," George said, picking up the little dead animal and biting into its soft, fleshy rump.

"I think I am going to be sick," said Bea, looking away and downing her pisco sour.

I signalled the overworked waiter and requested that he slice up Bea's and mine so that we would not have to endure looking into the poor creatures' eyes as we devoured them.

"I won't be eating it anyway," Bea said, excusing herself to go to the lean-to washroom outside. I hastily combed the sparse menu for a substitute.

I finally settled on Arros con Pollo (chicken and rice—how bad could that be?) for Bea and me, and handed our two guinea pigs to Ali and George who were slurping and washing their dinner down with more chicha.

The music got louder and so did the chatter as the drinks began to take hold. Other campers were pouring in; this camp was the last stop before the big discovery tomorrow and the disco was the only entertainment in town.

At first I thought nothing of it, but suddenly a chill crept down my spine. Manuel and three locals had entered the disco behind a tall blond man who looked like a trekker in his early thirties. The blond trekker, wearing a shirt unbuttoned down to his navel, was at least six and a half feet tall, with tattoos covering his arms and chest. They passed the bar without acknowledging Valdez and his porters who were nursing drinks and trading small talk with the bartender.

I had lost track of George and Ali; they had got up to dance before Bea and I finished our revised meal. Then I caught a glimpse of them in the tiny circle of dance floor, clinched tightly together, bumping through people, in a blissful world of their own. Occasionally, they would come out of their hug, and George would twirl Ali out onto the floor, then sweep her back into his arms and go bombing through the other dancers.

I sat timidly next to Bea, embarrassed, sheepish that once again I could not outdo George's antics. I sensed Bea's anticipation, despite her demure posture. I felt in her a kindred introverted soul waiting to burst out.

Finally, I downed my beer and said, "Would you like to dance?"

"I am not much of a dancer," she replied, looking out of place. She took a deep breath and finished her drink. "But I am willing to give it a try."

Holding a woman again was a great solace to me. For the second time that day, I felt that all was well. I felt free! For a few moments I was able to ignore the mounting sense of foreboding in me.

Disaster arrived with raised voices, and I recognized George's in the commotion. I stopped dancing and took Bea by the hand tightly.

George was pushing the big blond trekker. "You son-of-a-bitch! Who the fuck are you to feel up my girlfriend, huh?"

"Easy, old man," said the trekker, "That's not what happened. This place is pretty crowded."

"Old man! Old man ... I'll show you who's a bloody old man!" George was on tip-toe, yelling into the man's face.

And then, before I could get to him, George punched the trekker in the head. Ali screamed as another man, a local, grabbed her from behind, his hands squeezing her breasts. George swung around to wallop the second man when the trekker took him down in a Half Nelson. Someone broke a bottle and brought it down on George's head. And where was I while all this was happening? Frozen, watching déjà vu overcome my impulsive friend.

"We've got to help him," Bea's voice stirred me into action. I looked around for help. Valdez and his porters had not moved from the bar, they weren't even paying attention to the fight—perhaps this occurred all the time between gringo tourists.

"Help! Valdez, help!" I shouted, waving to get the man's attention. Fortunately, he caught my actions, and in an instant, he and his men were launching themselves off the bar. Meanwhile, Bea ran scratching and screaming at the man who was holding onto Ali. "Let her go you ... you...bastard!" I followed her, but one of the guys in the crowd caught me by the throat and threw me down on the floor. Coughing and spluttering, I flailed with my fists, connecting only with air. Then I felt myself being picked up and thrown. I went sailing off my feet to land on a group of dancers who broke my second fall to the floor. Bedlam broke loose as Valdez and his men joined in the fray, and I heard people screaming "Poliz! Poliz!" A push from somewhere landed a pile of bodies on top of me. I was drowned in the smell of faded perfume, sweat and alcohol breath. As I struggled upward for air, someone farted in my face.

Swearing, grunting and yelling filled the air. In the melee, a kid began tugging at my wristwatch. I recognized him as one of Manuel's sons. "Vamos!" I screamed. He quickly retreated and went seeking other loot in the press of crushed bodies. It took me awhile to crawl out from under the bum of a fat woman, navigate around two drunken tourists who were supine on their backs, and move an overturned table with its contents of food that had smeared me.

Back on my feet, there were many skirmishes to focus on, like a staged saloon fist fight in an old western movie. I caught sight of George; he was being set upon by three men and they were beating him with what looked like metal rods. Grabbing a chair, I advanced on them. It felt good breaking the chair over the back of the first man. He went down like a pole-axed steer. The other two men broke away from George and ran out the back door. Buoyed with confidence, I followed them with the crumbling chair as my only weapon. They were bundling into a familiar car that belched and coughed as it roared into life and sped away. I caught sight of Manuel behind the wheel. In the passenger seat, the blond trekker waved at me and winked. I gave chase but the car outdistanced me quickly. In frustration, I flung the broken chair after them.

The fight had broken up or moved elsewhere by the time I returned to the disco. George was still in his corner, staggering on his feet, blood streaming down his face. He was swinging at the empty air around him. "Where is that son-of a bitch? I'll kill that bastard."

Valdez was at my side. "Those people vamoosed. Manuel brought thugs from his village. My men scared them off."

"Where is the guy I clobbered?"

"He must have run away, or someone carried him away. These people do not like to leave traces behind, senor."

I did not bother to enlighten him further on the blond man's whereabouts. "Where are the ladies?" Bea and Ali were missing.

"In the washroom—cleaning up."

The room was a mess, people picking themselves up, some going to the bar for more drinks; loud guffaws, some swearing; and more onlookers pouring in from outside to see what had transpired. The bartender was shouting to no one in particular and straightening out the tables and fallen chairs. I recognized the boy who had tugged at my wristwatch; he was whistling and sweeping up the broken glass from the floor. The police hadn't arrived, and would not make an appearance, Valdez later told me. This incident, after all, had been started by two foreigners.

"Senor—" Valdez was looking at George. "You need a doctor."

"Bullshit," replied George holding on to a pillar by the dance floor. "I need to get my hands on those bastards."

"Cool it, George," I said. "You need to cut it out."

"Nearest hospital is miles away—downhill. We will have to rent a car." Valdez explained.

"I don't need a bloody hospital. Just get me some antiseptic and a bandage ... I will ... I will be okay." And with that, George collapsed.

Ali did not look pleased when she emerged from the washroom, with Bea trailing. The dirt marks on her white tee shirt that she had tried to wash away had ended up smearing more obviously.

We managed to haul an unconscious George onto a table that was still standing on all its legs while a crowd of onlookers gathered around. His pulse was weak and he had a gash running from above his left eye right across his forehead. Someone had placed a bowl of water and a towel on the table. I soaked the towel and applied it to his brow, staying away from the caked blood as I did not want to reopen the wound. A heavy metallic smell emanated from him.

"Can you get us a car?" I asked Valdez.

"I will have to see, senor. At this time of the night, it is not easy. My men are trying." His men seemed to do all his work for him.

"Well, keep trying," I insisted.

"How is George?" Bea was at my side, and her hand was cool on my elbow.

As if in response to her, my friend groaned and showed signs of stirring.

"How's Ali?" I asked instead.

"Pissed off. She blames George for starting the fight."

"She can tell him that when she sleeps with him tonight."

"Oh, that will not be happening. She wants to move our tent away from you guys. I had a hard time restraining her. I think we will be reverting to our original sleeping arrangements."

There was a hint of regret in her voice, and I stopped my ministrations on George to look at her.

She was gazing directly at me, her guard down, and her brown eyes looked sad. "We always have to look after them, don't we?"

I turned to George again. "Yes."

Ali had barged through the crowd of onlookers. "Bea—let's go. I can't stand this place anymore." She scarcely looked at George.

I got out my frustration then; after all, I was in the zone of Letting Go. "Do you always leave the ones who stand by you, Ali?"

She froze, those icy blue eyes narrowing. I decided to go in for the kill. "Is that how you left your husband? When the chips were down? George tried to save your honour, for Christ's sake."

"My ass!" she finally got out. "George was showing off! Showing me off!"

"And you were enjoying it too!"

"Ali, we've got to go," Bea cut in. "Jeremy—good night. We will talk with you tomorrow."

"There might not be a tomorrow. I have to get George to a hospital. We may never get to Machu Picchu, after coming this close."

Then a voice from behind brought us up sharp. "What the hell are you talking about?" It was George, stroking his forehead with the towel, smearing the uncongealing blood all over his face.

"You are not going anywhere in this shape, George." I said.

"The hell, I am!" he said rolling off the table and steadying himself against it. "I did not come this far to quit."

I held him as he put his weight evenly on both feet. "Thanks, buddy," he grinned gritting his teeth. "You're still getting me out of scraps, aren't you?"

The women were edging away, using the diversion to make an exit.

George called after them. "Goodnight ladies. Good night Ali! Tonight I will sleep with my only true friend—and it's not you."

"Go with them," I said to Valdez, worried that the troublemakers who had fled the scene would be lurking somewhere in the campground, looking for a repeat encounter.

I slung George's arm over my shoulder and we staggered out of the disco, as the music was starting up again and the dancers began returning to the floor.

"I'll be up at four o'clock, Jimmy—just as we planned."

"You've got five hours of sleep ahead of you George—better make the most of it."

"You hurt?"

"My throat hurts. Somebody grabbed and hauled me to the floor."

"I'm sorry, Jimmy. Guess I fucked up again, eh?" His hands were soothing my throat as we tiptoed like two drunks, down the stone pathway to our tent, where Valdez was waving to us with his lantern.

I realized how bad a shape he was in when I laid George out in his sleeping bag. His cheeks were an ashen pallor and his breathing was shallow and raspy. The blood on his forehead was clotted. I washed and dressed his wound but he waved away any further offers of assistance. "I'll be okay. It's the blows from the goddamned pipes that hurt. A good sleep will help."

"You have to get to a hospital, George."

"I was too ambitious this time, eh? Younger women don't come our way anymore."

There was a shuffle of footsteps outside the tent, and its flap opened. Ali peeked inside, a look of worry creasing her face.

"George?" She stood hesitantly, as if waiting to be invited in.

Seeing her, he tried sitting upright, and that sent him into a spasm of pain. His widening smile ended in a grimace and he fell back into his sleeping bag, gasping.

"He's had enough for one night," I said. "Can we pick this up again tomorrow?"

"I have to see him," she returned coolly. "Can I be with him for a few minutes?"

George began waving frantically, urging me to leave.

I glared at her. "Five minutes."

We brushed shoulders as we exchanged places inside the narrow space.

Outside, Bea was pacing.

"I'm sorry for what happened," she said without looking up. "I gave Ali a piece of my mind. She came to apologize."

"Is she doing this for George, or for herself?"

"You said unkind things to her, although they were mostly true." In the darkness, I made out her folded hands.

"I was upset. Wouldn't you be? When your friends walk out on you? And blame you?"

"Your point about her husband hit home. She divorced her last one after an illness left him impotent."

"She is the running kind. She's quitting on you and Tamaya, isn't she?"

"How do you know?"

"I can guess," I lied.

Bea wrung her hands. "I don't know what to do, Jimmy. I can't force her to make this commitment."

"I'll sign in her stead."

She stopped and stared at me.

"You will do...what?"

"I'll sign."

"You ... you will?"

"Yes." I was letting go and enjoying every minute of it.

"Do you know what this means? Debts, commitments, time away from other matters. Hospital visits, schoolwork, sports programs, summer camp, sleepless nights. Do you know, Jimmy?"

"Yes, I know. It also means giving up the cocoon I insulated myself in where no one else could enter. I told you that I lost something once. This was it. I have just been offered a second chance."

"But I hardly know you."

"Well, you can get to know me—starting now."

Before she could answer, Ali resurfaced from the tent looking relieved. She ignored me and made her way towards her tent.

Bea quickly broke off our conversation. "Good night. This is so overwhelming. I ... I need to think this over. So much has happened today." She joined Ali, and they slipped back into their tent.

***

George

He was grateful when Ali stepped inside the tent. This scene had been familiar on the campaign trail years ago. It usually took place in his hotel room or trailer, after dark, carefully scrutinized and filtered by handlers. Young political groupies, falling for his gift of oration, swayed by his charm, seeking the real man, hoping some of his greatness would rub off on them; some were just opportunists seeking influential allies to further their personal agendas. But now, he did not have to watch out for the blackmailers and the glory seekers—he had no more glory to protect or offer.

She stood hesitantly, crouched inside the tent flap. He raised the flame of the portable lamp, dispelling the shadows.

"How bad are your cuts?"

"On my forehead? Or on my soul?"

She flushed. "George, I didn't mean to be so ... "

"Mean?" He laughed.

"Was I mean? I just felt so out of my depth back there."

"Come here. Closer. Let me look at you. Don't worry, in this state I am quite harmless."

She stepped closer and knelt beside him. Yes, the shape of the eyes was the same; the curve of the lips, the blond hair at the right length that Denise had kept it. But there was something missing: the sensitivity, the depth. Only Bea seemed to have those attributes, not Ali. A voice inside him said—*you deserve Ali, you bastard, that is all you looked for in a woman— the physical.*

"Would you be terribly upset if I asked you a favour," he said.

Her eyes narrowed and her breath quickened, sensing a trap, perhaps.

"It's not something to embarrass you," he said quickly.

"That will depend," she said. "I just came to apologize, for what happened back there."

"You haven't apologized yet. But I'll let that one pass if you do me this one favour."

She remained hesitant. She made to rise. She paused by the tent flap and turned around. "What *do* you want?"

"Lie beside me for ten minutes. Flat on the floor."

She chuckled, a twisted smile of disdain.

"I thought better of you, George. That pick-up line is really weak."

"It's not a pick-up line. I guess you figured out my potency, or the lack of it, down at the waterfall."

"That was an unnatural situation. I was prepared to give you a second chance. I didn't give my former husband one."

"And I would have let you down again. Does that make you more comfortable?"

She inched forward.

"Just here? By your side?"

"Yes." He made room for her by moving on his side facing the tent wall, the pain shooting through his forehead with the movement.

The sides of their bodies touched as she straightened out on the sleeping bag.

"Thank you," he said, closing his eyes, thinking back to how it had been once, a long time ago.

"I couldn't do this with Brad...my ex. After he got ill."

"Well, this is just a sampling. I'll never see you again, after tomorrow."

"That's what makes this easier. I turned down Bea's adoption plan today."

"I figured you would. Physical beauty is important to you. I can relate."

"I guess that's the way I was made. Call it a talent or a failure. I'd like to think it's a talent to seek out the beautiful things in life."

He remained silent before saying, "There was a woman once. My wife. She looked a lot like you. She would have stood beside me in that disco."

"Sorry I disappointed you."

"It's all right. Sometime we only get one chance."

The time passed in silence after that; the beating of their hearts was asynchronous. When the ten minutes were up, she rose to her knees. "I have to go now. Have I paid my dues?"

He turned to face her, wincing in pain. He let the pangs subside then smiled at her. "Yes, thanks. It was wonderful having you lying beside me, even for this short while. A man in my position has to be grateful for these fleeting moments."

She shook her head. "I wish you wouldn't be so ... so extreme. It needn't have ended like this."

"You got away lightly," he said, and she shivered.

"Goodbye, George. Try to get some sleep," The flaps fell in place, and she was gone.

"Goodbye, Ali," he whispered to himself. "Goodbye, *all* my fair ladies. I've loved you all in my strange way...and I have feared you like I have never feared any man..."

***

Jimmy

When I got back inside the tent, George was staring at the roof.

"Patched up?" I asked.

"She said she was sorry. That's all."

"Old guys like us *do not* get younger women, George."

"We get sympathy."

"And you had great plans to bed her."

Suddenly, looking at him helpless in his rumpled sleeping bag, I felt I had earned my lifelong victory over George—time and hard living had made him less of the physical man I had envied.

He did not reply; he simply turned over on his side and faced the wall.

That night I slept as fitfully as George did; he moaned most of the time, and I woke up every time he made a sound. I had hatched a plan for getting him through this "last mile" to our destination, but I was going to need Valdez's team's co-operation, and George's too. Once we got to Machu Picchu, I was sure George would relent and let a doctor see him. If he could get to Machu Picchu, that is.

I heard the women taking their tents down before dawn. I knew then that they were not going to accompany us any further. It's easy to break up transient relationships despite the deep depths we may plunge into them during brief, intense interludes. But they were strangers who had crossed our paths, like we had done theirs. Bea hadn't responded to my offer although it was still open. As their footsteps, laden with knapsacks and tents, receded, I fell into a troubled sleep. I felt that another ship was leaving harbour and I was not on it.

When I awoke to more camp-breaking sounds, I found George, propped up against his knapsack, writing in a leather bound journal.

"I thought you were supposed to be asleep," I said, rubbing my eyes and yawning. "You groaned all night."

"I decided to stop complaining and finish my novel. I wrote the last chapter while you slept." George looked rested and reconciled despite the rough night. Perhaps the writing had helped.

When Valdez extended his hands into our tent with two steaming mugs of Coca tea, I knew it was time to put my plan into operation. I went out and spoke to him for a few minutes. He summoned his men and gave them instructions, and they nodded in agreement.

Valdez lingered for a few minutes over the fire after the rest of his men returned to their tasks of taking down our camp.

"Senor, I am sorry about yesterday. Manuel—he is a difficult man. But he is my sister's husband."

"He's not good for tourism."

"We will discipline him, senor."

"How?"

"We have our ways."

Like hell you have. As much as I had taken a liking to Valdez on this trip, I did not trust him. Why did he have to discipline Manuel? The gringo who'd had the cheek to beat up one of their own, in their own village, had been given a sound thrashing. And now the half-breed son would be adopted by the white woman and taken away, and the Inca can come into their own again. Why discipline anyone?

"And senor, one more thing...I am sorry to have compared you and Senor George to the conquistadors. You really care about each other, more than you care for the women."

I nodded and went back into the tent to pack.

A thin drizzle had started and the temperature had dropped. I had to put on a sweater under my rain poncho. At 5 a.m. I helped George outside, and there, before our eyes, assembled and manned by the porters, was a makeshift stretcher, more like a palanquin.

"You're riding in that, George. Otherwise, we are not leaving," I said. He stood weakly, one hand holding the side of the tent, the other gripping his hiking stick.

He was all excuses. "But what about the rest of the gear? How will the men carry that?"

"We are leaving the gear behind. The men will pick it up when they return to the camp. They are from the area and will disband after we finish our tour in Machu Picchu."

I think he was secretly relieved for the ride, even though he made a fuss.

At the urging of Valdez that we needed to get to the Gateway of the Sun before sunrise, we set out in the strengthening rain. George was strapped to the stretcher, waving his stick above his head as if summoning the heavens to stop their downpour and allow us the magical sight of sunrise at Machu Picchu, the nirvana we had come through all this travail to experience. "I feel like Atahualpa going to his doom in Caxamalca," he shouted at one point, but I did not want to ask him to elaborate.

"It's not going to rise," George cursed under his breath. The porters had laid his palanquin on the highest step of the stone Gateway of the Sun, the entrance to Machu Picchu. The trip by stretcher had worn him out, and now with the rain gods soaking us, and with his inability to move, he was shivering and miserable.

We had traveled for over an hour through thickening rain and mist. There were more travelers on the trail; everyone was trying to get a view of sunrise on Machu Picchu. And now we were holed up in this tall rock gateway with a circular cupola like a giant truck wheel, through which the sun would shine and then move onto the ancient city which supposedly lay before us. But everything was covered in a wet curtain, and you couldn't see ten feet in front of you.

Valdez smoked a cigarette and kept humming to himself. He walked over to George and me, politely elbowing through other hopeful tourists who were standing wet and ragged. "Don't worry, senor, maybe the sun has already risen. The mist hides everything—like a curtain before the show, no? But you will see Machu Picchu, and it will be magnificent!"

Then it began to blow: great gusts of wind swirling in front of us. George, who was slumped in exhaustion, raised himself on his elbows. A murmur ran among the tourists; more and more of them kept coming off the trail and piling into this rocky portal.

"It's lifting, Jimmy!" George yelled, and I was drawn to the thick white cloud we were standing in, rising up over our bodies and up over the trees and beyond. A great gasp from the crowd, and there, towering in front of us, much closer than I had expected, lay the giant mountain Huayna Picchu, the poster card landmark that dominates the lost city—we had been literally standing inside Machu Picchu all the time!

"Hah, Hah!" came George's triumphant roar behind us. "We've arrived!"

Despite my prior reading and the anticipation of what I was about to witness, the sight of the city, with its geometrically precise buildings and monuments nestling beneath two mountain peaks, Huayna Pichu and its smaller cousin, took my breath away. The pent up release of days on the trail was another catalyst to the sense of euphoria that coursed through me, and I shared George's desire to shout and thank whoever for bringing us through safely. Everyone began to rush through the gate in a bid to get to the ruins as quickly as possible in case another downpour came our way.

The next couple of hours were spent visiting various outer buildings and inner ones, understanding the history, learning some of the ancient arts and sciences practiced here, and taking of lots of photographs while obliging fellow tourists who wanted their pictures taken. I was swept away with the stream of visitors going from sight to sight, learning why the windows in certain buildings faced in directions such that the equinox and solstice suns would hit precisely at points indicating the coming of those seasons; learning how rocks were split using wood and water. There were some sections of the site at a slant, testament to a sinking city. I lost track of George in my zeal to check out the sights. I knew he was safe in the hands of the porters, so I did not worry. Valdez had finally gone to arrange for a doctor.

As I walked among the ruins and absorbed the story of Machu Picchu, I realized that much of this city and its history was based on legendary interpretation that made it larger than it must have been; there was a legend for everything: why rocks were placed at certain angles, why the water zigzagged downhill, why the giant stone Condor stood in its position in the temple, why the majority of mummies found were those of women, why certain rooms showed signs of a hurried exodus—a tumbled bag of grain, books strewn on the floor—even though there was no sign of Spanish occupation. I wondered whether the people of Machu Picchu had been like me, people who had required order in their lives; and when they sensed that order under threat with the coming of the Spaniards, they had fled to try and regain their balance elsewhere? And their evolving culture at Machu Picchu had been permanently paused in mid brush-stroke, like Denise's painting, never to grow again. Time provides the luxury for conjecture and romanticising, for mystification, even deification and demonizing. The Inca living in this site had been scholars, and the Spaniards were plunderers. Might was Right in this era, and the Spaniards had prevailed, and the city had died under the passing shadow of the conquistador, much like the rest of the Inca empire.

Finally, coming out of the last stretch of thatched dwellings that had housed the city's inhabitants, and relieved to find that the rain had actually given way to a cautious sun, I went in search of George.

He was easy to spot, lying in the sun on his stretcher on one of the terraces. He was taking pictures of the structures that hovered around him. The porters must have taken a break, for none were around. I threw my knapsack on the ground beside him. He had his leather notebook open by his side.

"Well, George, are you glad you came?"

He looked amused. "Very glad." He clicked another picture from his new camera, still functioning despite the many soakings it had endured during the trek.

"The journey up here was better than the arrival. This is anti-climactic," I said.

"Like the moment of death," he replied, aiming his camera again.

"And you will see a doctor, now that you've achieved your goal?"

"Sure." He sounded dismissive, focussing another shot of Huayna Picchu and on some travelers who were braving a climb up its rugged face. "Not sure what they can do for me, though, Jimmy."

"What do you mean?"

"I am past it. The doctors told me in Vancouver a couple of years ago. The old prostate—something's been growing there for some time. Now it's spread elsewhere."

A chill ran through me, despite the sun that was warming us by the minute.

"George—"

He interrupted me. "It's okay, buddy. I was scared of getting it taken out—you know—you can't get it up afterwards and all that."

"Oh, for Christ's sake!"

"But I've had a good time. Vancouver was a party town. Lots of pretty young things. And the bigger this damn thing grew, the more I wanted sex. Was scared of losing it. Grew into an obsession, Jimmy."

"Was that why you got fired? Non-consensual sexual behaviour with students? I think that's what they call it now. It's a different world, George."

"Yeah, that's what they called it. And they chose to ignore the starry-eyed invitations, the desperate demands. But I guess it was my fault too. I let it get out of hand. You don't think I am a dirty old man now, do you?"

"No, just a small boy who never grew up."

"And I'm definitely not Norma Desmond?"

I grinned, holding back tears. "I'd say you are more like a fallen conquistador."

"Thanks. I like that better. I wanted to take this trip before it got too late for me to travel. Wanted to know what made Dee puke at that lecture and send her into her death spiral. Besides, I wanted to see you. Now, if I'd had Ali last night that would have been a bonus. Still, I got a smidgeon of her company. Haven't had a woman in months now, Jimmy, ever since this thing started affecting my 'performance' ... you know. Yes, my sword—the essence of George Walton—had been drooping ever since. Soon, it will hang dead between my legs, never to strike again."

"You son-of-a-gun!" Underneath my swearing I wanted to hold him and keep him safe. Instead, I said, "You damn near killed yourself on this trip."

"It would have been glorious to go out that way. Up on the trail, it was very tempting, to step off the path on Dead Woman's Pass, for instance, and 'shuffle off this mortal coil.'"

He stopped taking pictures and put his camera away. "Now I'm in for the next big challenge: experiencing what Dee went through in her last days. Only, I think my death will be slow and drawn out. I'll pay for my sins in ample measure. But at least, I will be able to share something with her."

"You don't fail at your one-upmanship, even in tragedy."

He laughed. "By the way, when I ... go ... I'm bequeathing these pictures to you, okay?"

"I decided to co-sign the adoption with Bea. Ali backed out, you know."

His eyes brightened. "Oh, I am so proud of you, buddy. That's fantastic. Now I can die in peace."

"You're not dying yet."

"Oh yes, I am. You know Jimmy, we were a selfish generation. We took what we could, never gave back, and produced nothing of significance. And now we are dying of the scourges of our time, the cancers and other shit. There is no immortality, only history. The conquistadors were no different. Pizarro was a plunderer and a bastard, and you cannot humanize a bastard. I realized that when I wrote the final chapter last night. And now that he's helped me understand myself, this book," he hefted the leather journal and tossed it into a nearby pile of stones being readied for restoration, "will be buried here, unpublished."

I rushed over and retrieved the leather tome, smeared now with mud and plaster. "Mind if I keep it?"

"Suit yourself."

I cleaned the journal as best as I could and placed it in my knapsack.

"*Our* story must have a better ending, George. Or else we wouldn't have progressed in five hundred years."

He closed his eyes and sucked in the mountain air. "I am glad you are adopting that child. Maybe that's where the story...our story ... changes."

"Bea left camp with Ali early this morning, though. I am not sure if she will accept my offer."

"Oh yes, she will, old buddy. You are the best deal she has right now. Trust me."

I went over and hugged him. The suppressed tears poured out of me. His body was limp, his clothes smelled musty; and there was another smell coming out of him: that of a dying animal.

"I'm sorry for what happened with Denise. In the end, she was your wife, and I stole her from you. I guess, I never really apologized."

"There is no need to, buddy. Look around you. The Spaniards never apologized to the Inca, nor the Inca to the tribes they usurped. Just think, we would not be here if those two nations had not done what they did. Peru wouldn't be what it is—a mess of contradictions—interesting in its confusion, a traveler's dream. We make our history, however screwed up it is, and no apology is needed."

"I'm going to write this story, about our trip, including the pieces of our former lives that returned constantly during the trek."

"Make sure you include the nasty pieces too. I can fill you in."

I heard someone calling my name. I felt self conscious, holding George in a clench like that. I drew away from him and turned around. Bea was standing on one of the upper terraces, a few yards away, looking hesitantly at us. A surge of joy swept through me, and I ran over to her.

"I wanted to give you my contact information, Jimmy." She extended a business card. "I accept your offer, if it's still open, that is."

My spirits rose. "Great! And I promise to visit. Kitchener is not far."

"I think I can trust you." She smiled in profile, showing her unmarked side to me. "How's George?"

"He's seriously ill right now."

"Can I help?"

"No, it's ... it's taken care of. Valdez has gone for help. Where's Ali?"

"Down at the railway station. She is taking the train back to Cusco. I am returning to the village with Valdez."

"And we are going to find a doctor for George."

"I hope he gets well soon. Can I call you when I get the adoption details sorted out?"

"Sure." I hunted in my pockets for a card and found one, sweat-stained and dirty. I scribbled my cell phone number on it. "Call me as soon as you need me. I will be in Cusco for a few days until George is able to travel back home."

She paused for a moment, a weight settling on her. "You think this will work out? Us? Adopting a handicapped child? It sounds as surreal as this place. Perhaps we'll get back to Canada and think we were being impulsive."

"I wish I had been more impulsive all my life. Look at my friend George over there—he's had a more interesting life than I'll ever have. He never stopped to think, he just *did*, 'Wrote my history,' as he says."

She brightened up. "Perhaps it *will* work after all."

"It must. This is our last chance. I say it selfishly."

"I'd better go then, before I have second thoughts." With a quick peck on my cheek and a wave to George, she headed towards the exit gate from the ancient ruins. I gazed after her, long after she had vanished from sight, until I saw Valdez alighting from a taxi outside the gate down below us.

The wind swirled around me as I went down the steps again.

"Can you stand up, George? I think we are going to be taking a ride to the hospital."

He was dozing and mumbled something. I bent down to hear him better.

"Did you get a date, Jimmy?"

"A date?"

"Yeah. Bea ... "

"She gave me her business card. Asked me to call."

He nodded and slumped back. "Good—that's a promising start. Yeah, get me up, I need to piss."

He limply extended his hand. I pulled him up, staggered under his weight, steadied, and started our walk back towards Valdez and the taxi.

End

Acknowledgements

Many thanks to my beta readers who provided me valuable feedback on earlier drafts of this novel: Jake Hogeterp, (the late) Brian Mullally, Sherri Cirra, Lorna Tucker, Ben Antao, Krista Asseltine Candela, Susan Statham, Dessy Pavlova, Maia Sepp, Christopher Canniff, Richard Joseph and Michael Daly.

To Juliet Mannock & Richard A Webb for their assistance with Quechua translations.

To my indefatigable designer, Joanna Joseph, who will work on draft upon draft of the cover until everything is just perfect. And to Susan Statham, for her fine depictions of Inca times in her pencil sketches found inside the book.

To Dessy Pavlova, for her editing and her eye for detail.

To my wife Sarah, who did not like the first draft, but who helped me persevere, and who endorsed the seventh and final version.

And last but not least, to Blue Denim Press, for continuing to give voice to writers struggling to be heard.

Shane Joseph
2015

Author Bio

Shane Joseph began writing as a teenager living in Sri Lanka and has never stopped. From an early surge of short stories and radio play scripts, to humorous corporate skits, travelogues, case studies and technical papers, then novels, more short stories and essays, he continues to pursue the three pages-a-day maxim and keeps writer's block at bay.

His career stints include: stage and radio actor, pop musician, encyclopaedia salesman, lathe machine operator, airline executive, travel agency manager, vice president of a global financial services company, software services salesperson, project manager and management consultant.

Self-taught, with four degrees under his belt obtained through distance education, Shane is an avid traveler and has visited one country for every year of his life. He fondly recalls incidents during his travels as real lessons he could never have learned in school: husky driving in Finland with no training, trekking the Inca Trail in Peru through an unending rainstorm, hitch-hiking in Australia without a map, escaping a wild elephant in Zambia, and being stranded without money in Denmark, are some of his memories.

Shane is a graduate of the Humber School for Writers in Toronto and studied under the mentorship of Giller Prize and Canadian Governor General's Award winning author David Adams Richards. His published works include the novels *Redemption in Paradise* (2004), *After the Flood* (2009) and *The Ulysses Man* (2011). His previously published short story collections are *Fringe Dwellers* (2008) and *Paradise Revisited* (2013). His short fiction has appeared in literary journals and anthologies internationally. His blog is widely syndicated.

After immigrating (twice), raising a family, building a career, and experiencing life's many highs and lows, Shane has carved out a niche in Cobourg, Ontario with his wife, Sarah, where he continues to work, write stories, and strum his guitar.

More details on Shane's work and blog can be found on his website at **www.shanejoseph.com**.

CPSIA information can be obtained at www.ICGtesting.com
Printed in the USA
LVOW07s0712091015

457604LV00006B/23/P